KU-506-381

Don't Tell Alfred

NANCY MITFORD

PENGUIN BOOKS

PENGUIN BOOKS

UK | USA | Canada | Ireland | Australia
India | New Zealand | South Africa

Penguin Books is part of the Penguin Random House group of companies
whose addresses can be found at global.penguinrandomhouse.com.

First published by Hamish Hamilton 1960
Published in Penguin Books 1963
Reissued in this edition 2015

001

Copyright © the Estate of Nancy Mitford, 1960

Printed in Great Britain by Clays Ltd, St Ives plc

A CIP catalogue record for this book is available from the British Library

ISBN: 978-0-241-97470-4

www.greenpenguin.co.uk

MIX
Paper from
responsible sources
FSC® C018179

Penguin Random House is committed to a
sustainable future for our business, our readers
and our planet. This book is made from Forest
Stewardship Council® certified paper.

9.18
2/9/21

Please renew or return items by the date
shown on your receipt

www.hertsdirect.org/libraries

Renewals and   0300 123 4049
enquiries:

Textphone for hearing   0300 123 4041
or speech impaired

Hertfordshire

PENGUIN BOOKS
Don't Tell Alfred

Nancy Mitford (1904–73) was born in London, the eldest child of the second Baron Redesdale. Her childhood in a large, remote country house with her five sisters and one brother is recounted in the early chapters of *The Pursuit of Love* (1945), which, according to the author, is largely autobiographical. Apart from being taught to ride and speak French, Nancy Mitford always claimed she never received a proper education. She started writing before her marriage in 1932 in order 'to relieve the boredom of the intervals between the recreations established by the social conventions of her world' and had written four novels, including *Wigs on the Green* (1935), before the success of *The Pursuit of Love* in 1945. After the war she moved to Paris where she lived for the rest of her life. She followed *The Pursuit of Love* with *Love in a Cold Climate* (1949), *The Blessing* (1951) and *Don't Tell Alfred* (1960). She also wrote four works of biography: *Madame de Pompadour*, first published to great acclaim in 1954, *Voltaire in Love*, *The Sun King* and *Frederick the Great*. As well as being a novelist and a biographer she also translated Madame de Lafayette's classic novel *La Princesse de Clèves* into English, and edited *Noblesse Oblige*, a collection of essays concerned with the behaviour of the English aristocracy and the idea of 'U' and 'non-U'. Nancy Mitford was awarded the CBE in 1972.

522 905 91 8

To Anna Maria Cicogna

I

On the day which was to be such a turning-point in my life, I went to London by the 9.07. I had planned to do a little shopping; somebody had told me of Chinese robes in the sales, perfect for dinner at home since they would cover up everything. I was also going to see my naughty boy, Basil, a perennial worry to me; Aunt Sadie begged me to look in on Uncle Matthew and there was something I had long wanted to put to him. I had appointments to lunch with the one and to have tea with the other. It was a Saturday because that was Basil's half-holiday – he was cramming for the Foreign Office. We were to meet at a restaurant, then go back to his lodgings, what used to be called 'rooms' and is now called a 'service flat'. My idea was to do a little, surely much needed, tidying up there, as well as to collect some dirty clothes, and bring them back with me to have them washed or cleaned. I took a large canvas hold-all to contain them and the Chinese robe, if I bought it.

But, oh dear, I don't think I've ever looked such a fool as I did in that Chinese robe, with my brown walking shoes, enormous beneath the hem, hair untidy from dragging off a hat, leather bag clasped to bosom because it had £28 in it and I knew that people snatched bags at sales. The assistant earnestly said think of the difference if I were carefully *coiffée* and *maquillée* and *parfumée* and *manicurée* and *pedicurée*, wearing Chinese sandals (next department, 35/6) and lying on a couch in a soft light. It was no good, however – my imagination could not get to work on all these hypotheses; I felt both hot and bothered; I tore the robe from me and fled from the displeasure of the saleswoman.

I had made my plan with Basil some days before, on the telephone. Like all the children he is quite incapable of either reading or writing a letter. I was rather more worried about him than usual;

last time he had come to Oxford his clothes had been distinctly on the Teddy side while his hair combed (or rather pulled) over his forehead and worn in a bob at the back gave him a curiously horrible look. This, no doubt, is now the fashion and not in itself a cause for alarm. But when he was alone with me he had spoken about his future, saying that the prospect of the Foreign Service bored him and that he thought he could put his talent for languages to better account in some other career. The sinister words 'get rich quick' were uttered. I was anxious to see him again and ask a few questions. It was a blow, therefore, though not a great surprise, when he failed to turn up at the restaurant. I lunched there alone and then went off to find his service flat. The address he had given me, in Islington, turned out to be a pretty old house, come down in the world (soon no doubt to come down altogether). There were five or six bells at the front door with cards attached; one bell had no card but somebody had scribbled Baz on the wall beside it. I pressed it, without much hope. Nobody came. I went on pressing at intervals.

A sharp lad in Teddy costume was lounging in the street, eyeing me. Presently he came up and said, 'If it's old Baz you're after, he's gone to Spain.'

Rain, rain, go to Spain. 'And when will he be back again?'

'When he comes for the next batch. Old Baz is a travel agent now, didn't you know? Joined up with his Grandad – some people are lucky in their relations. Baz herds them out to the Costa Brava, goes into hiding while they live it up there and brings back the bodies a week later. Or that's the general idea – he's only just started the work.'

Travel agent – Grandad – what did the child mean? Was not this a line of talk intended to keep me here until a man who was walking up the street should be out of sight? There was nobody else about, this dread Teddy, armed, no doubt, with blades, was clearly after my bag and the £28. I gave him a nervous, idiotic smile. 'Thank you very much,' I said, 'that's just what I thought. Goodbye and thank you.'

Upper Street was near and very soon I was in a good old No. 19 sagely ambling towards Piccadilly. This sort of thing always happened when I tried to see Basil. Oh well, one must put oneself in his shoes. Why should he want to spend his Saturday afternoon with a middle-aged mother? What a bore for a young man, on his own for the first time, to have to watch this elderly woman messing about in his room and taking away his suits. All the same, it was not like him to throw one over quite so callously; what could have happened? How could I find out? Meanwhile here I was in London on a Saturday afternoon with nothing to do until tea-time. We were passing the National Gallery, but I felt too dispirited to go in. I decided to walk off my bad temper in the Park.

Though I have lived in London for longish periods at various times in my life, I have never been a Londoner, so that its associations to me are more literary and historic than personal. Every time I visit it I am saddened by seeing changes for the worse: the growing inelegance; the loss of character; the disappearance of landmarks and their replacement by flat and faceless glass houses. When I got off my bus at Hyde Park Corner, I looked sadly at the huge hotel where Montdore House used to be, in Park Lane. When first built it had been hailed as a triumph of modern architecture, but although it had only stood there for three years it had already become shabby, the colour of old teeth, and in an odd way out of date. I stumped off towards Kensington Gardens. Somebody had told me that Knightsbridge Barracks were soon to go, so I said good-bye to them. I had never looked at them very carefully – I now saw that they were solid and well built in a pretty mixture of brick and stone. No masterpiece, but certainly far better than the glorified garage that would replace them. Wendy's Wishing Well is horribly altered, I noted, and what has happened to the trees in the Broad Walk? However, Kensington Palace is still there, though probably not for long, and eccentric old men are still sailing boats on the Round Pond, which has not, as yet, been dried and levelled and turned into a car park.

Presently, drops of rain began to fall. It was half past three.

Uncle Matthew never minds one being early; I decided to make for his mews at once. If he were in he would be pleased to see me, if not I could wait for him in a little sheltered place where the dust-bins are kept.

Uncle Matthew had handed over Alconleigh to his only surviving son, Bob Radlett, keeping a small Regency house on the estate for himself. Aunt Sadie was delighted by this exchange; she liked being nearer the village; the new house got sunshine all day and it amused her to do it up. Indeed, newly painted from top to toe and containing what little good furniture there had been at Alconleigh, it had become a much more desirable residence than the other. But hardly had they moved into it than my uncle fell out with Bob: the eternal story of the old king and the young king. Bob had his own ideas about shooting and estate management; Uncle Matthew disagreed violently with every innovation. His son-in-law, Fort William, his brother-in-law, Davey Warbeck, and such neighbours as were on speaking terms with Uncle Matthew had all warned him that this would happen; they had been invited to mind their own business. Now that they had been proved right he refused to admit the real cause of his chagrin and persuaded himself that Bob's wife, Jennifer, was to blame. He pronounced his intense dislike for her; her vicinity, he said, was not to be endured. Poor Jennifer was quite inoffensive, she only wished to please and this was so obvious that even Uncle Matthew, when asked to explain the reason for his hatred, found himself at a loss. 'Meaningless piece of flesh,' he would mutter. Undeniable; Jennifer was one of those women whose meaning, if they have one, is only apparent to husband and children, but she certainly did not deserve such a torrent of hatred.

Of course Uncle Matthew could not remain in a place where he risked setting eyes on this loathed daughter-in-law. He took a flat in London, always known as The Mews, and seemed strangely contented in a town which he had hitherto regarded as a plague spot. Aunt Sadie remained peacefully in her nice new house, able to see a few friends and entertain her grandchildren without any fear of explosions. Uncle Matthew, who had been fond of his own children when they were young, took a very poor view of their progeny, while my aunt really liked them better, felt more at her ease with them, than she ever had with their parents.

At first domestic troubles raged in The Mews. There was no bedroom for a servant; daily women were found but Uncle Matthew pronounced them to be harlots; daily men smelt of drink and were impertinent. Luck favoured him in the end and he arrived at a perfect solution. One day, driving in a taxi to the House of Lords, he spied a pound note on the floor. On getting out, he handed it and his fare, plus, no doubt, an enormous tip (he was a great over-tipper), to the cabby, who remarked that this was a nuisance because now he would be obliged to take it round to the Yard.

'Don't you do any such thing!' said Uncle Matthew, rather oddly, perhaps, for a legislator. 'Nobody will claim it. Keep it for yourself, my dear fellow.' The cabby thanked him warmly, both for the tip and the advice, and they parted on a chuckling note, like a pair of conspirators.

The next day, by chance, Uncle Matthew, having rung up his local shelter (or, as it is probably now called, Drivers' Rest and Culture Hall) for a cab to take him down to the House, got the same man. He told my uncle that, though he had quite seen the good sense of his advice, he had nevertheless taken the pound to Scotland Yard.

'Damned fool,' said Uncle Matthew. He asked him his name and what time he started his day. The name was Payne and he was on the streets at about half past eight. Uncle Matthew told him that, in future, he was to put his flag down when he left his garage and drive straight to The Mews.

'I like to get to Victoria Street every morning in time for the Stores to open so that would suit us both.' The Stores (Army and Navy) had ever been a magnet to my uncle; Aunt Sadie used to say she wished she could have a penny for each pound he had spent there. He knew most of the employees by name and used to take his constitutional in the magic precincts, ending up with a view from the bridge, whence he would note the direction of the wind. No sky was visible from The Mews.

Presently Payne and my uncle came to a very suitable arrangement. Payne would drop him at the Stores, return to The Mews and put in a couple of hours doing housework there. He would then go back for Uncle Matthew and drive him either to his club or home, in which case he would fetch him some hot luncheon from the Rest and Culture Hall, where according to my uncle, the cabbies do themselves exceedingly well. (I often feel pleased to remember this when waiting in a bitter wind for one of them to finish his nuts and wine.) For the rest of the day Payne was allowed to ply his trade on condition that between every fare he should ring up The Mews to see if anything were wanted. Uncle Matthew paid him, then and there, whatever was on the clock and a tip. He said this saved accounts and made everything easier. The system worked like a charm. Uncle Matthew was the envy of his peers, few of whom were so well looked after as he.

As I was walking along Kensington Gore a cab drew up beside me, Payne at the wheel. Taking no notice of his fare, who looked surprised and not delighted, he leant over to me and said, confidentially, 'His Lordship's out. If you're going to The Mews now I'd best give you the key. I'm to pick him up at St George's Hospital after taking this gentleman to Paddington.' The fare now pulled down the window and said furiously, 'Look here, driver, I've got a train to catch, you know.'

'Very good, sir,' said Payne. He handed me the key and drove away.

By the time I arrived it was raining hard and I was glad not to be obliged to sit on the dust-bin. Although we were already in July the day was turning chilly; Uncle Matthew had a little fire in his sitting-room. I went up to it, rubbing my hands. The room was small, dark and ugly, the old business room at Alconleigh in miniature. It had the same smell of wood fire and Virginia cigarettes and was filled, as the business room had always been, with hideous gadgets, most of which my uncle had invented himself years ago and which, it was supposed of each in turn, would make him rich beyond belief. There were the Alconsegar Ash Tray, the Alconstoke Fire Lighters, the Alconclef Record Rack and the Home Beautifier, a fly trap made of fretwork in the form of a Swiss chalet. They vividly evoked my childhood and the long evenings at Alconleigh with Uncle Matthew playing his favourite records. I thought with a sigh what an easy time parents and guardians had had in those days – no Teddy boys, no Beards, no Chelsea set, no heiresses, or at least not such wildly public ones; good little children we seem to have been, in retrospect.

Tea was already laid out, silver hot-dishes containing scones and girdle cakes and a pot of Tiptree jam. You could count on a good tea, at The Mews. I looked round for something to read, picked up the *Daily Post* and fell upon Amyas Mockbar's Paris Page. Provincials like myself are kept in touch with fashionable and intellectual Europe in its last stronghold of civilized leisure by this Mr Mockbar who, four times a week, recounts the inside story of Parisian lives, loves and scandals. It makes perfect reading for the housewife, who is able to enjoy the chronicle without having to rub shoulders with the human horrors depicted therein; she lays down the paper more contented than ever with her lot. Today, however, the page was rather dull, consisting of speculations on the appointment of a new English Ambassador to Paris. Sir Louis Leone, it seemed, was due to retire after a mission of unusual length. Mockbar had always presented him as a diplomatic disaster, too brilliant, too social and much too pro-French. His beautiful wife was supposed to have made too many friends in Paris; reading between the lines, one gathered that Mockbar had not been among them. Now that the Leones were leaving, however, he was seized with an inexplicable tenderness for them. Perhaps he was saving his ammunition for the new Sir Somebody whom he confidently tipped as Sir Louis's successor.

I heard the taxi crawling into The Mews. It stopped, the door slammed, the meter rang, my uncle rattled some half-crowns out of his pocket, Payne thanked him and drove off. I went to meet Uncle Matthew as he came slowly up the stairs.

'How are you, my dear child?'

It was comfortable to be my dear child again; I was so accustomed to seeing myself as a mother – poor, neglected mother today, left to have her luncheon all alone. I looked at myself in a glass while Uncle Matthew went to the little kitchen to put on a kettle, saying 'Payne got everything ready, there's only the tea to make.' No doubt there was something in my appearance which made 'my dear child' not too ridiculous, even at the age of forty-five. I took off my hat and combed my hair which was as springy as ever, turned up all over my head and was neither faded nor grey. My face was not much lined; my eyes looked bright and rather young. I weighed the same as when I was eighteen. There was an unfashionable aspect about me which came from having lived most of my life in Oxford, as much out of the world as if it had been Tibet, but no doubt some such drastic treatment as a love affair (perish the thought) or change of environment could still transform my appearance; the material was there.

'Very civil of you to come, Fanny.'

I saw Uncle Matthew but seldom these days and never really got accustomed to finding him old, that is to say, no longer in the agreeable, seemingly endless autumn of life but plunged in its midwinter. I had known him so vigorous and violent, so rampageous and full of super-charged energy that it went to my heart to see him now, stiff and slow in his movements; wearing spectacles; decidedly deaf. Until we are middle-aged ourselves, old age is outside our experience. When very young, of course, everybody grown up seems old while the really old people with whom we come into contact, never having been different during the few years – short to them, endlessly long to us – of our acquaintance, seem more like another species than members of our own race in a different condition. But the day comes when those we have known in the prime of life approach its end; then we understand what old age really is. Uncle Matthew was only in his seventies, but he was not well preserved. He had gone through life with one lung, the other having been shot away in the Boer War. In 1914, on the reserve of officers, he had arrived in France with the first hundred thousand and spent two years in the trenches before being invalided home. After that he had hunted, shot and played lawn tennis as though he had been perfectly fit. I can often remember, as a child, seeing him fight to get his breath – it must have been a strain on the heart. He had known sorrow too, which always ages people. He had suffered the deaths of three of his children and those his three favourites. Having lost a child myself I know that nothing more terrible can befall a human being; mine, having died as a baby, left no gap comparable with the disappearance of Linda and the two boys he was so proud of.

When he came back with the tea, looking like some old shepherd of the hills who had invited one to his chimney-corner, I said, 'Whom were you visiting at St George's?'

'Why, Davey! I though you couldn't have known he was there or you would have come.' Davey Warbeck was my uncle, widower of Aunt Emily who had snatched me from my own, unmaternal mother and brought me up.

'Indeed I would have. Whatever is he in for now?' There was no terror in my voice as I asked; Davey's health was his hobby and he spent much of his life in nursing homes and hospitals.

'Nothing serious. It seems they have got a few human spare parts, frozen, don't you know, from America. Davey came up from the country to give them the once over. He says it was hard to know what to choose, they were all so tempting. A few yards of colon, some nice bits of membrane, an eye (but where could he put it? Even Davey would look rather odd with three) – finally he picked on a kidney. He's been after a suitable one for ages – he's having it grafted. It's to give the others a chance. Now who else would have thought of that? Wonderful fella – and all for nothing, don't you know? We pay – health service.'

'It sounds rather terrific – how did he seem?'

'Strong as a bull and having the time of his life. Doctors and

9

nurses so proud of him – exhibit A. I asked if they couldn't give me a new lung but they wouldn't touch it. Kill me stone dead they said, with my heart in the state it is. You want to be in the pink, like Davey, to have these graftings.'

'Delicious girdle cake.'

'Comes from the Shelter – they've got a Scotch cook there now. Davey's been telling me about your mother's new husband. You know how he likes to be in on things – he went to the wedding.'

'No – how could he! Weren't the papers awful?'

'I thought so too, but he says not nearly as bad as they might have been. It seems to have been a thick week, luckily for us, with all these heiresses running to leper colonies and the Dockers docking at Monte Carlo. What they did put in they got wrong, of course. Have you seen him, Fanny?'

'Who? Oh, my mother's husband? Well no, she has rather stopped asking Alfred and me to meet her fiancés. They've gone abroad now, haven't they?'

'To Paris, I believe. He's only twenty-two, did you know?'

'Oh dear, I can easily believe it.'

'She's as pleased as Punch, Davey says. He says you must hand it to her, she didn't look a day over forty. It seems your boy Basil was at the wedding – he introduced them in the first place.'

'Goodness! Did he really?'

'They both belong to the same gang,' said Uncle Matthew, adding rather wistfully, 'we didn't have these gangs when I was young. Never mind, though, we had wars. I liked the Boer War very much, when I was Basil's age. If you won't have wars you must expect gangs, no doubt.'

'Does my stepfather, aged twenty-two (oh, really, Uncle Matthew, it is past a joke. Why, he is the boys' step-grandfather, you realize?), does he do any work or is he just a criminal?'

'Davey said something about him being a travel agent. That's why they've gone abroad, most likely.'

The words of that Teddy boy came back to me. 'Old Baz is a travel agent . . . he's joined up with his Grandad.' I became very thoughtful. What was I going to tell Alfred when I got home?

I said: 'At least that sounds fairly respectable?'

'Don't you believe it. A chap in the House was telling me about these travel agents. Bandits, he said. Take people's money and give them ten days of hell. Of course, going abroad in itself would be hell to me. Now how many would you say that makes, Fanny?'

'What, Uncle Matthew?'

'How many husbands has the Bolter had now?'

'The papers said six –'

'Yes, but that's absurd. They left out the African ones – it's eight or nine at least. Davey and I were trying to count up. Your father and his best man and the best man's best friend, three. That takes us to Kenya and all the hot stuff there – the horsewhipping and the aeroplane and the Frenchman who won her in a lottery. Davey's not sure she ever married him, but give her the benefit of the doubt: four. Rawl and Plugge five and six, Gewan seven, the young man who writes books on Greece – relatively young – old enough to be the father of this one – eight and the new boy nine. I can't think of another, can you?'

At this point the telephone bell rang and my uncle picked up the receiver. 'That you, Payne? Where are you now – East India Docks? I'd like the *Evening Standard*, please. Thank you, Payne.' He rang off. 'He can take you to the station, Fanny. I suppose you're catching the 6.05? If you wouldn't mind being a bit on the early side so that he can be back here in good time for the cocktail party.'

'Cocktail party?' I said. I was stunned. Uncle Matthew loathed parties, execrated strangers and never drank anything, not even a glass of wine with his meals.

'It's a new idea – don't you have them at Oxford? You will soon, mark my words. I rather like them. You're not obliged to talk to anybody and when you get home, it's bedtime.'

Timidly, without much conviction, but feeling it my duty to do so, I now broached the subject which was the reason for my visit. I asked him if he would like to see Fabrice, Linda's child whom Alfred and I had adopted. He was at school with our Charlie; they had been born on the same day and in the same nursing home; Linda had died; I had survived and left the home with two babies instead of one. Aunt Sadie went to Eton sometimes and took the boys out but Uncle Matthew had not set eyes on his grandson since he was a baby, during the war.

'Oh, no, my dear Fanny, thank you very much,' he muttered, embarrassed, when he understood what I was trying to say. 'I don't set great store by other people's children, you know. Give him this and tell him to keep away, will you?' A pocket book lay beside him – he took out a fiver. This unlucky idea of mine was a cold spoon in the soufflé; the conversation lapsed and I was thankful when Payne arrived with the *Evening Standard*.

'Eighteen and six on the clock, m'lord.'

My uncle gave him a pound and two half-crowns. 'Thank you, Payne.'

'Thank you – much obliged, m'lord.'

'Now, Payne, you'll take Miss Fanny to Paddington – no scorching, I beg, we don't want her in the ditch, we are all very fond of Miss Fanny. While you are there, would you go to Wyman's, present my compliments to Mr Barker of the book-stall and see if he could oblige me with a ball of string? Come straight back, will you? – we are going to Lord Fortinbras in Groom Place. I am invited for six-thirty – it wouldn't do to miss the beginning.'

When I arrived at Oxford I was startled to see Alfred waiting for me on the platform. He never came to meet me as a rule – I had not even said what train I would take. 'Nothing wrong?' I said. 'The boys – ?'

'The boys? Oh dearest, I'm sorry if I frightened you.' He then told me that he had been appointed Ambassador to Paris.

2

It may be imagined that I got little sleep that night. My thoughts whizzed about, to begin with quite rational; more and more fantastic as the hours went on; finally between sleeping and waking, of a nightmare quality. In the first place, of course, I was happy to think that my dear Alfred's merits should have been publicly recognized at last, that he should receive a dazzling prize (as it seemed to me) to reward him for being so good and clever. Surely he was wasted in a chair of Pastoral Theology, even though his lectures on the pastoral theme made a lasting impression on those who heard them. During the war he had filled a post of national importance; after that I had quite expected to see him take his place in the arena. But (whether from lack of ambition or lack of opportunity I never really knew) he had returned quietly to Oxford when his war-work came to an end and seemed fated to remain there for the rest of his days. For my part, I have already told* how, as an eager young bride, I had found University life disappointing; I never reversed that opinion. I was used to being a don's wife, I knew exactly what it involved and felt myself adequate; that was all. The years rolled by with nothing to distinguish them; generations of boys came and went; like the years I found that they resembled each other. As I got older I lost my taste for the company of adolescents. My own children were all away now: the two youngest at Eton; Basil – oh where was he and when should I confide my fears about him to Alfred? Bearded David, the eldest, was a don at a redbrick university, living with the times, or so he informed me. In moments of introspection I often thought that a woman's need for children is almost entirely physical. When they are babies one cuddles and kisses and slaps them and has a

---

* In *Love in a Cold Climate*.

highly satisfying animal relationship with them. But when they grow up and leave the nest they hardly seem to belong any more. Was I much use to the boys now? As for Alfred, detached from all human emotions, I thought it more than likely that if I were to disappear he would go and live in college, as happy as he had ever been with me. What was I doing on earth at all and how was I going to fill in the thirty-odd years which might lie ahead before the grave?

Of course I knew that this state of mind is common among middle-aged, middle-class women whose children have gone into the world. Its causes, both psychological and physiological, are clearly understood nowadays and so is the fact that there is no remedy. What can't be cured must be endured. But Alfred's miraculous appointment might effect a miraculous cure. I had often longed to leave behind me a token of my existence, a shell on the seashore of eternity. Here was my chance; Alfred might become one of those plenipotentiaries whose names are ever remembered with gratitude and respect, and some of the credit might be mine. At the very least I would now have a little tiny place in history as one of the occupants of a famous house.

All this was rather cheerful, if high-falutin', midnight stuff. But by the early hours doubts and terrors were crowding in. I knew little enough about Paris or diplomatic life, but I did know, like everybody else, that Sir Louis and Lady Leone, whom we were to replace, held a glittering court there, reminiscent of the great embassies of olden days. Lady Leone was universally admitted to be more beautiful, charming and witty than any other woman in public life. Absurd to think that I could compete with her – how could I fill her place even adequately? Not only had I no training, not the very slightest knowledge of diplomacy, but I had certain decided disabilities. I can never remember people, for instance, either their names or their faces or anything at all about them. I am a poor housekeeper. When I first arrived in Oxford as a young bride I had resolved not to be as other dons' wives in this respect; to begin with my dinners were decidedly better than theirs. However, my dear Mrs Heathery never improved beyond a certain point, I had four hungry boys to shovel down the

vitamins and a husband who never noticed what he ate. After the end of coupons, other people's food improved, mine did not. I had never presided over a large household or had more than three servants (one of them a daily) in my life. What would the domestic side of the Embassy be like, mismanaged by me? Visiting Ministers, or worse, visiting Royalty, would complain and this would be bad for Alfred. My clothes – better to draw a veil. So, with my absent-mindedness and ghastly food and ghastly clothes I should become the Aunt Sally of diplomatic life, a butt and a joke.

I only wished I could go to sleep for a bit and forget the whole thing. Yes, a joke. I began to see myself in farcical situations. This silly habit of kissing everybody – quite new since the war. My ex-undergraduates and other men friends kiss when they see me; it has become an automatic gesture. Mental picture: a party in some official building, very pompous and grand. Out of pure distraction I kiss the President of the Republic.

I suffer from weak ankles and sometimes topple over unexpectedly. When this happens in the Turl nobody minds; I am picked up by some friendly young chap, go home and change my stockings. Mental picture: The Arc de Triomphe, military music, wreaths, television cameras. Flop, down I come, extinguishing the Eternal Flame. Now I really must wake myself up properly from these half-nightmares, undermining my morale. I stood at the window and, watching the sun's first rays as they fell upon Christ Church, I let myself get very cold. Then I went back to my warm bed, and fell into a dreamless sleep.

In the morning when I told Alfred some of these unnerving thoughts (not the kissing and falling-down ones however) he said, 'I specially didn't want you to lie in bed working yourself up, that's why I never mentioned your side of the business last night. I'm glad to say Philip is in England and I've told him to come and have luncheon with you today. You'll be able to talk it all over with him and get these worries out of your system. I must go to London for a few hours.'

'Oh, of course we shall find Philip in Paris – I'd quite forgotten he was there. I say, what a comfort!'

'Yes, and a great comfort to me, too. Meanwhile do remember that the social side is quite unimportant. As I told you last night mine is intended to be a serious mission – sobriety, security the keynotes. The *ci-devants* have had their day with the Leones, I intend to concentrate on the politicians and people of real importance. And by the way, dearest, perhaps your – shall I say – flightier relations could be discouraged from paying us too many visits?'

'Yes, darling, I quite agree. But the boys –'

'The boys! Why of course it will be their home whenever they want to come. Nice to have a healthy youthful element, which has been lacking there of late.'

This was clearly not the moment to mention my worries about Basil. Anyhow, the holidays were about to begin, when he was supposed to be leaving the crammer to work on his own in some quiet place. I decided to wait and see what happened.

Philip Cliffe-Musgrave sauntered in at one o'clock. Ten years younger than me, he was by far my favourite of all the under-graduates who had passed through our hands, so to speak. Owing to the war, he had come late to Oxford, a man, not a boy. He had, I thought, been slightly in love with me and I might easily have returned this slight love had not the example of my mother, the Bolter, for ever discouraged me from such adventures which begin so cheerfully and finish so shoddily, I had noticed. However, we had trodden the pleasant path of a loving friendship and I had remained extremely fond of him. He was an elegant creature, the best-dressed man I have ever seen, and one of those people who seem to have been born with a knowledge of the world. Alfred thought him very brilliant.

'Well,' we said now, looking at each other and laughing.

'*Madame l'Ambassadrice*. Too interesting for words. There have been the wildest rumours about Sir Louis's successor, but truth is certainly stranger than fiction. The dinners I shall be asked to when it gets out that I actually know you!'

'Philip, I'm terrified!'

'No wonder. They'll gobble you up, all those smart women. At first, that is. I think you'll defend yourself in the long run.'

'You are horrid – Alfred said you would reassure me.'

'Yes, yes, I'm only teasing.'

'Be careful – I'm in a delicate state. Such a lot of things I want to ask; where to begin? Do the Leones know?'

'That they are leaving? Oh yes.'

'I mean about us?'

'When I came away, three days ago, he had been told it was a possibility. They'll be pleased, I think. That is, it will kill her to leave the Embassy but if she has to hand it over she'd rather it were to someone like you.'

'Oh. Dreary, d'you mean?'

'Different. And above all not the wife of a colleague. You don't know what the jealousy between wives is like, in that service. As for Sir Louis, he is a typical career diplomat. He despises the amateur and is certain that Alfred will make an unholy mess of the job. This, of course, will soften the blow of leaving quite considerably.'

'Philip, do tell me – why have they chosen Alfred?'

'Up to their clever tricks, you know.'

'Now what's coming?' I said, uneasily.

'Don't be so nervous. I only mean that when the war was comfortably over, the Entente doing all right, the allies in love with each other – not the rulers but the people – everybody busy with their own internal affairs, they sent Sir Louis to captivate the French. And oh, how he succeeded – they eat out of his hand. Now that we are running into choppy seas they send Alfred to puzzle them.'

'And will he puzzle them?'

'As he does everybody. His whole career has been one long mystery if you come to consider it. What was he doing with Ernie Bevin during the war? Have you ever understood? Nobody else has. Did you know that he lunches at No. 10, alone with the P.M., at least once a week? Bet you didn't. Or that the well-informed regard him as one of those people who really govern the country?'

'Alfred is very secret,' I said reflectively. 'I often think that's why I'm so happy with him. Plate glass is such a bore.'

'I shall be very much interested to see him at work. No doubt he will keep Bouche-Bontemps and his merry men in a state of chronic perplexity which may be very useful.'

'Who is Bouche-Bontemps?'

'My poor Fanny, you'll have to mug up the political situation a bit. Surely you must have heard of him – he's the French foreign minister.'

'They change so often.'

'Yes, but there are a few old faithfuls who reappear like the soldiers in *Faust* and he is one.'

'I know about M. Mendès-France.'

'Only because he's called France. Everybody in England has heard of him because the *Daily Post* goes on about Mr France, which makes it nice and easy.'

'I know about General de Gaulle.'

'Yes, well you can forget him, for the moment at any rate.'

'To go back to the Leones. She minds leaving dreadfully?'

'All Ambassadresses mind. They are generally carried screaming from the house – *"encore un instant, M. le Bourreau"* – poor Pauline, yes, she is in despair.'

'And you'll hate to lose her?'

'Yes. I adore her. At the same time, Fanny, as it's you, I shall be on your side.'

'Need there be sides? Must we be enemies?'

'It is never otherwise. You'd better know the form. By the time you arrive she'll have had an enormous send-off at the Gare du Nord – the whole of Paris – flashlights, flowers, speeches, tears. All her world will have heard – not directly from her but by a sort of bush telegraph – what brutes you and Alfred are. I suppose I shall swim against the tide, but I shan't exhaust myself – a few languid strokes – because it will turn so quickly. The point is that, until you arrive, Parisian society will curse upon your name and wish you dead, but from the moment you set foot in the Embassy you will become entirely delightful. Soon we shall hear that the Leones never really quite *did*, in Paris.'

'How cynical you are.'

'That's life, I guess. Mind you their friends will continue to love them, give dinners for them when they go back and so on. But people are always attracted by power and high office; a house like the Embassy, to which the rulers of the earth gravitate, is worth more to its occupant than the prettiest face, the kindest heart, the oldest friendship. Come now, Fanny, you know enough of the world to know that, I suppose. In this case you are the beneficiary. Soon it will be as though Pauline had never been there – Pauline Leone. Pauline Borghese never leaves and she is on the side of the sitting tenant.'

'Why Pauline Borghese?'

'It was her house, you know. We bought it from her, furniture and all, after Waterloo.'

'Oh, dear. You haven't really reassured me very much. There's another thing, Philip – clothes. Of course there's always Elliston's Petite Boutique but it's so expensive.'

'I shouldn't worry. As soon as you arrive, you'll make an arrangement with one of the dressmakers there. Aren't you rather rich now, Fanny?'

'Richer, yes we are. My father left me quite a lot – I was surprised. But what with the boys and so on I never feel I ought to spend much on myself.'

He then told me about the running of an embassy and calmed my fears in that direction. According to him, the comptroller and the housekeeper do the work. 'You will only need a social secretary – some nice quiet girl who won't get married at once.'

'I'd thought of that. My cousin Louisa Fort William has got the very one, Jean Mackintosh.'

'Yes, I know her. Not a ball of fire, is she? By the way, whom d'you think I saw at a cocktail party last night? Lord Alconleigh.'

'No! Do tell me what he was doing?'

'He was standing with his back to the wall, a large glass of water in his hand, glaring furiously into space. The rest of the company was huddled together, rather like a herd of deer with an old lion in the offing. It was impressive – not altogether cosy, you know.'

Alfred's appointment was well received by the responsible newspapers, partly no doubt because many of their employees had been at Oxford and known him there. It was violently opposed by the *Daily Post*. This little paper, once considered suitable for schoolroom reading, had been bought by a press peer known to the world as Old Grumpy and now reflected his jaundiced view of life. It fed on scandal, grief and all forms of human misery, exposing them with a sort of spiteful glee which the public evidently relished, since the more cruelly the *Daily Post* tortured its victims the higher the circulation rose. Its policy, if it could be said to have one, was to be against foreign countries, cultural bodies, and the existing government, whether Conservative or Labour. Above all, it abominated the Foreign Office. The burden of its song on this occasion was, what is the point of maintaining an expensive foreign service which cannot produce a trained man to be Ambassador in Paris but has to fall back on a Professor of Pastoral Theology.

The French papers were perfectly friendly, if puzzled. The *Figaro* produced a leading article by a member of the Académie Française in which the word pastoral was wilfully misunderstood and theology left out altogether. The Knight on horseback (Alfred) coming to the Shepherdess in her orchard (Marianne) was the theme. No mention of the Knight's wife and boys (Alfred was a Knight now; he had been to London and seen the Queen).

I received many letters of congratulation, praising Alfred, praising me, saying how well we were suited to the work we should have to do and then going on to speak of some child or friend or protégé of the writer's who would like to join our establishment in almost any capacity. Louisa Fort William, ever practical, cut out the praise and offered me Jean. Alfred knew this Jean, who had been up at Oxford, and did not include her among my flightier relations. With his approval I wrote and engaged her to be our social secretary.

At Oxford, Alfred's colleagues and their wives took but little account of our news. This was no surprise to me. Nobody who has not lived in a university town can have any idea of its remoteness from the world. The dons live like monks in a cloister, outside time and space, occupied only with the daily round; ambassadors to Paris do not enter their ken or interest them in the very least. To be Warden or Dean would seem to them a far greater thing. At this time, it is true, there were some rich, worldly dons whose wives dressed at Dior, and who knew about Paris and embassies, a tiny minority on the fringe of the University – in every way; they did not even live in the town itself as we did. They regarded Alfred as a bore; he disregarded them; their wives disregarded me. These Dior dons were not pleased by our appointment; they laughed long and loud, as kind friends informed us, at the idea of it and made witty jokes at our expense. No doubt they thought the honour would sit better upon them; how I agreed with them, really!

After twenty-five years of university life my outlook was more akin to that of the monkish than to the Dior type of don, but, though I had little first-hand experience of the world, I did know what it was. My cousin Linda had been in contact with it and my mother had always been of it, even during her wildest vagaries. Lady Montdore, though she saw real life through distorting glasses, had had the world and its usage at her fingertips; I had not been a sort of lady-in-waiting to her for nothing. How I wished she were still alive to see what fate had brought to me – like the Dior dons she would have mocked and disapproved but unlike them she would have been rather impressed, no doubt.

Our summer holidays passed as usual. Alfred and I went to stay with Davey Warbeck, in Kent, and paid one or two other visits. Our youngest boys, Charlie and Fabrice, were hardly with us at all. They were invited by a boy called Sigismond de Valhubert, who was at their house at Eton, to stay in Provence, after which all three went shooting in Scotland. Bearded David sent postcards from the Lakes – he was on a walking tour. As for Basil, he might have been dead for all I knew; I weakly told Alfred that he had gone to Barcelona to rub up his Spanish. Very soon we came to the last days of August and of our monotonous but familiar Oxford life.

3

I shall never forget my first impression of the Embassy. After the hurly-burly of our reception at the Gare du Nord, after the drive through Paris traffic which always unnerves those not accustomed to it, the large, beautiful, honey-coloured house, in its quiet court-yard, seemed a haven of delight. It has more the atmosphere of a country than a town house. For one thing, no town noises can be heard, only the rustle of leaves, the twittering of birds, an occasional mowing-machine, an owl. The French windows on the garden side fill the rooms with sunshine and air in amazing quantities. They open to a vista of trees; the only solid edifice in sight is the dome of the Invalides, a purple shadow on the horizon, hardly visible through summer leaves. Except for that and the Eiffel Tower, on the extreme right hand of this prospect, there is nothing to show that the house is situated in the centre of the most prosperous and busy capital on the continent of Europe. Philip took us straight up to the first floor. At the top of the fine staircase there is an ante-chamber leading to the yellow drawing-room, the white and gold drawing-room, the green drawing-room (to be our private sitting-room) and Pauline Borghese's bedroom, so recently vacated by the other Pauline. These rooms all face south and open into each other. Behind them, looking north over the courtyard, are the Ambas-sador's dressing-room and library and the social secretary's office. Well-wishers had filled the house with flowers; they made it look very beautiful, glowing in the evening light, and also reassured me. Many people seemed prepared, at any rate, to like us.

I believe it would have been normal for me to have paid a visit to the outgoing ambassadress soon after our appointment was announced. However, the said ambassadress had set up such an uninhibited wail when she knew she was to leave, proclaiming her misery to all and sundry and refusing so furiously to look on the bright side (a happy and respected old age in a Kensington flat), that it was felt she might not be very nice to me. Her attitude seemed rather exaggerated until I saw what it was that we were usurping; then I understood. Lady Leone had reigned in this palace – the word reign is not too much, with her beauty, elegance and great funniness she had been like a Queen here – for five whole years; no wonder she left it all with death in her heart.

As for me, my fears fell away and so did my middle-aged gloom. The house seemed to be on my side; from the very first moment I set foot in it I was stimulated, interested, amused and ready for anything. When I woke up next morning to find myself in Pauline's bed, the bed of both the Paulines, opening my eyes on the dark red walls and mahogany furniture, a curious contrast to the light gaiety of the rest of the house, I thought, 'This is the first day, the beginning.' Then I wondered how I should feel on the last day, the end. I was deeply sorry for Lady Leone.

Alfred appeared, in high spirits. He was going to have breakfast in his library. 'Philip will come and talk to you while you have yours. He says you must never get up too early. You'll have a tiring life here; try and be quiet in the morning.' He dumped a lot of papers on my bed and went off. There was nothing much about us in them – a small flashlight photograph in the *Figaro* – an announcement in *The Times* that we had arrived – until, at the bottom of the heap, I came to the *Daily Post*. The whole of the front page was covered with an enormous photograph of Alfred, mouth idiotically open, apparently giving the Hitler salute. My heart sank; horrified I read:

The mission of the former Pastoral Theologian, Sir Alfred Wincham, to Paris has begun with an unfortunate incident. As M. Bouche-Bontemps, who had interrupted his holiday to meet Sir Alfred at the Gare du Nord, came forward with a gesture of welcome, our envoy rudely brushed him aside and confabulated, at length, IN GERMAN, with a tall fair young man in the crowd . . .

I looked up from the paper. Philip was standing by my bed, laughing.

'Is this all right? One always used to see Pauline before she got up – it seemed a good moment.'

'Oh dear,' I said, 'you'll miss that lovely face under the baldaquin.'

'This is different,' he sat down on the end of the bed, 'and in some ways nicer. So, I see you've got to the incident.'

'Philip!'

'Don't say it has upset you. It's nothing to what there will be – the *Daily Post* man here, Amyas Mockbar (you mustn't forget that name), is preparing the full treatment for you; you're on Old Grumpy's black list.'

'But why are we?'

'The English Ambassador here always is; besides, Lord Grumpy personally dislikes Alfred, who seems unaware of his existence.'

'He is unaware. There's one blessing, Alfred only reads *The Times* and I shan't mind what the *Daily Post* says.'

'Don't you be too sure. Mockbar has a wonderful knack of making people mind. I've had to give up seeing him and I mind that – he's such a jolly old bird, there's nothing more enjoyable than drinking whisky with old Amyas at the Pont Royal bar.'

'But this incident,' I said.

'You see, you are minding already.'

'Yes, because it's entirely invented.'

'Not entirely – he never entirely invents, that's where he's so devilish.'

'Alfred talked to a German at the Gare du Nord?'

'While you were being introduced to Mme Hué, Alfred spied poor old Dr Wolff of Trinity peering at him under the arc lights. Of course, being Alfred, he darted off – then he came straight back and explained the whole thing to Bouche-Bontemps. The incident was of no consequence, but it wasn't entirely invented.'

'But Dr Wolff isn't a tall, fair, young German – he's a tiny little old dark one.'

'Mockbar never sees things quite like other people, his style is strictly subjective; you'll have to get used to it.'

'Yes, I see.'

'There are a lot of things you'll have to get used to here, but I think he is the worst. What have you done about a social secretary?'

'I've got Jean Mackintosh coming next week. I wanted to settle myself in first and Alfred thought you'd lend me a hand until then, though I know you are far too important.'

'Certainly I will. It amuses me and I can help you as I know the form. There's no other work at present – total lull on the international front and all the ministers are away. Bouche-Bontemps is off again tomorrow. So let's get down to it. First, here's a list of the people who have sent flowers; you'll want to thank them yourself. Then Alfred thought you had better see the arrangements for this week – rather hectic, I'm afraid. You have to polish off the colleagues – visit them, you know – and there are eighty embassies here so it takes a bit of doing.'

'Are there so many countries in the world?'

'Of course not – the whole thing is great nonsense – but we have to keep up the fiction to please the Americans. There's nothing the millionaires like so much as being ambassadors; at present there are eighty of them, keenly subscribing to party funds. We have to tag along. In small countries like the Channel Islands practically all the male adults are ambassadors, nowadays.'

I was looking at the list of names he had given me. 'I only know one of the people who have sent flowers – Grace de Valhubert.'

'She's still away,' said Philip. 'How do you know her?'

'Her boy and my two are friends at school. They've just been staying down in Provence with her. If they have kindly said they will come here for Christmas it's chiefly on account of Sigismond.'

'Sweet Sigi, fascinating child,' said Philip with a good deal of feeling. 'I may as well tell you, Fanny, since we are such old friends and anyhow you're sure to find out, that I'm in love with Grace.'

I felt a small, stupid pang when he said this. No doubt I would selfishly have preferred him to concentrate on me, as he used to when he was at Oxford.

'With what result?'

He said bitterly, 'Oh, she keeps me hanging about. She probably rather likes to show her husband, whom she is madly in love with, that somebody is madly in love with her.'

'Silly old love,' I said, 'bother it. Let's go on with the list. Who is Mrs Jungfleisch?'

'Mildred *Young fleesh*. The Americans have begun to copy our tiresome habit of not pronouncing names as they are spelt. She says you know her.'

'Really? But I never remember –'

'Nor you do. She's always going to Oxford so I expect you have met her.'

'With the Dior dons probably, though I hardly ever see them – not their cup of tea at all.'

'I suppose not.'

'There, you see yourself how I'm not. So how shall I manage here where people are twice as frightening?'

'Now – now!'

'Mrs Jungfleisch is a *femme du monde*, I suppose?'

'Yes, indeed. I've known her for years – we went to the same charm school in New York when I was with U.N.O.'

'You went to a charm school? I always thought you were charm personified!'

'Thank you. Mildred and I went to see if we couldn't pick up a little extra warmth of manner, but as you so kindly suggest we found we were too advanced for the course.'

'The person who needs it is me.'

'Wouldn't be any good to you, because of not remembering who people are. A memory for names and faces is the A.B.C. of charm, it's all built up on the pleased-to-see-you formula, but you must show that you know who it is you're being pleased to see.'

'I know so few Americans,' I said. 'Do you like them, Philip?'

'Yes, I'm paid to.'

'In your heart of hearts?'

'Oh, poor things, you can't dislike them. I feel intensely sorry for them, especially the ones in America – they are so mad and ill and frightened.'

'Shall we see a lot of them here? – I suppose so. Alfred has been told he must collaborate.'

'You can't avoid it, the place teems with them.'

'Any friendly ones?'

'Friendly? They make you long for an enemy. You'll like some of them though. They fall into three categories, the ones here. There are the business men trying to make a better position for themselves at home as experts on Yurrup. They are afraid there may be a boom in Yurrup. Of course they don't want to miss anything if there is. For instance, there's the art market – all these old antique objects to marry up to the dollar. (Art is booming so they love it, they even call their children it.) There are dollars in music too – Schu and Schu can be quite as profitable as Tel and Tel. Art and music are only to be found in Yurrup; they come over prospecting for them – at the same time they don't want to be left out of things at home, so they play an uneasy game of musical chairs between Yurrup and the States, hurtling to and fro in rockets, getting iller and madder and more frightened than ever.'

'Frightened of what?'

'Oh, somebody else being in on something first; falling down dead; a recession – I don't know, dreadfully fidgety. Then there are literally thousands of officials who are paid to be here. One never sees them, except for a few diplomatic colleagues. They are dreadfully unhappy; they huddle together in a sort of ghetto – terrified of losing their American accent.'

'What a funny thing to mind losing.'

'It would be ghastly for them if they did. They'd be branded for ever as un-American. Finally we have the Henry James type of expatriates who live here because they can't stick it at home – perfect dears. A bit on the serious side perhaps, but at least they don't jabber on about art and dollars – it's the future of mankind

27

with them. Mildred is in that camp – camp commandant you might say.'

'Shall I like her?'

'You won't get the chance. She adores Pauline and is preparing to be very cold and correct with you.'

'Then why does she send me flowers?'

'It's an American tic. They can't help doing it – they send them to friend and foe alike. Whenever they pass a flower shop their fingers itch for a pen to write down somebody's name and address.'

'I'm all for it,' I said, looking at the Jungfleisch sweet-peas on my dressing-table. 'Lovely, they are –'

After a few days in the Embassy I began to suspect that something was afoot. Of course in a new house one cannot account for every sight and sound; even allowing for this I sensed a mystery. From my bedroom I distinctly heard a gathering of people making merry, some sort of party which went on every evening until the early hours; I would wake up in the night to shriek upon shriek of laughter. I thought the noise must come from the next house until I discovered that this is a block of offices belonging to the American government. Surely their employees did not laugh all night? By my bed there was a telephone with a line direct to the public exchange, not through the Embassy, and a discreet little buzzing bell. This sometimes rang and when I answered it I would hear confused phrases like 'Oh Lord – I forgot', 'C'est toi, chérie? Oh pardon, Madame, il y a erreur' – or merely 'Aïe!' before the line went dead. Twice Alfred's *Times* arrived late with the crossword puzzle already done.

The courtyard always seemed to be full of elegantly dressed people. I presumed they had come to write their names in our book (whose pages, according to Alfred, read like a dramatis personae of the whole history of France). Why, then, were they so often grouped on the little outside staircase in the south-west corner of the courtyard? I could have sworn that I saw the same ones over and over again, people with famous faces known even to me; a bejewelled dressmaker like a puppet in a film cartoon, face composed of brown golf balls; a Field-Marshal; a pianist with a guilty look; an ex-king. A pretty young woman, vaguely familiar to me, seemed to live in the courtyard, constantly up and down the little staircase with flowers, books, or gramophone records; sometimes she was carrying a huge picnic basket. Catching my eye one day she blushed and looked away. Mockbar, whom I had now met, was often in the Faubourg peering through our gateway. No mistaking him; he had the bucolic appearance of some little old groom, weather-beaten face, curved back, stiff bandy legs, wildly flailing elbows and an aureole of fuzzy grey hair.

'I wonder if you would like to make a statement?' he said, rolling towards me as I was walking home from the dressmaker one afternoon.

'Statement?'

'On the situation in your house.'

'Oh you are kind, but no, thank you very much, you must ask my husband.' I went indoors and sent for Philip.

'Philip,' I said, 'I'm a paper. Would you like to make a statement?'

'Statement?'

'On the situation in my house.'

He gave me a whimsical look, half-amused, half-worried.

'Who has the rooms on the right-hand side of the courtyard – did I see them when you showed me round?'

'Yes, it's time you knew,' he said. 'The fact is, Pauline has dug herself in there and we can't get her to leave.'

'Lady Leone? But she did leave. I saw her on a newsreel, in floods. How can she still be here?'

'She left the Gare du Nord all right, but she had the train stopped at Orry-la-Ville and came straight back, still holding Bouche-Bontemps' roses. She said she was very ill, possibly dying, and forced Mrs Trott to make the bed in the entresol for her. There's a sort of little flat where the social secretary used to live. Naturally she's not ill in the least. She has the whole of Paris in there day and night – I wonder you haven't heard them.'

'I have. I thought it was the Americans next door.'

'Americans never shriek like that.'

'Now I understand everything. But Philip, this is very bad for Alfred. Such an absurd situation, at the beginning of his mission.'

'That's what the F.O. thinks. They tell us to get her out – yes, but how? I've just been on to Ashley again. You see, at the beginning one thought it was a lark – that in a day or two she'd get tired of it. So the idea was not to bother you. But now the Parisians have joined in the joke and it's the fashion to go and see her there. People are pouring back from their holidays so as not to be left out. The smart resorts are in despair – nobody left to be photographed on the beaches. So, of course, she's having the time of her life and quite honestly I don't see how we shall ever induce her to go. We're all at our wits' end.'

'Can't we tell the servants not to feed her?'

'They don't. Mildred brings her food, like a raven.'

'The one with picnic basket? We could stop her coming – tell the concierge not to let her in?'

'Very difficult – it would be awfully embarrassing for him to have to bar the way. He's known her for years.'

'Yes, I see, and of course we can't very well kidnap her. Then could we bribe her? What does she like best in the world?'

'English top policy makers.'

'What, M.P.s and things?'

'Ministers, bankers, the Archbishop, Master of the Belvoir, editor of *The Times* and so on. She likes to think she is seeing history on the boil.'

'Well, that's rather splendid. Surely these policy makers must be on our side? Why don't they lure her to England – luncheon at Downing Street or a place for the big debate on Thursday?'

'I see you don't understand the point of Mildred. They worship her in the House – they can hardly bear to have a debate at all until she's in her place there. She's the best audience they've ever had. As for luncheon at Downing Street, why, she stays there when she's in London.'

'Oh, bother – !'

'And now I come to think of it, she isn't really the clue to our problem.'

'You said she brought the food.'

'I know. Food means nothing to Pauline.'

'Still, she can't live without it.'

'The point is, she can. She's for ever going off to Tring for the starvation cure. It's a mystery to me, this starving. People on rafts begin eating each other after a week; Pauline and Mildred are sometimes at Tring for a whole month – not a nibble out of each other's shoulders.'

'Oh dear, we don't want her here for another month. Surely the policy makers must stand by their employees, Philip, and lend a hand? Have you spoken to any of them?'

'They are doing what they can. The P.M. had a word with Sir Louis at Brooks's last night. No good at all. Sir Louis just sat with his hand over his nose heaving with giggles in that endearing way he has,' said Philip affectionately. 'But after all, what can he do? Apart from the fact that it amuses him to death –'

'Some important person ought to come over and see her – tell her she's being unpatriotic and so on. She is, too.'

'We've tried that. Moley came between two aeroplanes. He arrived very strict, but he didn't keep it up. He said she lay there like a beautiful stag dying in the forest, and he hadn't the heart to be cross.'

'Why do you think she's doing it?'

'Oh, I don't think there's any very profound reason – it amuses her – she's got nothing else to do – and if it teases you she can easily bear that. She thinks Alfred got the job by plotting against Sir Louis.'

'You know he didn't.'

'Didn't he? In any case, Sir Louis wouldn't have stayed on – it was time for a change.'

'I saw Mockbar in the street.'

'He'll go to town on it all right.'

'Has he seen Lady Leone?'

'Certainly not. Even Pauline draws the line somewhere.'

'We shall have to tell Alfred before Mockbar's piece appears.'

'He knows. It's he who has been saying don't tell Fanny.'

Distant, derisive laughter assailed my ear. The evening was drawing on; the entresol was waking up. I felt quite furious.

'How is the Quai d'Orsay taking it?'

'Thrilled. Hughie has given out that no wives are to join in, but I'm not sure I didn't see –'

'Who is Hughie?'

'Jacques-Olivier Hué, head of the protocol. Always known as Hughie.'

I was getting more irritated every minute. I have a sense of humour, I hope; this situation was clearly very funny; it was maddening not to be able to join in such a good joke, to be on the stuffy, official side against all these jolly bandits. I said, spitefully, 'As far as Alfred can make out, your friend Sir Louis simply lived for pleasure when he was here.'

'Ambassadors always go on like that about each other,' said Philip. 'One's predecessor is idle and one's successor is an intriguer. It's a classic of the service. But Sir Louis was an excellent ambassador, make no mistake about it.'

'Oh all right,' I said. 'Let's try and keep our tempers. If we think it over calmly there must be a solution.'

A long silence fell between us. At last I said, 'I'm going to speak to Mrs Jungfleisch.'

'You can now if you want to – she's sitting in her car in the courtyard, reading the New Deal.'

'Why isn't she in there shrieking with the others?'

'I tell you, she's a very serious girl – she puts aside certain hours every day for historical study. Besides she says the room is too hot – twenty people in that tiny room on a day like this – it must be the Black Hole of Calcutta.'

'Then why not go home and read the New Deal there?'

'She likes to be in on things.'

'The cheek of it!' I said.

I stumped out into the courtyard, opened the door of Mrs Jungfleisch's Buick and boldly got in beside her. She was very fair and pretty with a choir-boy look, accentuated by the big, white, pleated collar she wore and straight hair done with a fringe. She turned her calm, intelligent blue eyes upon me, put down a document she was reading and said, 'How d'you do? I am Mildred Jungfleisch. We did meet, ages ago, at Oxford.'

I was agreeably surprised by her voice which was not very American, rather more like that of an Englishwoman who has once lived in the United States. Although I knew about the charm school prospectus being too elementary for her and guessed that this was the fully qualified charmer's voice, specially warm, for soothing an irate ambassadress in the grounds of her own embassy, it worked. Feeling decidedly soothed, I said: 'Please excuse me for getting into your motor without an invitation.'

'Please excuse me for sitting in your courtyard without an invitation.'

'I want to talk to you.'

'I'm sure you must, Lady Wincham. It's about Pauline, of course?'

'Yes – how long do you think she intends to stay?'

'Pauline is utterly unpredictable. She will leave when she feels inclined to. Knowing her as I do, I guess she'll still be here at Christmas.'

'With you still feeding her?'

'I'm afraid so.'

'If my husband were a private person, none of this would matter. As things are, I intend to get rid of Lady Leone.'

'How?'

'I don't know.'

'In my experience of Pauline it is impossible to deflect her from her purpose.'

'Aha! She has a purpose?'

'Please do not misunderstand me, Lady Wincham. Her purpose

is a simple one, she wants to have a good time. She has no desire to upset you, still less to damage the embassy or embarrass the Foreign Office. It all began because she had a sudden impulse to stop the train at Orry-la-Ville and spend one last night in this house which she worships – you can have no idea what she feels about it.'

'I quite understand, on the contrary. People do get like that about houses and this one is so very extraordinary.'

'You are under the spell already! Then she found she was having fun. She rang up a few friends, for a joke; they came around. It started to be the thing to do; one signs your book and then one goes in to see Pauline. Excuse me, please, there's the Nuncio – I think he's looking for her door.'

She got out of the motor, put the prelate on his way and came back again.

'Philip tells me that you are a very responsible person,' I said. 'Couldn't you explain to her that if she goes on like this she will undo all the good she and Sir Louis have done during their brilliant embassy?'

The honest choir-boy eyes opened wide. 'Indeed, Lady Wincham, I have told her. I've even pointed out that only one person, in the end, can reap an advantage from her action.'

'And who is that?'

'Why, Mr Khrushchev.'

I felt this was going rather far; still it was all on the right side.

'Unfortunately Pauline has no public conscience whatever. I find many European women are like that. They do not give a thought to the great issues of our time, such as the delicate balance of East and West – they will not raise a finger to ease the path of N.A.T.O., U.N.E.S.C.O., O.E.E.C. or the World Bank. Pauline is frankly not interested.'

'So there's nothing you can do?'

'Regretfully, no.'

'All right,' I said, 'I may look rather mousy but I must tell you that I very often get my own way. Good-bye.'

'Good-bye, Lady Wincham. Awfully nice to have seen you.'

4

'We must send for Davey,' I said.

This uncle of mine by marriage had long filled the same role in our family as the Duke of Wellington in that of Queen Victoria. Whenever some apparently insuperable difficulty of a worldly nature arose, one consulted him. While Alfred and I had been staying with him, we had of course talked of little else than our appointment and Davey had urged me not to forget that he understood the French. He had once lived in Paris (some forty years ago), had frequented salons and been the darling of the hostesses. He understood them. He had never liked them much, 'cross, clever things', and indeed, before the Nazis had taken over, during the decadent days of the Weimar Republic, he had greatly preferred the Germans. It was a question of shared interests; his two chief ones, health and music, were catered for better in Germany. As soon as the healthy, musical race began to show other pre-occupations, Davey left Berlin and all the delightful Bads he was so fond of and which did him so much good, never to return. He always said thereafter that he did not understand the Germans. But he continued to understand the French.

I don't know what magic wand I expected him to wave, since Lady Leone and Mrs Jungfleisch were not French and he had never claimed to understand them. True, he was a childhood friend of Lady Leone's but that was no reason why he should prove more persuasive than the head of the Foreign Office. It would, however, be a comfort to have him with me as I felt sure he would be on my side, more sure than I was about Philip whose loyalties must, in the nature of things, be rather divided. After my talk with Mrs Jungfleisch I had a long discussion with Alfred as a result of which I telephoned there and then to Davey.

'It's an S.O.S.,' I said. 'I'll explain when I see you.'

'You have run into storms,' said Davey, hardly bothering to conceal his glee, 'even sooner than I had expected. I'll let you know as soon as I've got a place on an aeroplane.'

The next morning, one read in Mockbar's page:

DUKES

Four French Dukes, three ex-Ministers, nine Rothschilds, and countless Countesses crossed the courtyard of the British Embassy yesterday evening. Were they going to pay their respects to our envoy, Sir Alfred Wincham? They were not.

ALONE

The former Pastoral Theologian and Lady Wincham sat alone in the great suite of reception rooms on the first floor, waiting for callers who never came. The cream of Parisian society, meanwhile, was packed into a tiny room off their back staircase.

TWO AMBASSADRESSES

It is no secret to anybody here that an unexpected and awkward situation exists at the Embassy where we now seem to have one ambassador and two ambassadresses. Lady Leone, wife of the last envoy, is still living there. Lady Wincham, though a woman of charm, cannot compete with her brilliant predecessor; she is left out in the cold. The Corps Diplomatique is wondering what the upshot will be.

I went to Orly to meet Davey. Although he was now past the middle sixties, his appearance had hardly changed since the day, nearly thirty years ago, when I first saw him with my sharp little girl's eyes at Alconleigh looking, as I thought, unlike a captain and unlike a husband. (On the second count, at any rate, I had been completely wrong. Nobody ever had a happier marriage than my dear Aunt Emily.) If his face had become rather like a portrait by Soutine of that other younger face, his figure was perfect. Elegant and supple, waving the *Daily Post*, he darted out of the group of arrivals from London. 'A pretty kettle of fish!' he cried cheerfully. 'Must see my luggage through the customs – wait for me in the motor.'

Then, getting in beside me, he said, 'Mind you, it's not a new situation, far from it. Lady Pickle kept the key of the Embassy garden in Rome and gave a garden party there weeks after the Betteridges had arrived. Sir George looked out of the window and saw her receiving the whole of the Embassy black list. Lady Praed opened a junk shop in the Faubourg here and nabbed people as they were going into the Embassy. Lady Pike went back to Vienna and then I seem to think she lived in a tree like a bird. English ambassadresses are usually on the dotty side and leaving their embassies drives them completely off their rockers. Alfred's statement is out in the evening papers – perfect, very dignified.' Alfred had said that Lady Leone not being well enough to travel, he was, of course, delighted to lend her the secretary's flat until she was better. 'You needn't worry, Fanny, the sitting ambassador holds all the cards – he can't help winning in the end.'

'If he doesn't win soon it may be the end,' I said.

'Yes, it's time she went. I lunched at Boodle's just now – Alfred's enemies are beginning to crow – you may imagine. *Daily Post* in great demand there.'

'We utterly count on you, Davey.'

'Quite right. As soon as we get back I must have a very strong cocktail and then I'll go straight to Pauline.'

'Good,' I said. 'I've got an ambassadress from some invented country (the real ones are all away still) coming to call on me at six. That fits in very well and we'll see you at dinner.'

As I sat with a little rat of a woman in black velvet with jet sleeves (dressed for the *thé dansant* I thought until I remembered what an old-fashioned notion that was), I heard the usual irritating sounds of distant laughter, punctuated now by Davey's well-known and rather specially piercing shriek. He was evidently enjoying himself. I found it even more difficult than usual to concentrate on the *thé dansant* lady's domestic problems. 'The Americans get them all because they don't mind what they pay.'

Davey reappeared in a black tie, at dinner-time.

'Nobody to meet me?' he said, seeing three cocktail glasses only. 'I thought you would be tired after the journey.'

'Now that I've got this extra kidney I'm never tired. No matter.'

'Whom would you like to see – anybody special? A lot of people are still away but Philip could find somebody for tomorrow, I expect, and of course, Davey, you must ask your own friends while you're here.'

'Well, tomorrow –' a little shade of embarrassment perhaps – 'I said I'd take pot luck with Pauline.'

'Don't tell me poor Mrs Jungfleisch has got to stagger here with a pot for a whole dinner party now?'

'Only for Pauline and me. The others will dine at home and look in after.'

'Perhaps you'd like my chef to send something up?' I said, sarcastically.

'Now, Fanny, don't be cross and suspicious. This is only a little exploratory operation – if I'm to effect a cure I must know all about the case, mustn't I?'

'Mm. Who was there?'

'They came and went – awfully elegant and pretty and funny, one must hand them that. I'd forgotten about French clothes being so different. They think it was very brave of you to beard Mrs Jungfleisch in her own motor.'

'She was in my own courtyard. Do they talk about me?' I said, not best pleased.

'My dear, you are topic A. They know absolutely everything you do, which dressmaker you've got an arrangement with, what the arrangement is, what clothes you have ordered ("*ça, alors!*"), what impression Alfred makes at the Quai ("*évidemment ce n'est pas Sire Louis*") and so on. When they heard I was your uncle they were all over me. Thought to be a new feather in Pauline's cap,

getting somebody who is actually staying with you and a relation to boot. By the way, Philip Cliffe-Musgrave – I suppose he is on your side? If you ask me he has been in communication with the enemy.'

'That's inevitable under the circumstances.' Alfred now appeared and we went in to dinner.

The next morning was spent trying to get in touch with Davey's Paris friends of olden times. He had lost his foreign address book, it seemed. I sent for Philip to assist; he looked carefully at the names but said he had never heard of any of them in spite of having had four years of intensive social life all over France. None of them were in the telephone book. 'That doesn't mean anything,' said Philip, 'you wouldn't believe how many people here aren't. There is the pneumatique, you see, for urgent messages.'

He and Davey sat on my bed surrounded by books of reference. 'To begin with,' said Philip, 'we'd better consult Katie.' Katie was Miss Freeman of the Embassy telephone exchange, a great dear, soon to become a key figure in our lives. He took my telephone and said, 'Have a look at your list, Katie, will you, see if you've got any of these people and ring me back.' He read out the names of Davey's friends. A few minutes later the bell rang and Philip answered. 'None? Not even on G.P.O.? Thanks, Katie.'

'What is G.P.O.?' I asked.

'Garden Party Only. It runs into thousands. If they're not on that it means they've never set foot here. Now we must start on these directories.'

At this point Davey took his list back and jettisoned several mysterious figures, saying he had not really known them so very well or even liked them so very much. He could die happy without having seen them again. But he absolutely clung to three who must be found at all costs. They were a Marquis, an Academician and a doctor. We began with the Marquis who was neither in the *Bottin Mondain* nor the *Cahiers Noirs de la Fausse Noblesse* nor the *Dictionnaire des Contemporains*. Two fellow Marquises whom

Philip rang up had never heard of him (though they said of course the name was that of a famous family) nor had George at the Ritz bar.

'What are his hobbies?' said Philip.

'He used to be the greatest living expert on Russian genealogies.'

'Try Père Lachaise,' said Philip.

'Not at all, he's quite alive, he sent me a *faire part* of his grand-daughter's marriage just the other day.'

'What address on the *faire part*?'

'I lost it. I can only remember the church – St François Xavier.'

Philip rang up the Curé of St François who gave him an address in Picardy. A telegram was duly dispatched there.

'That's one,' said Philip. 'Now, what about this alleged Academician?'

'Do you mean to say his name means nothing to you?'

'No, and furthermore I'll take a huge bet he's not in the Académie Française. I know those old Forty by heart and oh how I despise them. There they are, supposed to be looking after the language, do they ever raise a finger to check ghastly misuses of it? The French wireless has started talking about Bourguiba Junior – Junior – I ask you – why not Bourguiba Fils?'

'That's awful, but what could the Forty do?'

'Make a fuss. Their prestige is enormous. But they don't care a bit. Anyway, as I was saying –'

'But I've got a photograph of him in his uniform – I sent a pound to help buy his sword – I know he is a member.'

'What's his subject?'

'He's the greatest living expert on Mauretanian script.'

'Aha!' said Philip. 'Then he'll be of the Académie des Inscriptions. English people always forget there are five academies under the same cupola and mix them up.'

Davey was displeased at being thus lumped together with ignorant English people but Philip was quite right. A pneumatique was sent off to the Institut de France.

As for the doctor, he seemed to have found the perfect hideout.

'Docteur Lecœur,' said Davey impatiently, 'the greatest living expert on the *vésicule bilière*.'

I asked what that was. 'It's a French disease we don't have in England,' said Philip, rather too spry.

Davey shot him a look of great dislike. 'It's not a disease at all, it's a part of the body. We all have it. You ought to see the stones that came out of mine.'

Philip giggled annoyingly. He then rang up several famous doctors and the École de Médecine; nobody had ever heard of this greatest living expert.

'He used to live in the rue Neuve des Petits Champs.'

'Doesn't exist any more.'

'Pulled down? Those lovely houses?'

'Not yet, thank goodness. Only rechristened.'

'Oh, it is too bad. What about the "Ballad of Bouillabaisse"?

> "A street there is in Paris famous
> For which no rhyme our language yields,
> Rue Neuve des Petits Champs its name is,
> The New Street of the Little Fields."

How cruel to give it a new name. The Academicians might well have protested about that.'

'Not they!'

'I wonder if Docteur Lecœur isn't still there? D'you know, I think I'll go round and see – I must have a little walk anyhow. Where is the best chemist?'

He went off in slight dudgeon. Philip said, 'The English so often have these unknown French friends, I've noticed. Collaborators one and all, mark my words. And talking of that, has it occurred to you that your uncle isn't perfectly sound? He seems to be keenly fratting with Pauline in her entresol.'

'The only person in Paris who isn't is me,' I said. 'I'm feeling thoroughly out of it.'

Philip looked guilty. 'Oh well,' he said, 'that's the whole

morning wasted. How thankful I shall be when Miss Mackintosh arrives.'

I was sorry that he and Davey were not quite hitting it off. I never saw my uncle again all day. Alfred and I had to lunch with the American Ambassador, who was passing through Paris between two holidays, and my evening was again taken up with ambassadresses from improbable lands which I could certainly not have pin-pointed on a globe; as I discussed the disappearance of the genus footman with them I again heard those shrieks which undoubtedly meant that Davey was keenly fratting in the entresol. I began to be very downhearted indeed.

To add to my trials, the morning post brought news that good, clever, plain Jean Mackintosh, not attractive to men, unlikely to get married, whose sensible support was going to facilitate my task in such a variety of ways, was now not coming. She had married, suddenly, not sensibly at all, a member of the Chelsea Set; Louisa wrote to tell me this news, evidently thinking herself more to be pitied than I was.

'Her godmother left her £4,000 and a tiara. It seems this Chelsea setter is always marrying or deed-polling people for little things like that. Oh Fanny!'

Jean, I knew, was her favourite child. She ended up a perfect wail of despair: 'PS. I am sending you Northey instead but it won't be the same.'

I had a feeling it would not be at all the same. I racked my brains to remember what I could about Northey, whom I had not seen since the early days of the war when Louisa and I were living at Alconleigh with our babies. A flaxen-haired toddler, she used to be brought to the drawing-room at tea-time and made to sing loud, tuneless songs, 'S'all I be p'etty, s'all I be rit?' We all thought her tremendously sweet. Louisa once told me that she was conceived in the Great Northern Hotel – hence her curious name. My children knew her well as they often stayed with the Fort Williams in Scotland; I seemed to have noticed that their verdict was rather scornful. 'Northey is old-fashioned.' 'Northey, brimming as usual.'

'Brimming?'

'Yes, her eyes are always brimming over with tears.'

'What about?'

'Everything.'

Basil could have given me an account of her, he was good at describing people. Naughty Baz, in Spain, in Spain. I had at last received a sheet of paper from him, dirty and crumpled, having spent many a week in a trouser pocket, with a Barcelona postmark, on which was written, 'I shan't be able to lunch Saturday, all news when we meet. Love from Baz.'

I wondered if I should not do well to put off this Northey, in spite of the fact that I had no other candidate and was beginning to feel the need of a secretary. Then my eye fell on the envelope of Louisa's letter and I saw that she had scribbled something almost illegible on the back of it, by which I understood that the child was already on her way, in a cattle boat going from Glasgow via I couldn't read what.

'Good luck to her,' said Philip, when I told him this. 'What time do you think your uncle left the entresol last night?' he added sourly.

'About half past three,' I said. 'I heard them. Mrs Jungfleisch brought champagne, by the sound of it.'

'I've been talking to Mildred, she says it was absolutely hilarious – Pauline and Mr Warbeck are wonderful together, telling tales of the 1920s. If I were you I should put a stop to all this, it's only prolonging the agony. Mildred says Pauline, who had been getting rather bored, has taken on a new lease of life.'

'We must give him time, Philip. He's only been here two days – I'm sure he'll fix it in the end, he is so clever.'

'Hm – I feel very doubtful.'

So, in my heart of hearts, did I.

Davey now appeared, bright and bustling, not at all like a man in the late sixties who had been up until half past three. 'Sorry I'm late. Docteur Lecœur has just been round to give me an injection of bull's brains.'

'Oh, so you found him then.'

'He's dead. But his son carries on in the same old house, with the same concierge. Paris is extraordinary the way nothing changes. If I hadn't lost that address book I would have found all those nice friends of mine, or at least their children.'

'And what about the Marquis and the Academician?'

'Both away. Hope to see me next time I come. Anyhow, Lecœur was the important one – goodness, I felt exhausted this morning – the lives you lead here – I wasn't in bed till four!'

'I heard you shrieking,' I said, reproachfully.

'I wished you'd popped down. Pauline was at the peak of her form. We had the life cycle of the Bolter, among other things, and now of course they are all longing to meet you.'

Philip looked at me significantly.

I said, 'I hope you had a good dinner?' Davey was fussy about food.

'Not very. Coarsely mashed potatoes – there's no excuse for that, nowadays. However, enough of this frivolity, agreeable as it has been. I was quite right to go into the thing thoroughly and in fact I only thought of the solution to our problem late at night after several glasses of wine.'

'You have thought of a solution?'

'Yes. It's very simple but none the worse for that, I hope. As Philip so truly says, one can't starve Pauline out and one certainly can't lecture her out. We must bore her out. The problem is how to stop all these Dukes and Rothschilds and countless Countesses from going to visit her. Now I suppose the social life here is built up on "extras", those men in white coats who go from party to party handing things round?'

'Indeed it is,' said Philip, 'more so every day.'

'You must get hold of one who is seen at all the big receptions. IS SEEN are the operative words. He must know everybody by sight, but above all they must be well aware he does. Post him at the steps to the entresol, paper and pencil in hand, and tell him to write down the names of Pauline's visitors – he might ask them as they go in – it must be very much underlined, what he is up to.

At the same time, Philip, you must put it about on the grape vine that those who are found frequenting the entresol will not be invited to anything here during The Visit. I think you'll find that will do the trick all right.'

Philip gave a great shout of laughter – Davey joined in and they rocked to and fro. 'Wonderful,' Philip said.

'I think it's rather neat myself.'

'But what Visit?' I was considerably unnerved.

'Not necessary to specify,' said Philip, who now showed the true niceness of his character by accepting Davey's scheme with whole-hearted appreciation, 'the word Visit, with a capital V, is magical in Paris. To the *gens du monde* it is as the din of battle to the warrior. They will never risk missing it, like brave Crillon, simply in order to have a few more jolly evenings with Pauline. Hitherto it has been a sign of social failure not to be seen in the entresol – from now on it will be social death to go there. I'd have given anything to have thought of your scheme myself – what a genius you are. The decks will be cleared in half an hour.'

'It must be properly organized,' said Davey.

'Yes, indeed. We won't allow it to go off at half-cock, that would never do. First I'll ring up the greatest gossips I know. Then I'll go and engage M'sieur Clément. He's our boy, he rules the concierges of the Avenue du Bois with a rod of iron and is the king-pin of that neighbourhood. All Paris knows him by heart. So I've got a busy day, better get on with it. I congratulate you keenly,' he said to Davey and went off.

Davey said complacently, 'I hope now you are sorry that you suspected me of changing sides.'

'Davey – I humbly apologize.'

'Not that I mind. But you realize how it was. I had to find out what sort of people she was seeing. There are many amusing and delightful people here who wouldn't care a rap about a Visit or even expect to be invited if there is one. Docteur Lecœur, for instance. Those friends of hers, however, would. As I told you before, I understand the French.'

45

5

Davey's plan could not be put into operation for a day or two. When M'sieur Clément understood what he was being hired to do he demanded an enormous bribe. He pointed out that Lady Leone's acquaintances all employed him in one capacity or another; if they suspected him of betraying them to *les Anglais* he might lose the many lucrative engagements and transactions on which his living depended. Philip, after a long session with him, came back to report and explained this to Davey and me but said that in fact no Parisian, especially not those who lived in M'sieur Clément's district, would dare get on the wrong side of him. He had been king of the black market during the war and was now indispensable for things like difficult railway and theatre tickets and for his ability to produce any requirement, from unlimited whisky to a trained nurse, not to speak of other, more sinister commodities, at a moment's notice. Undoubtedly very thick with the police, he knew all about the private lives of a vast section of the community. Philip had suggested to him that he would not really be risking very much by undertaking our assignment and had said that we, for our part, were obliged to take into account the remuneration he would receive from people wanting him to keep dark the fact that they had been about to visit Lady Leone. After long, hard bargaining and double bluffing on both sides, Philip got him down to £500. They shook hands on this. M'sieur Clément, wreathed now in smiles, said it might seem rather expensive but he guaranteed that the work would be impeccable. Philip then flew to London and, with some difficulty, persuaded the powers that be to disburse this amount from the secret funds. All these negotiations had to take place without the knowledge of Alfred who would certainly never have allowed them for a single minute.

At last the stage was set. Davey, Philip, and I were the audience, established behind muslin curtains at Philip's bedroom window. His flat, which was over one of our lodges, had good views both of the courtyard and the street and was therefore in a commanding position. One could see and not be seen.

'I haven't been so excited since chub-fuddling days with Uncle Matthew,' I said to Davey.

M'sieur Clément, a lugubrious individual with a bottle nose, had posted himself by the staircase of the entresol. For some reason he was not only dressed in inky black from head to foot but the sheets of paper which he held ready for the guilty names were black-edged like those put out, for the congregation to sign, at a French funeral. No doubt, in fact, pinched from one, according to Philip, since M'sieur Clément was, of course, a beadle. (Another of his part-time jobs was that of executioner's assistant.)

Presently a group of Lady Leone's gossips sauntered elegantly into the courtyard. There were five or six of them, all seemed to have arrived together and they were deep in talk. A tall, commanding man began to recount something, the others clustered round him, savouring his words. Two more people came in from the street; they joined the group, shook hands and were evidently put into the picture, after which the teller continued his tale. Suddenly, looking round as if to illustrate some point, his eye fell on M'sieur Clément. He stopped short, clutched the arm of a young woman and pointed; they all turned and looked. Consternation. Hesitation. Confabulation. Flight. Never had chub been more thoroughly fuddled; they flapped off, mouths open, and disappeared into the main stream of the Faubourg.

After this, incidents succeeded each other. A well-known pederast fainted dead away on seeing M'sieur Clément and was heaved, like Antony to the Monument, into the entresol. Women screamed; very few kept their heads and demanded to sign our book. Nobody else went near Lady Leone. Gradually, the intervals between visitors became longer; at eight o'clock, when the entresol was usually at its liveliest, a whole hour had gone by without a single soul coming through our gate.

'It's done the trick,' Philip said, 'all the telephones in Paris must be engaged. I'd better go and give the old fiend his ill-gotten gains and then we can dine. Good work!' he said to Davey.

'I must say I never saw £500 so easily earned.'

'M'sieur Clément would reply, like Whistler, that we are paying for the knowledge of a lifetime.'

Lady Leone was now deserted by her friends, except for faithful Mrs Jungfleisch, but greatly to my disappointment she showed no signs of leaving us. She lay on in her bed, perfectly contented, according to Davey, with her embroidery, the crossword puzzle and a very loud gramophone. When I suggested that we might take the gramophone away, since it did not belong to her at all but had been presented to the Embassy by a visiting rajah long ago, Davey and Philip made me feel like some cruel gaoler trying to remove the last solace of a lovely, unfortunate, incarcerated princess. It was less irritating, certainly, for me to hear strains of Mozart or the war speeches of Sir Winston Churchill, which she was inordinately fond of and which she played at full blast, than shrieks of laughter; at least Lady Leone could not be discussing me and my mother with a gramophone. The sting of her presence had been drawn by Davey's clever manoeuvre – now that nobody went near her any more the fiction of illness could be maintained. Alfred's face was saved. All the same it annoyed me that she should still be under my roof and so did the fact that Davey was in the habit of slipping downstairs for a game of scrabble before dinner. However, both he and Philip were rather reassuring. They said she was bored and restless; furthermore Mrs Jungfleisch was anxious to go to London for a debate at Chatham House. Their view was that Lady Leone would not be with us much longer, that she was merely biding her time in order to make a suitable exit. 'Pauline won't sneak out unobserved, you can be very sure. I expect she is hiring the Garde Républicaine to conduct her with trumpets and drums.'

I had various preoccupations at this time, still without a secretary, Philip much busier than he had been at the beginning. The days seemed too short for the hundred and one things which I must see to, among others our first entertainment, a cocktail party for the Dominions' Ambassadors. I was terrified at the thought of it, nightmares crowding in. I had not felt so nervous since the first dinner party I gave at Oxford, many years ago, for Alfred's professor. This was rather unreasonable since I had very little to do with the organization. Philip made out the lists and Major Jarvis, our comptroller, saw to the drink and the food of which there was to be a mountain. 'How can people eat anything at all between an enormous luncheon and an even more terribly stuffing dinner?' I asked.

'You'll see how they can. Are you going to do the flowers, Lady Wincham?'

The day came. I bought a lot of pink carnations (my favourite flowers) and stuck them into silver bowls. They looked so pretty, I was quite amazed at my own cleverness. Then I went upstairs and put on my cocktail dress. Nobody could have said that it looked pretty; hideous it was and very strange. My maid, Claire, pronounced it to be 'chic', but without much conviction. I had never liked it, even when worn by a wonderfully elegant Indo-Chinese mannequin, and had only been persuaded into ordering it because my vendeuse, in urging it on me, seemed to have the backing of a prominent English writer on fashion.

'Make no mistake,' asserted this pundit (photograph appended), with her usual downright authority, 'waists have gone for good.'

Having no wish to make a mistake over a dress which cost what had formerly been my allowance for a whole year, I had plumped for this waistless creation and oh! how I loathed it. However, there was nothing to be done; I was in it now, I must hope for the best and only try not to see myself in a glass.

The party was to take place in the state rooms on the ground floor. I went down and found Philip and Davey in hilarious mood, having had, I thought, good strong cocktails. I hurried towards them. They were kind enough not to remark on my dress but began making silly criticisms of the flowers.

'So like you, Fanny – why didn't you ask us first?'

'Carnations dumped in vases simply don't do any more. Haven't you ever heard of Arrangements? Don't you know about the modern hostess and her clever ways? Still-lifes – imaginative – not only flowers but yards of red velvet, dead hares, pumpkins, wrack from the seashore, common grasses from the hedgerow and the Lord knows what rubbish! Or else Japanesey, one reed by itself cunningly placed is worth five dozen roses, nowadays.'

I did know what they meant. Once, asked to the house of a Dior don, with other wives (women in Oxford have no identity, they are lumped together as wives), I had noticed a lot of top-heavy old-man's-beard in an urn surrounded by cabbages on the floor, and thought it all looked like a harvest home. People were saying, 'Utterly divine, your Arrangements.'

'Did Lady Leone go in for them?'

'Yes, indeed. Her feeling for colour and sense of form were the despair of all the hostesses here.'

'Shall I tell you something? – I intend to stick to pink carnations.'

Alfred joined us, saying, 'What's that dress, Fanny?' in a falsetto voice he sometimes used to denote that he was being quizzical.

'It's the fashion.'

'We are not here to be fashionable, you know.'

There were voices in the hall now, our guests were beginning to arrive; Alfred and I stood by the fireplace waiting to come forward effusively when they were announced. Philip had suggested that warm American rather than cold English manners might be adopted on this occasion and that we must do our best to look as if we were pleased to see the people.'

'I can't say it, it wouldn't seem a bit real.'

'Don't force yourself then, but do just bare the gums.'

So there we were, preparing to simper, under the eyes of King George and Queen Mary, bad copies of bad portraits. I felt them disapproving of the fashionable dress, of the grins and of the whole notion of a cocktail party but approving of the carnations. Nobody came into the room. I felt perfectly idiotic planted there like a waxwork, horrible dress and artificial smile. There were clearly a lot of people in the hall; a curious silence had fallen on them. Davey and Philip went over to the door; when they got there they looked left towards the entrance and then, as though following the gaze of others, they sharply turned their heads to the staircase. They remained quite still, looking up it, with a stupefied expression.

'What is this all about?' said Alfred, going over to join them. He too stood eyes to heaven, with his mouth slightly open. I followed him. The hall presented a scene like a picture of the Assumption: a mass of up-turned faces goggling at the stairs down which, so slowly that she hardly seemed to be moving, came the most beautiful woman in the world. She was dressed in great folds of white satin; she sparkled with jewels; her huge pale eyes were fixed, as though upon some distant view, over the heads of the crowd. Following her, two of my footmen were carrying a large gramophone; then came Mrs Jungfleisch, elegant in white linen, a basket on her arm. All the time, more guests were arriving. When Lady Leone got to the bottom of the stairs they divided into two lanes; she shook hands, like a royal person, with one here and there as she sailed out of the house for ever.

6

Charming Northey, how to describe her? Can this creature of *commedia dell'arte* really have resulted from the copulation on a hard, brass, hotel bed, trains rumbling below, of dear old Louisa and terribly dull John Fort William? Some pretend that the place of conception, that of birth, and also the Christian name have a bearing on personality. Northey, product of King's Cross and Hill View Clinic, Oban, and with that name, must be a living refutation of this theory. Nothing of the northerner about her, no vague mistiness, no moments of absence; she was not romantic nor did she yearn after the unknown. She was the typical product, one would have said, of an ancient civilization beneath cerulean skies. Impossible to believe that she had a Scotch father, old enough to be her grandfather, and Pictish ancestors; yet surely good Louisa – oh no, perish the thought! She was incapable of inventing such a wealth of detail to cover up a sin. I incline to think that Northey must have been a changeling; that carelessness occurred in Hill View Clinic, Oban, by which the child of some noble Roman lady and a strolling player was exchanged for Louisa's brat. Physically she bore no resemblance whatever to the other Mackintoshes who all had solid frames, ginger heads and freckles. She was like a small exquisite figure in enamelled glass, with hair the colour of a guinea; her eyes the liveliest and most expressive I ever saw, not very large, brilliantly blue. In moments of excitement or distress they became diamond-shaped. When she talked she used her whole body in the concentrated effort of expressing herself, gesticulating, wriggling, as babies and puppies do. Her little thin hands never lay still in her lap. Furthermore, there was something indescribably lovable about her, she radiated affection, happiness, goodwill towards men. From the first moment we set eyes on her Alfred and I were her slaves.

She exploded into our household as we were dining alone together, tired and depressed, after the Dominions party. Davey had gone off saying that his friend the Marquis was now in Paris; it seemed that Philip was obliged to dine with his London stock-broker; both, I suspected, had really joined Lady Leone at Mrs Jungfleisch's. I thought the party had been a total flop, though I heard afterwards that it was the most successful ever given at the Embassy in the sense that those who had missed it were wild with fury while those who had been present were sought after by the whole of Paris and supplied with free meals for weeks. But as Alfred and I could not discuss the great topic of the evening with our guests we were naturally the last people they wanted to talk to. They were longing to compare notes with others who had witnessed Lady Leone's exit, to buttonhole newcomers who had not and tell them about it, above all to leave as soon as they decently could and get on to the telephone. Everybody was very polite; indeed I was finding out that diplomats are diplomatic, it is one thing you can say for them. After the frank and outspoken rudeness I was accustomed to in Oxford this made a pleasant change. There were, too, moments of encouragement as when somebody said, 'Ah! The Irish Ambassador! That is a feather in Sir Alfred's cap – he never came to the Leones.'

The Ambassador of the Channel Islands praised my carnations, a major export, so he told me, of his country. A marvellous-looking Othello of a man gorgeously draped in pale blue taffeta (slightly marred by boots sticking out below, as my walking shoes had stuck out from beneath the Chinese robe) had invited me to go lion shooting in his. But the party had had a restless undercurrent and was certainly not much fun for the hosts.

So now it was over and we were dining. All of a sudden Northey was there, in the doorway, an inquiring look on her face. 'It's me,' she said.

'Darling!'

'I'm so sorry, I had to ask them to pay the taxi. No money at all. The station-master had to lend me a ticket. Yes I did, but I lost it.'

'Nothing matters now you're here. You must have had a beastly journey.'

'Oh Cousin Fanny (oh, you are kind, may I really), oh Fanny –' the soft skin of her forehead crumpled like tissue paper, her eyes took on a diamond-shaped, tormented expression which was to become very familiar to me and they brimmed. I saw exactly what Basil had meant about the brimming. 'You can't, you can't imagine. There were sweet bullocks on board. You don't know the sadness – the things they do to them. Their poor horns had been cut off – imagine the pain – and all because they get a pound more for them without horns and that's because then they can pack them tighter. I'd like to drop a hydrogen bomb on Ireland.'

'And kill millions of cows and all the birds and animals and the Irish also who are so charming?' Alfred said, gently.

'Charming!'

'Oh yes, they are. They have to export these bullocks in order to live. They have no industries, you see.'

'I hate and loathe and execrate them.'

'Darling, you mustn't be so worked up.'

'But I must be. These little creatures are put in the world for us to look after them. We are responsible. How do we treat them? They don't sleep you know, cows, they never have a moment of forgetting. Their comfort is to chew the cud – nobody feeds them properly on the journey – not enough water – fourteen hours in the train after the boat, with no water in this weather. And when they get to the – you know – dreadful place, does anybody give them water there?'

These things have worried me all my life; as I despise myself for not having the strength of character to do more than give an occasional pound to the R.S.P.C.A., I try to put them out of my mind.

'Come and have your dinner, dearest.'

'No, I couldn't,' she said, when the butler put a plate of consommé before her, 'nothing made of meat – I won't prey on them – never again.'

Alfred said, 'But if nobody ate meat the whole race of cows and

54

sheep and pigs would become extinct. They have happy little lives you know and death is never agreeable, it won't be for us, either. It's the price we all have to pay.'

'Yes, but not torture. That's too much. Fanny, do promise you'll never have cruel food here.'

'What is cruel food?'

'For instance, lobsters and Irish horses and foie gras. A Frenchman on board told me what they do to sweet geese for pâté de foie gras.'

'Very wrong and stupid of him.'

'He told to make me care less about the bullocks.'

'This journey has been a nightmare. Now you must forget it.'

'But if people always forget these things they go on and on. All right, I suppose I'm boring you.'

'You're not boring us,' said Alfred, looking at her with love, 'but we don't like to see you so upset.'

'But you understand why, don't you? There we were, all travelling together – I used to go and chat to them, they looked so sad and good, poor little creatures – then I come to this lovely house and you, while they –' she was eating the remains of a cheese soufflé now, evidently very hungry. 'The captain of the *Esmeralda*,' she said, with her mouth full, 'was a most unpleasant person. He was ghastly to the bullocks and he offered to – you know – to hug me. But the sweet Frenchman who was there got me off.'

'Weren't there any women on board?'

'Only me.'

'And this Frenchman – he didn't want to hug you himself?'

'M. Cruas? He might have liked to but he didn't offer. He *is* kind. So is the station-master. When we got on shore and I looked for my ticket, quelle horrible surprise – there it wasn't. M. Cruas is poor, you know, so he couldn't buy me one, he could only carry my luggage to save porters. So the station-master lent. Can we pay him back at once, Sir Alfred – oh you are kind, may I really? Alfred? He knows about us because Lady Leone never has a ticket, or any money, or a passport – just a basket he says. Sacrée Lady Leone. Why sacred I wonder?'

55

'It only means that blooming Lady Leone,' said Alfred, in his falsetto. 'How's your French, Northey?'

'Very nice. M. Cruas is a teacher, so he taught me.'

'Did you not learn it at school?' An embarrassed, pouting wriggle was the answer to this. 'You went to school, I suppose?'

'I went. Only I didn't stay.'

'Why not?'

'It was too dread.'

'You'll have to learn quickly you know or you won't be any good to Fanny.'

'Yes. I've thought of that. So M. Cruas will come here and go on with the lessons.'

Alfred said to me afterwards, 'Your cousin Louisa is a fool. Imagine letting that child go alone on a cattle boat and sending her to a school where she was so unhappy she had to leave. I've no patience with such people. The poor little thing seems to have been utterly mismanaged.'

Implacable where his own contemporaries were concerned, Alfred had infinite indulgence for the young; in fact I sometimes thought he was too much on their side – hoodwinked by them. It was plain to see that Northey would twist him round her little finger.

Presently Philip came in. Perhaps he felt sorry for us, all alone as he thought, dwelling on that horrid party. When he saw Northey, he said, 'Don't tell me, I'm going to guess. I suppose this must be the wonderfully efficient young lady who is going to make life easier for all of us? Northey, in fact. How d'you do? How was the cattle boat?'

Alfred and I began talking simultaneously to change the subject. Northey made a sad little noise like a kitten but went on eating; the food, and the sight of Philip (that, perhaps most of all, she was gazing at him as if she had never seen a young man before) seemed to be taking the edge off her sorrow.

'This is Philip,' I said, 'he is busy, he mustn't be put upon, but in real emergency you'll find that he will come to the rescue.'

'Each for each is what we teach,' said Northey, looking at him from under her eyelashes. Oh bother, I thought, silly old love, again. Why does he have to be in it already, with Grace? Like all happily married people I am inclined to make matches; Philip and Northey seemed, on the face of it, such an ideal couple.

'What would a real emergency be?' she asked him.

'Let me think. Well, if you invited the Tournons to the same dinner party as les faux Tournons, that would be a pretty kettle of fish.'

'Please explain.'

'There is a couple here called M. et Mme de Tournon – social butterflies, pretty, delightful, perfectly useless. They are the real Tournons. Then there are M. et Mme Tournon. He is a deputy, a brilliant young man who specializes in finance, hard-working, ambitious, a parliamentary under-secretary. His wife is a prominent physicist. In spite of the fact that he is almost bound to become Prime Minister, while she may well end up with the Nobel prize, they are known to the whole of Paris as the false Tournons. Now if you had the two couples here together, protocol would demand that the false Tournons, elected by the people, should take precedence of the others. Thereupon the real Tournons would turn their plates upside down and say, *"il y a erreur"*. I suppose you have understood every word? What a look! Never mind, in six months' time all this will be second nature to you.'

'You know, Philip,' said Alfred, 'I don't wish to fill this house with the ornaments of society.'

'No, sir. If I may be allowed to make an observation, all ambassadors begin by saying that. The fact is, however, that if you don't have a sprinkling of them the others don't care to come. By the way, I really looked in to tell you that Bouche-Bontemps has just telephoned. He wants to know if he can see you tomorrow.'

I liked M. Bouche-Bontemps very much, felt natural and at my ease with him. 'He's a dear,' I said.

'Yes. The old-fashioned kind – a jolly Roman Catholic. All the up-and-coming young men seem to be Protestants – makes them so priggish.'

'I thought the old ones were free-thinkers?'

'It's the same as far as jollity goes.'

'Let's ask him to luncheon, shall we?' I said.

'Tomorrow? I don't know if he could with this crisis impending.'

'Of course, there's a crisis. I've been too much occupied with our own to take much notice.'

'All the same it might just suit him. I'll go and see.'

'What crisis?' said Northey, following him out of the room with her eyes.

'One of your duties here will be to read the papers,' said Alfred. 'You can read, I suppose?'

'I can read and I have a certain native intelligence. Don't be sarcastic with me, I beg.'

'Well, then, there's a parliamentary crisis going on and it looks as if this government may fall.'

'Then there'll be a general election? You see, I know about politics.'

'The point is that there will not. Fanny must give you some books to read about the state of France.'

Philip came back and said the Foreign Minister would be very much pleased to lunch, but he had business to do with the Ambassador and must see him alone.

'Northey and I can eat in the Salon Vert,' I said, 'and you can have your secrets in the upstairs dining-room. But do bring him in for a cocktail first, if you think he has time.'

'They always have time in the middle of the day,' said Philip. 'They can be up all night and start intriguing again before breakfast but the hours between one and three are sacred. That's why they are all so well – one never hears of a French politician dying – they live for ever, haven't you noticed?'

'I've come to say good-bye,' said Davey, arriving with my tray in the morning.

'Davey, don't go. It's so comfortable to feel you're here. Why don't you stay on in some capacity – comptroller? I think Major Jarvis is leaving us. Take his place – oh do!'

'Sweet of you, Fanny, but I couldn't live with the French.

I understand them too well. Besides, I have fish to fry at home. New curtains for the drawing-room. And I can't live for ever without Mrs Dale. Tea-time at home is delightful – blinds are drawn at the witching hour of 4.30 and I have her on the wireless.'

'We've got a wireless; you can have her here.'

'I've tried. She doesn't sound the same.'

'I wanted you to see Northey.'

'I have. We had our breakfast together just now. Rocks ahead there. So, I'm off. When you're next in trouble send for me, won't you? See you very soon in that case.'

When the Foreign Minister saw Northey he said we must all lunch together. He could do his business with Alfred in two minutes on his way out – he had never meant that the charming Ambassadress should be excluded from their talk. Mees Nortee was no doubt aware that her job demanded enormous discretion and indeed he could see by her face that she was a serious woman. During luncheon he addressed himself to her in a tender, avuncular, bantering tone of voice.

'So you are studying French. But why? Everybody here speaks English. And reading books on the state of France by English experts? I know these experts. They are all in love with Arabs.'

'No,' said Alfred firmly, 'respectable, married men.'

'The English who specialize in French affairs fill me with misgivings. Why are there so many of them and why must they concentrate on my poor country – are there no others in the world whose state is worth considering? Why not the state of Denmark for a change?'

'You ought to be flattered,' said Alfred. 'The publishers know they can sell any amount of books about France – in fact France, like Love, is a certain winner on a title-page.'

'Ah! So Mees Nortee is to learn about France and Love. I shall teach her, I know more than the English experts.'

'You are kind,' said Northey, 'because I can see that these books are a bore. No pictures, no talk and such terribly long sentences.'

'You told me you could read,' said Alfred.

'Like all of us she can read what interests her. When you have been here for a year, Mees, you will probably find yourself enjoying books about the state of France – though what this state will be by then, who can say?' He sighed deeply. 'Now, we will begin our lesson. Your uncle, the Ambassador here, has two bones to pick over with the French government, whenever there is a government. There are Les Îles Minquiers, a very nice point. You will hear more of them in due course – hats off to the Intelligence Service! And there is the European Army, known as C.E.D. or E.D.C., nobody can ever remember why. One of your uncle's assignments is to persuade us to merge our army, which is overseas, fighting, with that of the Germans which is non-existent. This merging is desired by the Americans who see everything in black and white – with a strong preference for black.'

'M. le Ministre –' said Alfred sharply.

'Your protest is registered, M. l'Ambassadeur. The English are really indifferent, they don't care, but whenever they can please the Americans without it costing anything they like to do so. Armies have never meant much to them in times of peace – one army – another army – zero they think, anyhow, in the face of the Bomb. At the same time they have never been averse from weakening the Continental powers. All their Generals and Field-Marshals tell them that a European force would be quite unworkable so they say come on, the Americans want it, it rather suits us, let's have it. Now, if it were a question of commerce, M. l'Ambassadeur, I believe the nation of shopkeepers would sing a very different song? Suppose we wanted a European market, Excellency, what would you say to that?'

This lesson seemed to be more for the benefit of Alfred than of Northey who, crumpled forehead, looked extremely puzzled.

Alfred said, 'My American colleague tells me that you are going to accept the European Army, however.'

'Your American colleague has a beautiful wife whom everybody wants to please. No Frenchman can bear to see somebody so exquisite looking sad for a single moment. So wherever she goes, in Paris or the provinces, the deputies and mayors and ministers and IGAMEs say "of course" to whatever she tells them. And she tells them, most beguilingly, that they are going to accept the European Army. We shall never accept. This government, as you see, is tottering. It will fall during the night, no doubt. But no French government could pass such a measure. We may be weak – nobody can say we are very strong at present – but we have an instinct for self-preservation. We shall appear to be about to give way, over and over again, but in the end we shall resist.'

'And over the Minquiers,' said Alfred, 'you will appear to resist, but in the end you will give way?'

'You have said it, M. l'Ambassadeur, not I.'

'And then what about Europe? If the C.E.D. fails?'

'It will be built up on a more peaceful and workable foundation. My great hope is, that when the time comes, you will not oppose it.'

After luncheon M. Bouche-Bontemps said, 'Shall I take Mees to the Chambre? She could then see the state of France in action.'

'Oh, you are kind. The only thing is, M. Cruas said he would come at five.'

'Who is M. Cruas?'

'He teaches me French.'

'Ring him up. Say you have another lesson today.'

'He's poor. He hasn't got a telephone.'

'Send a pneumatique,' said the Minister, impatiently.

He had a word on the staircase with Alfred and then left the house accompanied by Northey, who hopped, skipped and jumped across the marble paving of the hall, Alfred said, like a child going to a pantomime. I saw no more of her that day. Philip, in and out of the Chambre, reported during the evening that she seemed perfectly entranced, determined to stay to the end. The government fell in the early hours and Northey slept until luncheon-time.

'So what was it like?' I said, when she finally appeared.

'Terribly like that dread school I went to. Desks with inkpots and a locker. From where I sat you could see there are lollipops in the lockers and when they are pretending to listen to the lecturer or read lesson books they are really having a go at the illustrated mags. All the same they do half-listen because suddenly all the Madames get up and stamp and roar and shout and the master has to ring a bell and shout back at them.'

I had a vision of ghastly women, Erinyes, *tricoteuses*, obstructing the business of the Chambre. 'Madames? Women deputies?'

'No, Fanny,' said Northey as one explaining a well-known fact to a child. 'Madames are the Social Republicans, so called because their party headquarters are in the rue Madame. The Republican Socialists, whose H.Q. is in the rue Monsieur, are called les Monsieurs. They are each other's worst enemies. You see how sweet M. Bouche-Bontemps was quite right and going is better than reading.'

'What was the debate about?'

'Really, Fanny, I'm surprised that you should ask me that. Have you not seen your *Figaro* this morning? I hear that it is very well reported. Pensions for remarried war widows, of course.'

'Are you sure?'

'Quite sure. There was a nice person in the box called Mrs Jungfleisch who told me all about it. And an Englishwoman married to one of the deputies – a marquis I suppose because when he got up to speak the Communists chanted "*imbécile de Marquis*" and he became quite giggly and lost his place.'

'That must be Grace de Valhubert,' I said, pleased to think that she was back in Paris.

'Yes. She knows Fabrice and Charlie and she sent you her love. She talks with such a pretty French accent and Fanny! her clothes! Sweet M. Bouche-Bontemps came and took me out to dinner. He said if he fell he would be able to devote himself to my education. Well, he has fallen, so – Philip brought me home,' she added, nonchalantly.

I thought I understood now why she had stayed so late.

7

Now that the French were comfortably without a government, Alfred received instructions from the Foreign Office to make strong representations at the Quai d'Orsay about Les Îles Minquiers. These islands, which were to occupy his waking thoughts for many a long month to come, are described in Larousse as dangerous rocks near St Malo and given no independent notice in the *Encyclopaedia Britannica*. There are three of them and at high tide they are completely submerged. During the liberation of France, General de Gaulle found time to have a tricolour run up, at low tide, on the Île Maîtresse or middle island. Never has the adage 'let sleeping dogs lie' been more justified. This flag was immediately spotted by the Argus-eyed Intelligence Service and the Admiralty found time to send a frog-man, at high tide, to haul it down again. Now that the attention of Whitehall was drawn to the existence of the Minquiers, some busy-body with a turn for international law began to study the complicated question of their ownership. It transpired that the Traité de Brétigny (1360) which gave Normandy to the Kings of France, and Calais, le Quercy, le Ponthieu, Gascony, etc., to the English crown, made no allocation of the Minquiers. They were not covered by the various Channel Island treaties and have existed throughout history as a no-man's-land. As they are within sight, when they can be seen at all, of the French coast, no doubt they were always assumed to be part of France, but nobody seems to have minded one way or the other. It was bad luck for Alfred that the government which appointed him to Paris should be determined to paint the Minquiers pink on the map; nothing could have been more calculated to annoy the French at that particular juncture.

'But what is the point of these islands?' I asked as Alfred was about to leave for the Quai d'Orsay.

'Islands are always rather desirable – the Royal Yacht Squadron would like them to be English; our fishermen could use them, I suppose. The Foreign Secretary says the question must be settled now in the interests of Western solidarity. I must say, I'm not delighted to have to make a nuisance of myself at such a time.'

The President of the Republic, M. Béguin the outgoing Prime Minister, and the heads of the parties, one of whom was M. Bouche-Bontemps, had been up for several nights trying to resolve the crisis; tempers were beginning to be frayed. The English newspapers were pointing out the impossibility of relying on an ally who never seems to have a government. In decidedly gloating tones they inquired: will France be represented at the Foreign Ministers' Conference next week or shall we, as usual, see an empty seat? Can the Western Alliance afford these continual tergiversations? The people of England look on with dismay; they have but one desire, to see our French friends strong, prosperous and united.

The French papers urged the political parties to settle their differences with the least possible delay since '*nos amis britanniques*' were clearly about to make use of the situation to further their own sinister schemes. The two old neighbours are not always displeased by each other's misfortunes, nor do they trust each other not to take advantage of them.

'And you will notice when you have lived here for a bit,' said Grace de Valhubert, 'that it is the English who are the more annoying. The French never sent arms to the Mau-Mau, that I heard of.'

Grace counted herself as a sort of supernumerary English ambassadress; like most people who have been accredited for years to a foreign country she could only see one side of every question and that not the side of her own, her native land. Everything French was considered by her superior to its English equivalent. She was inclined to talk a sort of pidgin English, larded with French words; she slightly rolled her r's; at the same time her compatriots in Paris noted with glee that her French was by no means perfect. She was a bit of a goose, but so good-natured, pretty and elegant that one could not help liking her. It was the fashion to say that she had a terrible time with her husband but when I saw them together they always seemed to be on very comfortable terms. She was evidently quite uninterested in Philip.

She had come to call on me, sweet and affectionate, bringing me flowers. 'So sorry not to have been here when you arrived but I always stay at Bellendargues as long as I can. It's what I like best in the world. Anyway, who knows that I would have resisted the entresol? Too awful if you hadn't been able to ask me when next there is a Visit!'

'Oh Grace, the rules would be quite different for you!'

I took her to my room to see the fashionable dress I hated so much. She transformed it instantly by putting a belt on it, after which it became the prettiest I had ever had. 'Never believe that we have seen the last of the waist – the English have been saying it ever since the New Look went out – wishful thinking I suppose. An Englishwoman's one idea is to get into something perfectly shapeless and leave it at that.'

I thought of the Chinese robe.

'As a matter of fact,' she went on, 'if you're like me and get fond of your clothes and want to wear them for years the first rule is to stick to the female form. Everything that doesn't is dated after one season. Perhaps I'd better take you to my dressmaker – he's in the Faubourg – very nice and convenient for you – his clothes are more ordinary and far more wearable. I always think Dolcevita really wants to make one look a figure of fun.'

I thanked her for this advice, on all of which I acted. 'Come back to the Salon Vert and we'll have some tea.'

'You've moved the furniture about – it's better like this,' said Grace, looking round the room. 'It never seemed very much lived in. Pauline used that gloomy bedroom more.'

I poured out the tea and said I hoped the boys had behaved themselves at Bellendargues.

'We never saw them except at meals. They were very polite. Do you know about Yanky Fonzy?'

'I don't think so – is he at school with them?'

'He's a jazz biggy,' said Grace, 'he sends them. All that lovely weather they were shut up with a gramophone in Sigi's room being sent by Yanky. Haven't you seen their shirts with Yank's the Boy for Me printed on them? It's a transfer from Disc.'

'What does that mean?'

'I don't know, I'm quoting.'

'How did your husband take it?'

'Don't ask,' said Grace, shutting her eyes. 'However, it's entirely Charles-Édouard's own fault for insisting on Eton instead of letting the child go to Louis-le-Grand like everybody else. Then he'd never have heard of this ghastly Yanky.'

'Any news of him since they all arrived in Scotland?'

'*Silence de glace*. But as a matter of fact I have never received a letter from Sigismond in my life – I wouldn't know his writing on an envelope if I saw it. I pity the women who fall in love with him. When he first went to Eton I gave him those printed postcards: I am well, I am not well – you know, *rayer la mention inutile*. Of course he never put one in the box. Steamed off the stamps, no doubt. Afterwards he said the only thing he wanted to tell me was that his fag-master had stolen £5 from him and he couldn't find that on the list. They went back yesterday, didn't they?'

'Day before, I think.'

'I rang up my father in London this morning – thick fog over there, needless to say – look at the glorious sun here, it's always the same story – yes, so I begged him to go down and see them. No good worrying, is it? Charles-Édouard doesn't in the least. He says if Sigi is ill they'll have to let one know and when he's expelled he'll come home. He'll be obliged to, if only to worm some money out of us.'

'I suppose so, at that age. Later on they don't seem to need money and then they vanish completely.' I was thinking of Basil.

'What d'you hear of the crisis?' said Grace.

'Can you explain why the government fell at all? It seems so infinitely mysterious to me. War widows or something?'

'They were already bled to death on foreign affairs. The pensions for remarried war widows only finished them off. It's always the same here, they never actually fall on a big issue – school meals, subsidies for beetroot, private distilling, things of that sort bring them down. It's more popular with the electorate (they like to feel the minorities are being looked after) and then the deputies don't absolutely commit themselves to any major policy. *C'est plus prudent.*'

'Does your husband like being in the Chambre?'

'He gets dreadfully irritated. You see he's a Gaullist; he can't bear to think of all these precious years being wasted while the General is at Colombey.'

'Nobody seems to think he'll come back.'

'Charles-Édouard does, but nobody else. I don't think so, though I wouldn't say it, except to you. Meanwhile all these wretched men are doing their best, one supposes. M. Queuille has failed – did you know? – it was on the luncheon-time news. Charles-Édouard thinks the President will send for M. Bouche-Bontemps now.'

The telephone bell rang and Katie Freeman said, rather flustered, 'I've got M. Bouche-Bontemps on the line.'

'But the Ambassador is in the Chancery.'

'Yes, I know that. It's Northey he wants and I can't find her – she's not in her office and not in her room. He's getting very impatient – he's speaking from the Élysée.'

'Let me think – Oh I know, I believe she's trying on something in my dressing-room.' She had borrowed two months' wages from me, bought a lot of stuff and had turned my maid, Claire, into her private dressmaker. 'Just a moment,' I said to Grace, 'it's M. Bouche-Bontemps.' I went to look and sure enough, there was Northey being pinned into a large green velvet skirt. 'Come quickly, you're wanted on the telephone.'

She gathered up the skirt and ran into the Salon Vert. 'Hullo, oh, B.B.?' she said. 'Yes, I was working – not in my office – my work takes many different forms. That would be lovely. Ten o'clock would be best – I'm dining with Phyllis McFee but then I'll say I must go to bed early. Ten, and you'll pick me up? Oh, poor you, you must really? Never mind, soon be over.' She rang off.

Grace looked very surprised at this conversation.

'B.B. has to see the President now, which is a bore he says. But when that's over he'll take me to Marilyn Monroe.'

'That means he's going to refuse,' said Grace. 'The crisis will go on and the English will bag the Îles Minquiers, you mark my words. It's intolerable.' She said to Northey, 'You must come and dine one evening and we'll go dancing. I'll arrange something as soon as the household is a bit organized.'

'The utter kindness of you,' said Northey and trotted back to Claire.

'What a darling!'

'Oh, isn't she! You can't imagine how much I love her – so does Alfred.'

'And Bouche-Bontemps, it seems.'

'He's very kind to her. Don't look like that, Grace, he's a grandfather.'

'Mm,' said Grace.

'And she's as good as gold.'

'All right, I believe you.'

'Yes, you must. I sometimes think I would swap all my naughty boys for one daughter like Northey.'

'I've got three little girls, you know, but they are babies. The eldest is only six. I wonder – they are heavenly now, but people say girls can be so difficult.'

These words of Grace's soon came true. Adorable as she was, Northey was by no means an easy proposition. She was now in love, for the first time (or so she said, but is it not always the first time and, for that matter, the last?) and complained about it with the squeaks and yelps of a thwarted puppy. Her lack of reticence astounded me. When dealing with the children, I always tried to think back to when my cousins and I were little; any of us would have died sooner than admit to unrequited love, even in a whisper to each other, in the Hons' cupboard, while the grown-ups never had the smallest idea of what went on in our hearts. But with

Northey there was no question of concealing the worm, the canker and the grief; she displayed them. The loved one himself was not spared.

'Oh, Philip, I worship you.'

'Yes, I know.'

'Shall I chuck B.B. and dine with you instead?'

'No, thank you. I'm dining out.'

'Chuck!'

'No fear. It's a most amusing dinner.'

'The pathos! Well, if you won't take me out to dinner you might throw me a civil word.'

'If you go on like this, I'll throw something blunt and heavy. I must explain, m'lord, that my life had been made a purgatory. My work was suffering, I gave way to an uncontrollable impulse – it may have been wrong; it was inevitable. Fanny will be a witness for the defence, won't you?'

The fact that every Frenchman who saw her fell in love made her no easier to deal with and considerably complicated my task as ambassadress. Instead of a nice, sensible, methodical secretary ever at my elbow to help and support me I had this violent little fascinator flitting about the house, bewailing her lovelorn condition to anybody who would listen, or paralysing Alfred's private line as she wailed down it to one of her new friends. They were not spared the desperate state of her heart any more than we were. How could sobriety and security, the keynotes of our mission, be maintained under these circumstances? Northey created a circumambience of insobriety and doubtful security. Nothing could have been more unfortunate than her choice of followers. Such personages as the first Vice-President of the Chambre, the Secretary-General of the Élysée, an ex-Minister of Justice, the Ambassador of the Channel Islands, the Governor of the Bank of France, the Prefect of the Seine, not to speak of the outgoing Foreign Secretary who looked like being the next Prime Minister, could hardly be treated as ordinary young dancing partners. Difficult for Alfred to insist that they must not come to the house until they were invited or that they should at least limit themselves to the usual hours for calling on young ladies. They were all busy with the crisis, so they came when they could or else lengthily telephoned.

Perhaps unwisely, we had given Northey the entresol recently vacated by Lady Leone, with its own entrance to the courtyard. At all hours of the day and night one was apt to see French government or C.D. motors there whose owners were not transacting business with Alfred, while motor-bicyclists dressed like Martians continually roared up the Faubourg to stop at our concierge's lodge with notes or flowers or chocolates for Northey. She had taken to the social and political life of Paris with an ease more often exhibited nowadays by pretty boys than by pretty girls. Philip, who knew that esoteric world better than anybody else in the Embassy, said it was almost incredible how quickly she was picking up its jargon and manners. While I was still feeling my way through a thick fog, not knowing who anybody was, summoning small talk with the greatest difficulty, Northey seemed completely at home with the different groups which make up French society.

In one respect, however, she remained the same little Scotch girl who had arrived on the cattle boat. Her passion for animals was in no way modified and, as might have been foreseen, she began to accumulate pets which she had rescued from some misfortune.

'Yes, I saw this group of children in the Tuileries. Now I've always noticed that if you see children clustered round something and looking down at it fixedly it's going to be a creature and they are going to be cruel to it. Sure enough, they had got hold of this sweet torty. They kept picking her up and waving her about and putting her down again. You know how it's dread for a tortoise to be waved because she naturally thinks she is in the clutches of an eagle. So cruel, to bring them here from Greece – thousands of them – and wave them about all the summer and then leave them to die in the winter. Ninety per cent die, I read. Oh Fanny, the world! Anyway I bought her from those ghastly children for 1,000 francs, which I luckily had on me (we must have a little talk about money) and now she can be happy until the cold weather. Just look at the way she walks though, anybody can see her nerves are in ribbons.'

'Would you like to see my cat? She's old. She's bandaged up like this because her abscesses keep breaking out. The Duke's vet comes every morning when he has finished with the pugs and gives her penicillin. How d'you mean, kinder? Can't you see she's enjoying her life? She lies there purring, quite happy. Could I borrow a little money? Yes, well, penicillin is expensive, you know. You are kind – I'm keeping a strict account.'

Then she went for a walk on the quays and saw a badger asleep in a cage on the pavement outside an animal shop. 'The cruelty – they hate daylight – they live all day in a sett and only come out when it's dark. Imagine keeping it like that – why bring it here from its wood, poor little creature? So I came back for Jérôme and the Rolls-Royce and borrowed some money from Mrs Trott (darling, could you pay her for me if I promise to keep a strict account?) and together we lugged Mr Brock into the motor, huge and heavy he is, and brought him to the Avenue Gabriel, through that gate, and he's in the garden now. Do come and look –'

'Oh Northey, was that a good idea? As it's broad daylight in the garden – I don't see much difference.'

'Oh, the dear fellow will manage somehow.'

He did. The next morning there was an enormous, banked-up hole like an air-raid shelter in the middle of the lawn.

She was wildly unrealistic about money; each for each, her favourite adage, was evidently the keynote of her faith in such matters. She borrowed from any and everybody out of whom she could wheedle the stuff and then made Alfred or me pay them back, saying, 'I'm keeping a strict account. I've had my wages now until June of next year.'

'Dearest,' I said one day, 'what about M. Cruas? Ought we not to pay him for his lessons?' He came every afternoon for at least an hour, so Northey told me; he was evidently a good teacher as her French progressed amazingly.

'No, Fanny, it's not necessary, he comes for love. But if you have got a few thousand francs to spare, Phyllis McFee and me did a little recce in Main Street and saw un cocktail, prix shock, which is just my affair. Sharpen your wits, darling, it's French for a cheap afternoon dress.'

This Phyllis McFee was a Scotch friend of Northey's, from Argyllshire, who also had a job in Paris. So far I had not met her. I was glad that Northey had somebody to run round with, other than elderly cabinet ministers.

'Oh you are kind, now I can go and buy it. So I've had my wages until August I think – anyway I keep a strict account you know, it's all written carefully down.'

It could not exactly be said that Northey's work suffered from all these distractions, she had such a genius for delegating it. 'Each for each is what we teach' meant that Alfred and I, Mrs Trott the housekeeper, Jérôme the chauffeur, Major Jarvis and Philip did practically all her various jobs for her. Our reward was 'You are kind, oh the kindness of you.' But quite apart from extraneous calls on her time and attention, she was not cut out to be a secretary, nobody has ever been less of a career woman. She lived, quite frankly, for pleasure.

'I see what my boys mean when they say she is old-fashioned,' I observed to Philip, 'she is as frivolous as a figure of the twenties.'

'Thank goodness for that anyway. These new ones make me despair of the female sex. I belong to the old world, that's what it is, I talk its language – I'd sooner marry a Zulu woman of my own age than one of these gloomy beauties in red stockings.'

Quite good, I thought, as far as it went, but I was sorry to see that Philip showed no sign of falling in love with Northey. He burned for Grace and I feared that when that flame died down for want of fuel it would never be relit by Northey whom he regarded as a charming, funny little sister. I told her so. She had discovered that Grace was his love (enlightened, probably, by one of the followers, hoping to further his own suit) and came, eyes like diamonds, to communicate her dismay.

'Horrible, horrible Grace, how could he?'

I thought it better to be astringent, not too sympathetic. 'Last time we talked about her you said she was so fascinating.'

'Never! Idiot, rolling her r's and dressing up French. Besides, she's as old as Time.'

'As old as Philip.'

'It's different for a man as you know very well. Fanny, I can't understand it.'

'I'm afraid we never understand that others may be preferred to ourselves.'

'Has Alfred ever preferred anyone to you?'

'Yes, and very boring it was.'

'But you managed?'

'As you see. I think it's a good thing, really, that you know about Philip and Grace.'

'Why is it? I was much happier before.'

'Because now you won't go on harbouring dangerous illusions.'

'More dangerous for me to despair.'

'Don't despair, but don't be too hopeful, either. Remember that it would be a miracle if Philip fell in love with you, under the circumstances.'

'Well, there are miracles. Why shouldn't God do something for me?'

'Yes, I only say don't count on it.'

Philip, overhearing these words as he came into the Salon Vert, said, 'If you're after a miracle St Expédite is your boy. He's a dear little Roman saint who deals with lost causes and he hangs out at St Roch. Only he doesn't like it if you begin asking before the cause is really lost; you must be quite sure before you bother him. I thought we might get him on to the European Army soon. What do you want a miracle for, Mees?'

'It was love and love alone that made King Edward leave his throne.'

'Oh, love! Don't tell me you're keenly running after Bouche-Bontemps?'

'You know I'm not, you brute.' Brimming. 'You know quite well who it is.'

'By the way, I'd forgotten! That is a lost cause, I can tell you and I should know. There, there, mop them up. Are you going to the Chambre to see the old boy present his ministry?'

'Of course. I'm his Egeria.'

'Don't be up until five again,' I said.

'No. He's going to make one of his nutshell speeches – not more than two hours – he says they'll have thrown him out by midnight.'

'Oh, that's how it is?' said Philip. 'I wasn't sure. Excellent. Then we can get on with the Îles Minquiers.'

'I wish I understood about these islands,' said Northey.

'So do I,' said Philip.

'Why do our papers keep saying the French should be urged to give them up for their own sake?'

'Because we want them.'

'If it's good for us to have them, why is it good for the French to get rid of them?'

'In the first place they almost certainly belong to us. Then there's our altruism. In our great, true, sincere love for the French, knowing they will be better without the islands (and a great many other places as well) we are willing to take the responsibility for them off their shoulders. Now, put that in your pipe and stop asking questions. I'm a civil servant, policy is nothing to do with me, I am there to obey orders. I may add that I wish to heaven the bloody thing could be settled and forgotten – it's poisoning my existence.'

The telephone bell rang. 'Answer,' I said to Northey, 'and ask who it is.'

'Hullo – oh – yes, he's here – who is it? Quelle horrible surprise! It's for you, an affected foreign voice,' she said loudly, handing the receiver to Philip.

'Grace? Oh, don't pay any attention, she's not quite all there, you know. *The Times*? No, I haven't. There's a leader? Well, it won't be the last, they've got to fill that space every day – ghastly for them. And a letter from Spears? Not a bit surprised. But, Grace,

I've told you it's nothing to do with me. I don't approve or disapprove, I'm not meant to have an opinion. No, I won't resign, it never does any good and then one is unemployed. Do you want me to leave Paris? And all because of a few rocks which honestly don't matter either way. We'll talk about it presently. Yes, of course I will, I'd love to.' He rang off and said to me, 'We're both dining there, aren't we, Fanny? She wants me to take her to the Chambre later on.

'You said you'd pick me up and take me,' Northey brimmed.

'But we will. Grace won't mind a bit.'

'I mind.'

'Ah! Then you'd better tell them to send the Presidential motor, with its moon, for you.'

'Very funny and witty.'

'Jérôme can take you, darling. Send him on to the Valhuberts', that's all.'

'It's because – I don't like going in there alone. I know.' She took the telephone and said, 'Katie, love, put me through to the Bureau of the Assemblée, will you? I'll speak in my own room.'

8

Alfred had gone to London for a day or two, so Philip took me to the Valhubert dinner. I was beginning to lose my fear of such social occasions now that I knew some of the people likely to be present. They were all very nice to me. I was dazzled by the French mode of life; they keep up a state in Paris which we English only compete with in country houses. A Paris dinner party, both from a material point of view and as regards conversation, is certainly the most civilized gathering that our age can produce, and while it may not be as brilliant as in the great days of the salons, it is unrivalled in the modern world.

The Hôtel de Valhubert, like the Hôtel de Charost (the English Embassy), lies between a courtyard and a garden. It is built of the same sandy-coloured stone and, though smaller and of a later date, its ground plan is very similar. There the resemblance ends. The Embassy, having been bought lock, stock and barrel from Napoleon's sister, is decorated and furnished throughout in a fine, pompous, Empire style very suitable to its present use. The Hôtel de Valhubert is a family house. The rooms still have their old panelling and are crammed with the acquisitions of successive Valhuberts since the French revolution (when the house was sacked and the original furnishings dispersed). Beautiful and ugly objects are jumbled up together, and fit in very well. Grace's flowers were perfection; no yards of velvet, no dead hares, not a hint of harvest home, pretty bouquets in Sèvres vases.

After praising my dress, which was, I thought myself, quite lovely and which came from her dressmaker, Grace introduced me to various people I did not know already. 'It's pouring in London tonight,' she said, 'I've just had a word with Papa. He'd been to Eton and taken the boys out – you'll be glad to hear they are all three alive. He says he never saw such rain!'

Mrs Jungfleisch said the weather had been perfect when she was in London, much better than in Paris.

'Come off it, Mildred. You see London through rose-coloured specs, though I notice you don't go and live there.'

I had not met Mrs Jungfleisch since she came down my staircase, in white linen, actively participating in the rapine of the gramophone. She showed no signs of embarrassment but said, 'Nice to see you again.' I felt as if I had behaved badly in some way and had now been forgiven.

At dinner I sat next to Valhubert and we talked about the children, a ready-made topic whenever he and I saw each other.

'Poor Fabrice,' he said, speaking of my Fabrice's father. 'He was my hero when I was a little boy and as soon as I grew up we were more like brothers than cousins. I must say the child has a great look of him. I was telling my aunt – naturally she is anxious to see him – will you allow me to take him down there when he comes for Christmas? It could be to his advantage, she is rich and there is nobody left of the Sauveterre family. She might adopt him – no – you wouldn't care for that?'

'I don't think I would mind. After all, she is his grandmother. In another five years I suppose he will have gone out of my life. These boys seem to vanish away as soon as they are grown up.'

'And then what do they do?'

'I wish I knew. Alfred and I have always acted on the principle with them of never asking questions.'

'Like the Foreign Legion?'

'Exactly. Now I sometimes wonder if it has been a good plan. We have no idea what goes on; the two elder sons might be dead for all we see or hear of them.'

'Where are they – in diplomacy?'

I began telling him about Beard and Ted, but I could see that he was not listening. He was interested in his own Sigi and in his cousin's Fabrice while accepting our Charlie as inseparable from the others. Bearded professors, whiskered travel agents (if that was what Basil had become) were out of his ken. I knew that my encounter in the street with Basil's accomplice would have seemed strange and dreadful to any man of my own generation; I had never told Alfred of it.

'Aren't you going down to the House?' I said, to change the subject. I knew that the session began at nine o'clock.

'My father-in-law always says down to the House – I like it very much. Yes, presently I will. There's no hurry, we know to a minute what is happening. Jules Bouche-Bontemps at this moment is launching a pathetic appeal – no, pathetic is not the translation, it is one of those trap words which mean different things in the two languages. Rousing, perhaps, a rousing call, or a moving speech. (Nobody will be roused or moved by it, but let that pass.) I could make this speech for him if he fell ill in the middle, I know it as well as he does and so does the whole of his audience. He will begin by saying that our divisions suit nobody except certain allies who had better be nameless. Here we shall have a long digression on Les Îles Minquiers, their history and moral attachment to France. (Those islands are a bore, I can't listen to anything which concerns them, it is too dull.) This will be put in so that if we lose them – and who, except, of course, Grace, cares if we do? – he will be able to say that it is the fault of my party and les Madames who are all preparing, as he very well knows, to vote against him. He will pretend to be deeply shocked by the unholy alliance between les Madames and the Gaullists, all playing London's game. Well, that's a change from Moscow's game, isn't it, which he generally accuses us of playing? Then he will move on to next week's railway strike. The rotting vegetables and stranded tourists will also be the fault of ourselves and Mesdames. Of course all these gloomy prophecies and reproaches and upbraidings will have not the slightest effect and he knows it. He knows to a vote where he will be at the end of the session, that is to say out, not in, so he really might save himself the trouble of making this speech. But he is fond of speaking, it amuses him, and above all it amuses him to publish the iniquities of his fellow-countrymen. Do you like him?'

'Oh yes – very much.'

'I love him – I really love old Bouche-Bontemps.'

Philip leant across the table and said to me, 'All French politicians love each other, or so they say. You see, they never know when they may want to join each other's governments.'

Everybody laughed. Conversation became general, people shouting remarks at each other in all directions. I like this lively habit which enables one to listen without the effort of joining in, unless one has something to say. When the babel died down again I asked M. Hué, my other neighbour, what would happen if the crisis went on.

'René Pléven, Jules Moch and Georges Bidault, in that order, will try and form governments and they will fail. Anglo-French relations will deteriorate; social troubles will multiply; North Africa will boil. In the end even the deputies will notice that what we chiefly need is a government. They will probably come back to Bouche-Bontemps who will get in with the same ministers and the same programme they will have rejected tonight. Is it true that Sir Harald Hardrada is coming over to give a lecture?'

'So Alfred tells me.'

'That's bad.'

'Oh – I was looking forward –'

'I don't mean the lecture. There is nothing on earth more enjoyable than listening to Sir Harald. But it is a storm signal – the first in a sequence of events only too well known to us at the Quai d'Orsay. Whenever your government is planning some nasty surprise they send over Sir Harald to lull our suspicions and put us in a good humour.'

'What's the subject of the lecture?' Valhubert asked me.

'I think I heard it was to be Lord Kitchener.'

The two Frenchmen looked at each other.

'Nom de nom – !'

'We always think we can tell what is coming by the subject, you see. How well I remember "A Study in Allied Solidarity". It was intensely brilliant – delivered in Algiers just before the Syrian affair. "Lord Kitchener" can only mean good-bye to Les Îles Minquiers.

Well, if it's that, it's no great surprise. Let's hope the Intelligence Service is not preparing something much worse.'

'Talking of the Service,' said Valhubert, 'when do I meet the irresistible Mees Nortee?'

'Oh, poor Northey, so she's a spy, is she?'

'Of course. And such a successful one. It was devilish work sending her.'

'Well, you'll be able to see for yourself at our dinner party next week.'

'Good. Can I sit next to her?'

'Certainly you can't,' said Philip.

'Why not? If it's an official dinner, I get the *bout de table* anyway.'

'No – we have other candidates – me for one – it's a big dinner and you'll be well above the salt.'

'I thought the English never bothered about protocol?'

'When in Rome, however, we do as the Romans do – eh, Hughie?'

'Put me next to Mees –'

'After dinner,' said Philip, 'you may have a tête-à-tête with her on a sofa. It's as far as I can go.'

As we left the dining-room Valhubert and two or three other deputies took themselves off, leaving a preponderance of Anglo-Saxons. Philip looked sadly across the room at Grace. I noticed that when she was present Philip became unsure of himself in his anxiety to please her and, as a result, lost much of the charm which lay in his lounging, bantering, casual, take-it-or-leave-it manner. It was rather pathetic to see him sitting bolt upright, hands folded on his knees like a small boy. Presently Mrs Jungfleisch moved over to join him. She began questioning him about what all the Americans in Paris seemed to call the Eels. I listened with half an ear. I had got M. Hué again and he was telling a long, probably funny story about Queen Marie of Roumania. It was the kind of thing I often have trouble in listening to; this time, I had a feeling he had told it to me before and that I had not listened then, either.

Mrs Jungfleisch was saying, 'This parochial squabble over a few small rocks hardly seems to fit into the new concept of a free and balanced world community, does it?'

'Does it?' Philip spoke mechanically, his eyes on Grace.

'A certain absence of rationalism here?'

'To say the least of it.'

'If there are no inhabitants, how does auto-determination apply?'

'It can't.'

'But the modern concept of sovereignty is built up, surely, on auto-determination?'

'That's what we are told.'

'Another query which comes to mind. Where there are no inhabitants how can one know whether the Eels are French- or English-speaking?'

'One can't.'

'And yet language is a powerful determinant of the concept of sovereignty?'

'It's a question of law, not of language.'

'The French say they will soon have a Bomb.'

'Makes no odds. They won't drop it on London because of the Îles Minquiers.'

'I don't believe I have a perfectly comprehensive grasp of this problem from the point of view of you Britishers. Could you brief me?'

'I could. It would take hours. The whole thing is very complicated.'

I saw that Philip was longing for the party to break up so that he could drive Grace to the Chambre, having her alone with him for a few minutes in his motor. I was dying to go to bed. Although it was rather early I put on my gloves and said good-night.

9

Bouche-Bontemps' ministry was rejected by the Assembly. *'L'homme des Hautes-Pyrénées'*, as the French papers often called him, as if he were some abominable snowman lurking in those remote highlands, made his pathetic or rousing or moving oration to about three hundred and fifty pairs of dry eyes and flinty hearts. The two hundred and fifty who were sufficiently moved to vote for him were not enough to carry him to office. It was rather annoying for Alfred and me, because, shortly before M. Béguin fell, we had invited him and most of the members of his cabinet to a dinner party. Now it looked as if our first big dinner would be given to a lot of disgruntled ex-ministers.

The railway strike duly occurred. As always in France, the human and regional element played a part here. The northern workers came out to a man; their meridional colleagues, more whimsical, less disciplined, by no means as serious, brought quite a lot of trains into Paris. This caused a bottleneck; tourists on their way home from late holidays got as far as the capital and could get no further. Amyas Mockbar said:

STRANDED

Thousands of Britons are stranded in strike-torn Paris. They are camping round the idle stations, foodless, comfortless, hopeless. What is the British Embassy doing to alleviate their great distress? Organizing a lorry service to take them to the coast where British ships could rescue them? Arranging accommodation? Lending them francs with which to buy themselves food? Nothing whatever.

Miss Northey Mackintosh, niece and social secretary to Ambassadress Lady Wincham, told me today: 'My aunt is far too busy arranging a big dinner party to bother about the tourists.' N.B. Estimated cost of such ambassadorial entertainments, £10 a head.

'Did you tell him?' I asked, handing her the *Daily Post*. I was having my breakfast and she was perched on the end of my bed. She came every morning at this time for orders – those orders which were carried out by anybody but herself.

'Quelle horrible surprise! Of course I didn't tell him – would I have said my aunt when you are my first cousin once removed?'

'But do you see him, darling?' I knew that she did. Philip had met them walking up the Faubourg hand in hand looking, he said, like Red Riding Hood and the grandmother.

'Poor little Amy, he's a good soul,' said Northey, 'you'd love him, Fanny.'

'I doubt it.'

'Can I bring him here one day?'

'Certainly you can't. Whenever he sees Alfred or me he writes something utterly vile about us. You ought to be furious with him for this horrible invention. And now I must scold you, Northey. It's partly your fault for mentioning a dinner party at all, though of course I know quite well you didn't say those words. When one sees inverted commas in the paper these days it means speech invented by the writer. If you must go out with him, which I greatly deprecate, please remember never to tell him anything at all about what goes on here.'

'Oh the pathos! It's Lord Grumpy who forces the poor soul to write gossip. What interests him is political philosophy – he says he wants to concentrate on the Chambre but Lord Grumpy drags him back to the Chambre *à coucher*. You see, he's a witty soul!'

'I wonder if he's really such a good political journalist? It's rather a different talent from gossip writing, you know.'

'Oh, don't tell poor little Amy that – he might commit –'

'I only wish he would commit –'

'He's a father, Fanny.'

'Many revolting people are.'

'And he has to feed his babies.'

'So do tigers. One doesn't want to be their dinner, all the same.'

'Fanny,' wheedling voice.

'Mm?'

'He wants to do a piece on Auntie Bolter. He says when she got married he had a thick week with the Dockers and the Duke of Something and couldn't do her justice. He'd like to know when she's coming to stay here so that he can link her up with you and Alfred.'

'Yes, I expect he would love that. Just the very thing for a political philosopher to get his teeth into – now, Northey, please listen to me,' I said, in a voice to which she was quite unaccustomed. 'If we have trouble with Mockbar and if it turns out to be your fault I shall be obliged to send you back to Scotland. I am here to protect Alfred from this sort of indiscretion.'

Northey looked mutinous, her eyes brimmed and her mouth went down at the corners.

The door now burst open and a strange figure loomed into the room. Side whiskers, heavy fringe, trousers, apparently moulded to the legs, surmounted by a garment for which I find no word but which covered the torso, performing the function both of coat and of shirt, such was the accoutrement of an enormous boy (I could not regard him as a man), my long-lost Basil.

'*Quelle horrible* surprise!' said Northey, not at all displeased at this diversion from her own indiscretions, past and future.

Basil looked from one to the other. When he realized that we were both delighted to see him, the scowl which he had arranged on his face gave way to a particularly winning smile.

'Well, Ma,' he said, 'here I am. Hullo, Northey!'

'This is very exciting. I thought I'd lost you for ever.'

'Yes, I expect you did. What about breakfast – I could press down some bacon and eggs – in short I am starving. I say, this is all very posh, isn't it! Cagey lot of servants here, Ma – I had to show them my passport before they would let me in.'

'Have you caught sight of yourself in a glass lately?' said Northey, taking the telephone to order his breakfast.

'They must have seen a Ted before – how about *les blousons noirs*?'

'Not in embassies, darling, it's another world.'

'And what's this?' said Northey, fingering an armband he wore inscribed with the words: 'Grandad's Tours'.

'That's magic. Open sesame to the whole world of travel.'

'Where have you come from, Baz?'

'This minute, from the Gare d'Austerlitz. Actually from the Costa Brava.'

'Begin at the beginning, miserable boy. Do remember I've seen and heard nothing of you for three whole months.'

'Why, that's right, nor you have.'

'Not since you cut our luncheon that day.'

'But I wrote and put you off.'

'Six weeks later.'

'I wrote at once – I'm afraid there was posting trouble. Well, it's like this. You know old Grandad? Yes, Ma, of course you do, Granny Bolter's new old man.'

'I've never seen him.'

'Still, you know he exists. Actually, Granny met him with me – old Grandad and me have been matey for an age – he was the brains of our gang. I can tell you, Granny's got a good husband this time, just what she deserves. You can't think how well they get on.'

I had always noticed that, while my children regarded everybody over the age of thirty as old sordids, old weirdies, ruins, hardly human at all, the Bolter, at sixty-five, was accepted as a contemporary. She had an astonishing gift of youth due, perhaps, to a combination of silliness with infinite good nature and capacity for enjoyment. Physically she was amazing for her age; it was easy to see that her heart had never been involved in any of her countless love affairs.

Basil went on in his curious idiom, which consisted in super-imposing, whenever he remembered to do so, cockney or American slang on the ordinary speech of an educated person. 'Old Grandad found that Granny's money is earning a paltry four or five per cent on which she pays taxes into the bargain. Now that's not good enough for him, so 'e scouts round, see, and finds out about this travel racket – oh boy, and is racket the word? 'E lays down a bit of Granny's lolly for premises and propaganda and now he's all set for the upper-income group – tax free of course – and I'm on the band-wagon with him and soon I'll be about to give you and Father the whizz of an old age. Grandad's the brainy boss and I'm the brawny executive; the perfect combination. So you see now why I couldn't lunch that day – I had just embarked on my career.'

'Which is?'

'I'm the boy wot packs in the meat.'

'Here's your breakfast.'

'Thanks very much. It's many a day since proper food crossed my palate. Ever been to Spain? Don't! Well, to go on with my exposey – Grandad assembles the cattle and I herd it to and fro. In plain English, Grandad, with many a specious promise and hope-ful slogan – "No hurry, no worry if you travel the Grandad way" and so on – gets together parties of tourists, takes their cash off them and leaves me to conduct them to their doom. Ghastly it is – fifteen to a carriage across France and worse when we change for the peninsula. Then, when they finally disembark, more dead than alive after days without food or sleep, they have to face up to the accommodation. "Let Grandad rent you a fisherman's cottage" says the prospectus. So he does. The beds are still hot from the honest fisher folk prized out of them by yours truly! That's when the ruminants begin collapsing – disappointment finishes them off. Anyhow the old cows drop like flies when the temperature is over a hundred – Britons always think they are going to love the heat but in fact it kills them – we usually plant one or two in the bone-orchard before we start for home. I keep a top hat over there now, for the funerals, it looks better. Lucky I'm tough, you need to be for this work, I can tell you!'

'I wonder they don't complain?'

'Complain! But what's the good, they've got to go through with it once they are caught up in the machine. There's no escape.'

'How I should hate you!' said Northey.

'They hate all right – the point is they utterly depend. They can't speak any language bar a little basic British and they've got no money because Grandad bags whatever they can afford for the trip before they leave. So they are at my mercy. You should see the letters they write when they get home about "your tall, dark courier", threatening my life and everything. Bit too late then of course, I'm far away, packing in the next lot.'

'Whatever induces them to go in the first place, without making a few inquiries? It seems perfectly mad!'

'Ah! There you have the extraordinary genius of me Grandad. He literally mesmerizes them with his propaganda. All built up on smoothing the path of sex. "Let Grandad take you to the Land of Romance, Leisure and Pleasure." "Will you hear a Spanish lady, how she wooed an Englishman?" See the sort of thing? We've got a plate-glass window at the office, with life-sized dummies of a señorita riding behind a caballero. Inside it's lined with wedding snaps of people who have married Spanish grandees during Grandad tours (no funeral snaps of course). There's something in it, mind you, some of the girls do sleep with customs officers.'

'On those horrid tables?' said Northey, interested.

'But how do they have time?' I asked. 'I always seem to be in too much of a hurry to sleep with people at the customs.'

'Next time you must try Grandad's way – *no hurry*. The trouble is you travel soft. You don't know what a journey can be like when you go cheap – it beats imagination. The Leisure, the Pleasure! The waits are endless, whole days sometimes – hours to spare at every frontier you come to. Of course the douaniers, being in uniform, get the pick. The older ladies are obliged to pay waiters and beach attendants and such like.'

'I thought they had no money?'

'They tear off their jewels.'

'Well then, just tell the programme. You go sight-seeing or what?'

'Nothing whatever. The British female goes abroad for romance and that's that.'

'Ay de mi!' said Northey, 'how true!'

'And the men? Aren't Spanish women very much guarded?'

'The men usually arrive dead beat. They take the journey worse than the women do and fury tires their hearts. They just have the energy to strip and peel. I don't think they would ever manage – you know, in the state they are in. Besides, their emotions and energies, if any, are concentrated on revenge.'

'And how do you spend your time?' I vaguely hoped for an account of advanced lessons in Spanish.

'Me? I lie on my face on the beach. It's safer. Once we've arrived at the place and they've seen where they've got to doss down and when they've smelt the food, redolent of rancidol, which they are expected to press down, the younger male Britons have only one idea. Señoritas be blowed – they just want to kick my lemon – give me a fat lip, see? So I lie there, camouflaged by protective colouring. My back is black, but my face is white; they don't connect the two and I am perfectly all right providing I never turn over. When the day comes for going home they need me too much to injure me.'

'Goodness, Basil!'

'You may well say so. Where's Father?'

'He's been in London – back any time now. Look, darling, I haven't told him about your summer – I didn't know anything for certain – so let him think, what I rather hoped myself, that you were polishing up your pure Castilian. He might not like the idea of you – well –'

'Carting out the rubbish?'

'Oh dear, no, he wouldn't like it. But I don't think we need tell him. Now the holidays are over and you'll be going back to your crammer I think we might, without being deceitful, forget the whole thing?'

'Only I'm not going back to the crammer. That wasn't a holiday, Ma – funny sort of hol that would be – no, it's my career, my work, my future.'

'Lying on your face in the sand is?'

'Yeah.'

'You're giving up the Foreign Service?'

'You bet.'

'Basil!'

'Now listen, Mother dear, the Foreign Service has had its day – enjoyable while it lasted no doubt, but over now. The privileged being of the future is the travel agent. He lives free, travels soft – don't think he shares the sufferings of his people, he has a first-class sleeper, the best room in the hotel. Look at me now, washed, shaved, relaxed and rested. I only wish you could see my victims at this moment! Haven't taken their clothes off for days. Some of them stood the whole way last night while I lay at my ease. Even during a railway strike you've only got to exhibit the armband and the officials will do anything for you. You see we hold the national tourist industries in the hollow of our hands. There's nothing they dread more than a lot of unorganized travellers wandering about their countries exhibiting individualism. They'd never force a tourist on his own into those trams and hotels – he'd go home sooner. But you can do anything with a herd and the herd must have its drover. As he keeps the tickets and the money and the passports (no worry) even the most recalcitrant of the cattle are obliged to follow him. No good jibbing when the conditions are ghastly because what is the alternative? To be stranded without hope of succour. So the authorities need us; the tourists need us; we are paramount. Oh, it's a wonderful profession and I'm lucky to have the family backing which got me into it.'

My blood ran cold at these words. I have seen the promise of too many young men fade away as the result of taking a wrong step after leaving their university not to feel appalled at the prospect of this brilliant boy, easily my favourite child, thus jeopardizing his future. There is no sadder spectacle than that of a lettered beachcomber, a pass to which Basil seemed to have come in three short months.

'And your first in history,' I said, 'your gift for languages – all to be wasted?'

'It's no good, Ma, you'll have to be realistic about this. The world isn't like it was when you were young. There's more opportunity, more openings for a chap than there were then. You can't really expect me to swot away and get into the Foreign Service and put up with an aeon of boredom simply to end my days in a ghastly great dump like this? I love Father, you know I do, and I don't want to hurt your feelings, but I've no intention of wasting the best years of my life like he has and nothing you can say will persuade me to. So now, having partaken of this smashing breakfast, for which I'm truly grateful, I must wend my way back to the hungry sheep who will look up, poor brutes, and not be fed.'

'They must be fed. Where are they?'

'Sitting on bursting canvas bags at the Gare du Nord – at least I hope so. I put them into the metro, before taking a cab myself, and told them where to get out and that I'd be along. I said to meet at the bus stop of the 48 because I believe the crowds at the station are terrific and one sheep looks very much like another. I expect they'll be there now for days – only hope this fine weather will go on.'

'You horrify me. Can't we do something for them?'

'They're all right. Singing "Roll out the Barrel" like Britons always do at waits – wish they'd learn a new tune.'

'How many are there?'

'In my party? About twenty-five. You don't need to bother about them, Ma, honest.'

'Please go straight to the Gare du Nord and bring them here. I'll have breakfast for them in the garden, ready by the time they arrive.'

A wail from Northey. 'No, Fanny, you're not to – they'll petrify my badger.'

'Surely he's blacked out in his air-raid shelter?'

'He'll smell them down there and tremble. A badger's sense of smell is highly developed – people don't understand about creatures.'

'Don't you take on,' said Basil, 'they smell like badgers themselves. He'll be thrilled – he'll think his mates have arrived.'

'Go at once, Baz,' I said.

'But, Ma, this strike will probably last for days. You'll get awfully tired of "Roll out the Barrel".'

'Yes. As soon as you've brought them there you must see about a lorry to take them to the coast.'

'No fear. All our profit would melt away – Grandad would kill me.'

'I'll pay.'

'You're soft. Another thing – have I got to face all those posh butlers with that lot in tow?'

'Northey can go with you and bring you in through the Avenue Gabriel. It's nearer for the metro. Get the key of the garden, dearest, from Mrs Trott as you go out and tell Jérôme to be ready to help Baz find a lorry. Go on, Basil, twitch your mantle blue.'

I was not at all surprised when Basil's Britons turned out to be entirely delightful, very different indeed from the furious, filthy, haggard, exhausted, sex-starved mob which anybody not knowing Basil and not knowing England might have expected from his description. They were, in fact, sensible, tidy and nicely dressed, covered with smiles and evidently enjoying this adventure in a foreign land. There were rather more women than men, but it was unimaginable that any of them could have gone to bed with customs officers or waiters or indeed that they should commit fornication or adultery under any circumstances whatever. They looked more than respectable. I was glad to be confirmed in my suspicion that Basil's account of his own tough and unmerciful behaviour was an invention, to startle Northey and me. The Britons were full of his praises and when he explained that I was his mother they crowded round to tell me what a wonder boy or miracle child I had produced. They had no idea that they were in an embassy – not that they would have been impressed had they known it, since the English are less conscious than any other race of diplomatic status; they evidently thought I kept a hotel in Paris. 'Nice here,' they said, 'we must tell our friends.' Any strangeness in their situation they would put down to being abroad. 'Very nice,' they said of the breakfast, which they ate with the relish of extreme hunger.

When they had finished they told me, in detail, how splendid Basil had been. Hundreds of Britons, it seemed, many of whom had paid much more for the trip than they had, were left behind at Port-Vendres; Basil had literally forged a way through the mob, and, using his gigantic strength in conjunction with his mastery of languages, had lifted and pushed and shoved and lugged and somehow inserted every single member of his party on to a train already full to suffocation.

'Now all the others who were on it are stifling at that horrid Gare du Nord while here we are in these nice grounds.'

'Masterly organization,' said an elderly man of military aspect. 'He'll do well in the next war – a genius for improvisation – marvellous linguist – I think you should be proud of him. I could have done with more like him in the Western Desert. Now he's gone off to get a lorry to take us to the coast. What initiative! We are all going to subscribe for a memento when we get home.'

I said, 'You must be so tired.'

'Oh no.' A cheerful woman like a W.V.S. worker spoke up. 'After the holiday we've had, a night or two in the train seems nothing. Yes, forty-eight hours we've been since leaving. Quite an adventure!'

'And I suppose it wasn't too comfortable in Spain?'

'You don't go abroad for comfort exactly, do you? I always say, plenty of that at home. One likes to see how the foreigners live, for a change. There's no end to what they'll put up with. The toilet arrangements! You'd never believe!'

'Excuse me, but is that a badger's sett?'

'You are clever!' said Northey, twinkling and sparkling at the poor man whose head was turned there and then.

'Are there many badgers in this part of Paris?'

'I've never seen another but there may be. Do you have them where you live?'

'Oh no, not in the Cromwell Road. I knew what it was from the TV. I see you have a redstart, now that's a delightful bird.'

'Yes, and an owl at night. But we haven't got a TV.'

'Shame,' said the Briton. 'They don't seem to go in for them abroad we've noticed. Still, with so much nature about you hardly need one. That's what I have mine for, the nature. I didn't know Paris was like this, wouldn't mind living here myself.'

As Northey and I went back to the house we met Alfred. 'I was looking for you. Who are all these people?'

'Sweet Britons,' said Northey.

'Stranded by the railway strike,' I added. He seemed satisfied with this explanation. 'How was London?'

'Worrying. I'll tell you later – I must go to the Chancery now. Are we lunching in? Oh, thank goodness –'

I told Northey to see that the Britons got off all right, to have some sandwiches made up for them and to say good-bye to Basil for me. My business now was to protect Alfred, tired and preoccupied as he seemed, from the sight of his son in such a garb.

The Britons had a little nap on the grass. Then they began a sing-song. We had 'Lily Marlene', 'Colonel Bogey' (whistling only) and 'Nearer my God to Thee'. The noise was not disagreeable, thinly floating on a warm breeze. Just before luncheon-time I heard female voices sounding a cheer in the Avenue Gabriel.

Northey came running, to announce that they had gone, in a car.

'What, all twenty-five in one motor?'

'Car is French for charabang. Basil sends his love and he'll probably be back next week. He seems to think the Embassy can be his Paris H.Q. in future, if you're lucky. He's cooking a lot of schemes, I note. Then faithful Amy turned up.'

'You don't mean Mockbar?' I was horrified.

'Good little soul, indeed I do. But don't worry. I told Baz you wouldn't like to have him hanging about in the garden and he got rid of him in a tick.'

'How did he? That's a formula worth knowing.'

'It's not one you can use very often though. He pretended the Britons were all radioactive. Amy buggered off before you could say *canif.*'

'I absolutely forbid you to say that word, Northey. No, not *canif,* you know quite well. Wherever did you pick it up?'

'The Captain of the *Esmeralda.* He was a most unpleasant person, but I rather liked some of his expressions.'

'Well, I beg you won't use that one again.'

'All the same, do you admit it's perfect for describing the exits of Amy?'

I dreaded the *Daily Post* after that. Sure enough:

RADIOACTIVE

Some two score radioactive Britons sought the protection of our Embassy in Paris yesterday. Did Sir Alfred Wincham send for scientific aid? Are they now receiving treatment at a clinic?

DUMPED

No British officials went near them. They were hustled into a lorry by our amateur envoy's son Mr Basil Wincham and dumped at the coast. All efforts to get in touch with them subsequently have been fruitless. Where is this dangerous lorry-load now? Have the sanitary authorities been informed? If they went home on a British ship were the necessary precautions taken to see that their fellow-travellers were not contaminated? This whole incident seems to typify the slack and unprofessional outlook which permeates our Paris mission today.

I was quite terrified, envisaging awful developments. After a consultation with Philip we decided not to tell Alfred until something happened, knowing that he would never look at the *Daily Post* of his own accord. Nothing happened at all. The powers that be in England knew better than to believe an unsupported statement by Mockbar; the French were unaware of his existence and of that of the *Daily Post*. Philip said that even if their sanitary authorities should raise the question he could easily deal with them. 'You know what the French are, they don't quite believe in modern magic. They all go to fortune-tellers (M. de Saint-Germain is booked up for months), they read the stars every day and make full use of spells. But they don't get into a state about things like radioactivity.'

Old Grumpy, having failed to make any mischief for us, had to drop the story because Basil and his Britons, merged among thousands struggling home on Channel steamers, were never identified and therefore could not be interviewed.

In London, Alfred had submitted his own views on the likelihood of the French ever accepting the European Army; they were in direct contradiction to those of his American colleague. The Cabinet would naturally have preferred to be told what they wanted to hear and Alfred's prognostications were not well received. He was merely instructed to stiffen his attitude and informed that London regarded the C.E.D. as inevitable and essential. He was also informed that our government were going full steam ahead over the Minquiers and that he must make this perfectly clear in Paris. The Foreign Secretary announced that he would be coming over to see his opposite number, as soon as he had one. I believe that Alfred heartily wished himself back in Oxford, though he did not say so to me.

M. Moch, M. Pléven and M. Bidault all tried to form governments and all duly failed. Then Bouche-Bontemps tried again and was accepted by the Chambre the very day before our dinner party. Alfred and I were delighted. For one thing, he had become a friend and it was most fortunate for us to have him to help and even sometimes guide us while we were still finding our feet; besides which our dinner was, we thought, saved. Bouche-Bontemps was taking the direction of foreign affairs himself, anyhow for a while, so that the government was virtually the same as that which had been in power before this long crisis. M. Béguin was now Vice-Président instead of Président du Conseil, and one or two minor ministries were given to new men, belonging to groups hitherto in opposition. This procedure, known as *dosage* and frequently resorted to during the Fourth Republic, had ensured the extra votes necessary to put Bouche-Bontemps in.

I told Northey and requested Philip to come to my bedroom early on the morning of the dinner in order to talk over dispositions. Philip appeared, punctual as always. 'Isn't this a mercy!' I said. The morning papers hailed the end of the crisis, giving Bouche-Bontemps a friendly reception. In fact a naïf and optimistic reader, like myself, would suppose that a long term of stable government lay ahead. *The Times*, in a leading article, compared Bouche-Bontemps to Raymond Poincaré; the *Daily Telegraph* said he was the strongest man thrown up by the Fourth Republic so far and shared many characteristics with Clemenceau.

Philip looked sceptically at the headlines. 'You can thank the General for this. If he were not sitting like the rock of ages at Colombey we should never have a government here at all. As it is they are obliged to come to these little temporary arrangements simply in order to keep King Charles in exile. This ministry won't last six weeks. Hullo – have you seen Mockbar?'

'No – don't tell me – better not shake my nerve – !'

'Not too bad. It's headed: Paris Dinner Muddle. "Confusion – bungling – secrecy – lack of organization are casting a shadow over our amateur envoy's first official dinner." And so on. Zero, in fact. The old boy's losing his grip – he'll get the sack if he can't do better than that. Where's Mees – I thought she was to come for orders?'

'Naughty girl. I suppose she's overslept as usual.'

'She's not in her room – I banged as I came up the back stairs – nor in the bath, I banged there, too.'

'Are you sure? How very odd. I wonder if Katie knows anything?'

Katie knew everything, as she always did, in her cage and told what she knew with evident enjoyment. Philip listened in to her account with the earphone. It seemed that while Alfred and I had been out the evening before, rushing from the National Day of Iceland to a party for the Foreign Minister of Bali, ending up at a concert at the Costa Rican embassy, a hamper of live lobsters had arrived for me. They were a present from M. Busson, a deputy with a seaside constituency, one of the people invited to our dinner. The chef, overjoyed, unable to get hold of me, had informed Northey, saying that the menu would now have to be altered. It would then have been Northey's plain duty to send interim acknowledgment and thanks to M. Busson. No such thing. On seeing the dear lobsters, which were lurching about on the kitchen floor, she flew into a *fantigue*. She made Katie put her through to the Ministère de la Marine where, strange to say, she had no friend, and asked to speak to the Chef de Cabinet. Presenting Alfred's compliments she inquired at what point the Seine became salt. The answer was Rouen. She then ordered Jérôme for 8.30 a.m. When the time came she forced the furious chef to cram the lobsters back into their hamper, and made the footmen load them on to the Rolls-Royce (not in the boot, for fear of smothering the darlings, but inside, on the pretty carpet). By now she was well on the way to Normandy where the sweet creatures would duly be put back in their native element.

'Thank you, Katie.' I rang off and looked at Philip, suppressing a giggle as best I could. He shook his head, not very much amused.

'This Northey!' he said. 'In the first place the French navy, a thoroughly Anglophobe institution, will immediately assume that we are up to some monkey work. Why should Alfred want to know where the Seine becomes tidal, all of a sudden? In the second place Busson, who is the new Minister of Atomic Energy, is the leader of a small but powerful group in the Chambre. He is also a famous gourmet. He will be angry and disappointed when his lobsters fail to appear this evening – he may never forgive. In the third place, I think it's too irresponsible of Mees to go off like this on the one day when she might be some slight use to you!'

The telephone bell rang: Katie again. 'I forgot to say, she took a follower. At least I expect he is one by now –'

'Who?'

'The Chef de Cabinet. She arranged to pick him up at the side door of the Ministry in the rue St Florentin.'

'That's quite a good thing,' I said to Philip, 'at least he'll see for himself she's not spying.'

'My dear, they are madly suspicious of Mees – all the ones who aren't in love with her, that is. The sweet lobsters won't reassure them, I can tell you.'

'What time should you say she'll be back?'

'Who knows? Rouen is nearly 100 miles, I think. The Chef de Cabinet will spin it out as long as he can, no doubt. Oh well – it's not as if she'd be much use here, one can't trust her even to put cards round the table, let alone work out the seating. I should have had to do it for you in any case. I'll get on to old Hughie, presently.'

'Let's put M. Busson next to Northey so that she can explain about the lobsters in her own words – ?'

'And make an enemy for life? He has never been a minister before, he wouldn't at all relish sitting next to your social secretary. We must make her apologize to him before dinner – lucky she's so irresistible to French politicians. Now – business. Let's see who we've got. I suppose I shall have to have Mees – no hope of Grace for me, eh? Talking of Grace, why not ask her to come and give you a hand with the flowers and things? I know she'd love to.'

'Philip, what a good idea!'

'Yes, I'm going to telephone now – she'll turn up trumps, you'll see.'

He was quite right. Grace came for me in her motor after luncheon and took me to St Cloud to pick flowers for the party. Valhubert had a property there, just outside the park, an ancient garden on the site of a hunting-lodge which the Germans had destroyed in 1870. Here he grew flowers and fruit for his own use. It was a melancholy, romantic spot, especially in the autumn when the dark green leaves of the adjacent woodlands were flecked with yellow and the old fruit trees covered with apples and pears and peaches. Impossible to imagine that one was only ten minutes away from Paris. The flowers that were visible all grew in tubs and stone vases, while those for cutting were planted in regular rows, like vegetables, behind a hornbeam hedge. 'Charles-Édouard hates to see flowers growing in the earth,' Grace explained. 'Look how the hot summer has brought out the orange blossom and even ripened a few oranges; very rare, in this climate.' Wearing a dark grey linen dress with broderie anglaise collar and cuffs she looked exactly right there, as she always did whatever the circumstances. She gave me a pair of secateurs with which to cut the old-fashioned roses, lilies, hollyhocks, tuberoses, carnations, fuchsias and geraniums. 'We'll make a lovely mixture,' she said. 'Don't they smell better than those you buy in shops?'

'And no nursing-home flowers,' I said. 'That's rare at this time of year.'

'Those horrible gladioli, we don't dream of allowing them. Aren't English autumn flowers too loathsome!'

'Nursing homes here have them too.'

'Not quite such brutes. The English are for ever building themselves up as being so good at growing flowers, best gardeners in the world and all that, and what does it boil down to *en fin de compte*? Michaelmas daisies and chrysanths, *sentant le cimetière.*' Grace was off on her hobby-horse now. 'Have you ever noticed it's just those very things the English pride themselves on most which are better here? Trains: more punctual; tweeds: more pretty; football: the French always win. Doctors: can't be compared, nobody ever dies here until they are a hundred. Horses, we've got M. Boussac. The post, the roads, the police – France is far better administered –'

I felt quite furious. 'Well, come on, Fanny,' she said, 'I'm waiting for the answer – you're the Ambassadress, you're meant to know it –'

'It isn't fair. You've got these things all ready to trot out, and I suppose facts and figures to bolster them up if I begin to query them. Before I see you next I shall do a bit of prep, but for the moment my mind is a blank. Oh! I know – justice. Better and much quicker at home – admit?'

'We hurry people to the gallows all right. Fluster them up in the witness box and then swing them. Give me a dear old *juge d'instruction*, plodding away, when I'm in trouble –'

'No, Grace, we don't hang them any more.'

'Not even murderers?'

'Specially not them.'

'What are you telling me? I don't care for this news at all! Do you mean people can murder one as much as they like and nothing happen to them?'

'Yes. Unless you're a policewoman. I'm not sure they are meant to poison one either or perhaps it's shooting that's not allowed. I can never remember. But don't worry. If they know nothing will happen they don't murder so much.'

'Are you sure?'

'Yes, it was all in the papers. I say – I've thought of something else – the papers are better at home –'

'Are they? I can't say I ever see them except when Mockbar has a go at us, then some kind friend cuts it out and sends it. He's a delightful writer, such polish, such accuracy!'

'You take in *The Times*,' I said. 'I know you do. Try and be more truthful, Grace –'

'My father sends it, but we hardly ever open it. I keep it for covering the furniture in the summer.'

'I've thought of something else – digestives.'

'All right, I'll give you digestives and I'll give you Cooper's Oxford and if you're very good potted shrimps as well. Now that's rather typical. The only subject we agree on is food, which is not supposed to be an English talent at all. It's the things they pretend to be good at which are such flops.'

'It's THEY now, is it!' I said.

'Don't be angry, Fanny. After all, Charles-Édouard and the children are French –'

'That's no reason for downing the English.'

'I don't down them – not really, but they annoy me with their pretended superiority. And oh, how they chill me! Not only the climate –'

'Same as here.'

'Nonsense, darling, there's no comparison – but also the hearts. I was noticing that yesterday. I had to go to a wedding at the Consulate – cold as charity it was. Gabble gabble gabble – gabble gabble gabble – may I give you my best wishes? Over. Think of the difference between that and a wedding in a *mairie*! When the bride and bridegroom come in, M. le Maire, in his sash of office, throws up his arms like General de Gaulle: *"Mes enfants! Voici la plus belle journée de votre vie –"'*

'Yes, Grace. I dare say, but people must be themselves you know. Can you imagine poor Mr Stock throwing up his arms like General de Gaulle and saying "My children, this is the most beautiful day of your lives"? It would be simply ridiculous if he did.'

'Ridiculous, because he hasn't got a heart. That's what I complain of.'

'Anyhow it wouldn't have sounded very convincing at yesterday's wedding when you think that the Chaddesley-Corbetts are both nearly seventy and have been divorced I don't know how many times.'

We snipped away in silence. Presently Grace asked how the Minquiers were getting on.

'Nothing new, I think. Mr Gravely comes here next week to see M. Bouche-Bontemps. Partly about the Eels, I suppose.'

'Oh, does he? Bringing Angela?'

'No. Wives mustn't come too often because of foreign currency. It seems she was here in the summer.'

'So she was. Isn't it mad of the Treasury the way they drive these important politicians to the brothels just for the sake of the few pounds it would cost to bring their wives with them!'

'Darling! He's sixty, looks like an empty banana skin and is only coming for the inside of a week –'

'Some chaps can't stand more than twenty-four hours, you know.'

The Chef de Cabinet did indeed spin it out. Grace and I had done the flowers and done the table and she had gone home to dress when Northey reappeared. She seemed quite unaware of having done wrong and I saw no point in scolding as that particular misdeed was unlikely to recur. Besides, I was longing to hear about her day as much as she was longing to tell. The sweet lobsters having been returned to their native element the Chef de Cabinet had told Jérôme to make a little detour of about fifty miles which took them to a three-star restaurant. Here they ordered luncheon and then went for a walk in beautiful woods. The Chef de Cabinet, no doubt in an emotional state, had lost his head and ordered *homard à l'armoricaine*. When Northey discovered that this was French for lobster, and the cruellest sort at that, she was furious; she cried and sent him to Coventry for half an hour. They made it up again, ordered a different luncheon and got rather tipsy while it was being cooked. Back in Paris at last, the Chef de Cabinet, unable to endure the parting, put it off by taking her to see Notre Dame. 'Though really,' said Northey, 'when you know the outside you can guess what the inside is going to be like and he made me miss my fitting at Lanvin –'

'Fitting at Lanvin?'

'Didn't I tell you? M. Castillo has offered me Cecil Beaton. Oh, sharpen your wits, Fanny – Cecil Beaton, that heavenly dress with the bobbles –'

II

Our guests assembled under the gaze of King George and Queen Mary. When there is a large dinner at the Embassy it takes place in a banqueting-hall added on to the ground floor by Pauline Borghese. Though by no means beautiful, it is of an earlier date and therefore less catastrophically hideous than its equivalent at the Élysée which so torments the ghost of poor little Mme de Pompadour. The eighteenth-century dining-room on the first floor, with Flemish tapestries painful to a French eye, where we usually had our meals, only holds about twenty people.

When M. Busson arrived, Philip grabbed Northey by the shoulder and steered her towards him, saying that she had something to explain. She took him into a corner and I could see her launching into a pantomime, partly French, partly English, mostly dumb show, tortured expression and flying hands. He looked puzzled, though fascinated, and then amused. Finally, to my relief, he burst out laughing. He gathered his colleagues round him and gave a rapid résumé of Northey's statement. 'And now,' he ended up in English, 'these succulent crustaceans are no doubt swimming away to Les Îles Minquiers.'

'Swimming!' said Northey, scornfully. 'I have yet to see a lobster with fins.'

M. Béguin, who was always rather grumpy and more so now that he was no longer Président du Conseil, remarked sourly that these succulent crustaceans were more likely to be boiling away, at this very moment, in peasant cottages. Far better for them, he explained in his cold, clipped voice, had they been cooked at the Embassy, because the cottage saucepans would be smaller, the cottage fires weaker and the agony more prolonged.

Northey was unmoved by this argument. 'I could see on their sweet faces when they were bug – I mean making off – that they would never let themselves be caught again,' she said, comfortably.

Bouche-Bontemps said, 'Perhaps Mees is quite right, who knows? The Holy Office forbade the boiling alive of heretics – they tried it once, in Spain, and even Spanish nerves gave way at the sight. Ought we really to subject living creatures to such terrible cruelty in order to have one or two delicious mouthfuls?'

'M. le Président,' said Northey, 'je vous aime.'

'It is reciprocal.'

M. Béguin looked like a Nanny whose charges have gone too far in silliness. He said something to M. Hué about the frivolity of les britanniques being beyond endurance. M. Hué, a good-natured fellow, replied that while naturally deploring the waste of delicious lobsters, he found the whole thing funny, touching and plutôt sympathique. M. Béguin raised his eyes to heaven. His shoulders, too, went up until it seemed as if they would never come down again. He looked round for a partisan, saw that Mme Hué's gaze was also fixed to the ceiling and that she was clearly on his side. They went off together to a sofa where they sat talking very fast, throwing malignant glances in the direction of Northey.

The Valhuberts now arrived, raising the level of looks and elegance. I introduced him to Northey and had the satisfaction of seeing that this well-known ravager of the female heart fell there and then victim to the charm of Mees. The evening seemed to have begun extremely well; most of the guests, if not all, were there and were getting on famously. I am always struck by how easily a French party slides down the slipway and floats off to the open sea. People arrive determined to enjoy themselves instead of, as at Oxford, determined (apparently) to be awkward. There are no pools of silence, all the guests find congenial souls, or at least somebody with whom to argue. Even M. Béguin's disapproval had that positive quality which facilitates the task of a hostess; it led to lively talk and a reshuffling of the company.

At this point, Northey was supposed to count the guests and let me know if they were all there. However she was so completely surrounded by ministers that I could not catch her eye to remind her of her duty. Philip, with a resigned wink in my direction, performed it for her. 'That's it,' he said, presently.

The door opened. I supposed that dinner was going to be announced and vaguely wondered why by that door and not the one which led to the dining-room. For a moment nothing happened. Then my bearded son David came crab-wise into the room, pulling after him a blue plastic cradle and a girl attached to its other handle. He was dressed in corduroy trousers, a duffel coat, a tartan shirt and sandals over thick, dirty, yellow woollen socks. The girl was tiny, very fair with a head like a silk-worm's cocoon, short white skirt (filthy) swinging over a plastic petticoat, a black belt, red stockings and high-heeled, pointed, golden shoes.

In the silence which fell as this curious group came into the room I heard a voice (M. Béguin's I expect) saying something about 'cet individu à mine patibulaire' and another (Charles-Édouard de Valhubert probably), 'pas mal, la petite.'

I am always pleased when my children turn up. The sight of them rejoices me, I rush forward, I smile and I embrace. I did so now. David and the girl dumped the cradle on a precious piece by Weisweiller. He kissed me warmly (oh horrid, scrubbing-brush beard) and said, 'Ma, this is Dawn.'

Alfred's reactions were not as immediately enthusiastic as mine. With him it is not so much a physical instinct as a matter of principle that makes him welcome the boys whatever the circumstances of their arrival. Our house is their home, their shelter from the stormy blast. If they are naked they must be clothed; if hungry, fed; if the police of five nations are hot on their heels they must be hidden. No questions must ever be asked. Now he came forward and shook hands with his son, giving him a stern, grave, penetrating look. 'This is Dawn, Father.'

'How do you do?'

Alfred led Dawn and David round the room, introducing them, while I held a hurried consultation with Philip about fitting them in to our dinner.

He said, 'Do you really think it's a good idea? They are so travel-stained –'

Unfortunately I knew my David far too well to think that the stains had anything to do with travel.

'We can't possibly send them out when they have just arrived,' I said. 'Alfred wouldn't hear of it.'

'There's no room for them here. The table only holds fifty – it would take at least an hour to put in another leaf and re-do it.'

'Oh dear, oh dear,' I considered a moment. 'In that case, Philip, I'm most dreadfully afraid, and too sorry, that you'll have to take Northey out to dinner. Go to the Cremaillere – on the house of course. Do you mind?'

'Yes,' said Philip, displeased at this turn of affairs. Though he had not been able to arrange the seating so that he would be next to Grace (he was between Northey and Mrs Jungfleisch) he had been placed exactly opposite her so that he would be able to look at her all the time and occasionally lean over and exchange a remark. 'I mind but I bow to the inevitable.'

'What a funny little person,' I said, 'who do you imagine she is?'

'An heiress, by the look of her.'

'How too splendid that would be. Northey – come here – Philip is going to take you to dine at the Cremaillere to make room for David and the young lady.'

'Oh goody gum trees!' said Northey, eyes shooting out electricity.

'Yes, darling. And before you go, will you give that baby to Mrs Trott and ask her to keep an eye on it and also say I want two bedrooms got ready. Then come straight back after dinner, won't you?'

'We will,' said Philip.

Northey picked up the cradle, swung it round her, performed a pirouette and said, 'Come on, worshipful, let's bugger –'

The spontaneous sound of discontent rising from a dozen French throats as Northey left the room was silenced by the announcement of dinner. When at last I had got the women through the dining-room doors – all holding back politely and saying 'passez – passez' to each other – I led David and the young lady to the places designed for Philip and Northey.

'Why do you put me next my wife?' he said angrily. 'This seems most unusual.'

'But, dear duck, I'm not a fortune teller. How am I expected to know that she is your wife?' I said to Dawn: 'Please forgive me, but we can't do the table all over again. You must simply try and imagine that you are at a city banquet.'

She looked at me with huge, terrified, grey eyes, and I saw, what the extraordinary clothes had hitherto prevented me from realizing, that she was very pretty. I also noticed that she was pregnant.

I went to my place between Bouche-Bontemps and Béguin. They were already plunged in a violent political discussion; seeing that I was not really present in the spirit they continued it across me. David had Mrs Jungfleisch on his right. We had asked her because Philip had asserted that it was impossible to give a dinner party in Paris without her; how thankful I felt now that she had accepted. With a lack of inhibition which no European woman would have exhibited under the circumstances, she went straight to the point. I strained my ears and listened as hard as I could; this was made possible by the fact that, except for my two neighbours, everybody else was doing likewise.

'Your wife is quite beautiful,' she said, 'is she a model?'

'No. She's a student.'

'Indeed. And what does she study?'

'Modern languages.'

'How old is the baby?'

'I'm not sure. Not old at all.'

'Are you staying here long?' I held my breath at this.

'No. We are on our way to the East.'

'I envy you that. Provins and Nancy are at their best in the fall. Such interesting towns. Try and go to Cirey, it's well worth it, and just outside Paris don't forget to stop your car at Grosbois –'

'We haven't got a car. We are walking.'

'Walking to Provins? With the baby?'

'The baby? Oh yes, he's coming too. Not to Provins, to China.'

'My! That's quite some walk. China – let me see now – after

107

Provins and Nancy – don't miss the Place Stanislas – you can take in Munich and Nuremberg and Prague. I envy you that. Lemberg, they say, has charm. After Moscow there is the holy city of Zagorsk, the tomb of St Serge in solid silver. Are you looking for a special school of architecture or just going haphazard? By the way, I suppose you have your visas for China. I heard it was none too easy –'

David said they had no visas for anywhere. They were looking for Truth, he added.

'Aren't you afraid you may end up in gaol?'

He said, loftily, that Truth flourished in gaols, specially in Eastern ones.

'We are the bridge,' he added, 'between pre-war humanity with its selfishness and materialistic barriers against reality and the new race of World Citizens. We are trying to indoctrinate ourselves with wider concepts and for this we realize that we need the purely contemplative wisdom which comes from following the Road.'

Mildred Jungfleisch now had her clue. As soon as she realized that David was not on an ordinary House and Gardens honeymoon, but was in search of Truth, she knew exactly where she was and how to cope. She dropped the Place Stanislas and Grosbois and brought out such phrases as 'Mind-stretching interpretation of the Cosmos', 'Interchange of ideas between sentient contemporary human creatures', 'Explode the forms and habits of thought imposed by authority', 'I once took a course in illogism and I fully realize the place it should hold in contemporary thought', 'Atmosphere of positive thinking – change is life'.

One saw why she was such an asset in society; she could produce the right line of talk in its correct jargon for every occasion. She never put a foot wrong. David was clearly both delighted and amazed to find so kindred a spirit at his parents' table; they talked deeply until the end of dinner. Their neighbours lost interest in the conversation as soon as it moved from personal to eternal issues (the highlight having been the disclosure that David did not know the age of his own baby) and the usual parrot-house noise of a French dinner party broke out. As for the student of modern languages, she never opened her mouth. M. Hué, who was next her, tried all sorts of gambits in French, English, German, Portuguese and Norwegian. She merely looked as if she thought he was about to strike her and held her peace.

I now tried to put these children out of my mind for the present and do my duty as a hostess.

'What does *patibulaire* mean?' I asked M. Bouche-Bontemps. I thought M. Béguin had the grace to look embarrassed; he turned hurriedly to his neighbour.

'*Patibulum* is Latin for a gibbet.'

'I see exactly.'

M. Bouche-Bontemps was very kind and tactful. Instead of abruptly wrenching the conversation in an obvious manner from the subject which was clearly preoccupying me, he began talking about difficult young persons of former days. In seventeenth-century England there were the Ti Tyre Tu, educated gangsters who called themselves after the first line of Virgil's first eclogue. In the 1830s, 'the same length of time from Waterloo as we are from Dunkirk', young Frenchmen called Bousingos, like the Ti Tyre Tu, wore strange clothes and committed lurid crimes. I could have wished he had left out the lurid crimes, but I saw the connexion.

'I don't know about England,' he said, 'but in France mothers are frightened of making their children frown. They love them so much that they cannot bear to see a shadow on their happiness; they never scold or thwart them in any way. I see my daughter-in-law allowing everything, there's no authority outside school and the children do exactly as they like in their spare time. I am horrified when I see what it is that they do like. They never open a book, the girls don't do embroidery, the boy, though he is rather musical, doesn't learn the piano. They play stupid games with a great ball and go to the cinema. We used to be taken to the Matinée Classique at the Français and dream of Le Cid – that's quite old fashioned – it's The Kid now. How will it end?'

'I think you'll find they will grow out of it and become like everybody else.'

'Who is everybody else, though – you and me and the Ambassador or some American film actor?'

'You and me,' I said firmly. 'To our own children we must be the norm, surely. They may react from our values for a while but in the end they will come back to them.'

'But these grandchildren of mine are getting so big – they don't seem to change. They still throw that idiotic football at each other as soon as their lessons are over.'

'Good for the health, that's one thing.'

'I don't care. I don't want them to win the Olympic games. Furthermore healthy children are generally stupid. Those wise old monks knew what they were doing when they founded the universities in unhealthy places. I hate health – the more over-populated the world becomes the more people bother about it. *Hünde, wollt ihr ewig leben?* says I!'

'To your own grandchildren?'

'Specially to them!'

'I don't believe you.'

'I am very serious, however. This is a moment in the history of the world when brains are needed more than anything else. If we don't produce them in Western Europe where will they come from? Not from America where a school is a large, light building with a swimming-pool. Nor from Russia where they are too earnest to see the wood for the trees. As for all the rest, they may have clever thoughts about Karl Marx and so on, but they are not adult. If the children of our old civilization don't develop as they ought to, the world will indeed become a dangerous playground.'

I said, 'My two grown-up boys were perfect when they were little, very, very brilliant, longing to learn, all for Le Cid as opposed to The Kid. They both did well at Oxford. Now look at them. Bearded David there, with a first in Greats if you please, is walking to China in search of Truth. In other words he has given way to complete mental laziness. The other one, Basil, even cleverer, my pride and joy, lies on his face all day on a Spanish beach. How do you explain that?'

'I think they've got a better chance than my poor grandchildren because at least they have some furniture in their heads already.'

'If you ask me they'll all come out of these silly phases. They are nothing new – my cousins and I were quite idiotic when we were young. The only difference is that in those days the grown-ups paid no attention, while we concentrate (too much probably) on these children and their misdoings. How old are yours, by the way?'

'They must be quite seven, eight and nine by now.'

He was very much surprised when I laughed.

'At their age,' he said, 'I was reading the great classics in my spare time.'

'We all think that about ourselves, but it isn't always quite true!'

As soon as we left the dining-room, David took his wife away. He explained that they had an important rendezvous at the Alma. 'We are several days late – we must go at once.'

'But you'll come back for the night?'

'Possibly, or we may sleep there.'

'Where?'

'Under the bridge, where we are meeting our friend.'

'Oh, don't do that. You must be tired.'

'The great Zen Master, Po Chang, said when you are tired, sleep. We can sleep anywhere.'

'And the baby?'

'He'll come too. He sleeps all the time. Good night, Ma.'

'Shall we see you tomorrow?'

'Possibly. Good-night.'

Philip and Northey reappeared. Valhubert sprang from his chair beside Mme Hué and in a rapid and skilful manoeuvre he whisked Northey to an unoccupied sofa. They sat there for the rest of the evening, laughing very much. Grace, half-listening to Philip who had made a bee-line for her, looked at them imperturbably, quiz-zically, even, I thought. At the usual time and in the correct precedence, the guests came and thanked us for a delightful evening and went their way. I have seldom felt so exhausted.

12

I sat on my bed, looking at Alfred.

'Do we laugh or cry?' he said. 'Did you see the baby?'

'Not really. It seemed to be asleep. I saw the cradle all right.'

'Whose do you think it is?'

'Oh, surely theirs?'

'It's yellow.'

'Babies often are.'

'No, darling. I mean it's an Asiatic baby.'

'Heavens! Are you quite sure? I thought it was our grandchild.'

'It may be. A throw-back. Had you a Chinese ancestor of any sort, Fanny?'

'Certainly not. Perhaps you had?'

'I doubt it. The Winchams, as you know, were yeomen in Herefordshire, in the same village since the Middle Ages. If one of our ancestors had gone to the East and brought back an exotic wife it would have become a thrilling legend of the family – don't you think? The little young lady didn't look Mongolian, did she?'

'Not a bit. How very mysterious. Well, if they're taking it to China that will be coals to Newcastle, won't it?'

For two days we saw nothing of David, Dawn or the cradle; on the third day they turned up again. Alfred and I were having our tea in the Salon Vert. 'It looks as if they've gone for good,' I was saying. 'Weren't we nice enough to them?'

'I don't see what more we could have done.'

'I suppose not. I have this guilty feeling about David, as I've often told you, because of loving him less than the others.'

'One must see things realistically, my darling. You love him less because he is less lovable – it's as easy as that.'

112

'But may it not be because I loved him less from the beginning – I lie awake, trying to remember –'

'He has always been exactly the same,' said Alfred, 'he was born so –'

Then they sidled, crabwise, cradle between them, through the door.

'Oh good, oh good,' I said, 'there you are. We were beginning to be afraid you had gone East.'

David pressed his beard into my face and said, 'On the contrary we went back a little – West – to Issy-les-Moulineaux. But now we are really on the road. We've just called in to say good-bye.'

I rang for more tea cups and said to Dawn, hoping to bring her into the conversation, 'Issy-les-Moulineaux is such a pretty name. What's it like when you get there?'

She turned her headlamps on to me, dumb, while David scowled. He despised small talk and civilized manners.

'It's just a working-class suburb,' he said. 'Nothing to interest anybody like you. We went to see a practising Zen Buddhist who's got a room there.'

'And where did you stay?'

'In his room.'

'For three whole days?'

'Was it three days? How do I know? It might have been three hours or three weeks. Dawn and I don't use watches and calendars since we have no [voice of withering scorn] "social engagements"!'

'I thought you said he lived under a bridge.'

'He used to, but they have turned the embankment into a road. Imagine motor-cars speeding through your bedroom all night. He says the French are becoming simply impossible –'

The baby now began to scream. 'I expect he wants changing,' said David.

Dawn got up and bent over the cradle as if to do so there and then. 'Come upstairs,' I said. We each took a handle and went to the lift. 'I got this room ready for you hoping you would stay for a night or two. It's called the Violet Room. Mrs Hammersley and Mr Somerset Maugham were born here, imagine –'

She smiled. She was a duck, I thought – I did so wish she could speak. When she picked up the baby I saw that Alfred was quite right, it was as yellow as a buttercup, with black hair and slit black eyes, certainly not European: a darling little papoose of a baby.

'The pet!' I said. 'What's its name?'

At last the pretty mouth opened. ''Chang.'

I saw that a canvas bag with a broken zip fastener had been deposited on a folding table meant for luggage. 'I'll send my maid, Claire, to unpack for you.' She shook her head vehemently.

'She's not frightening a bit and she'd love the baby – very well, if you'd rather not. Have you got what you need, dearest?' She nodded. 'Come down again when you are ready.'

I went back to the Salon Vert. David was saying, 'Zen forbids thought' and Alfred was looking sad, no wonder, at these words which were the negation of his whole life's work. 'It does not attempt to be intelligible or capable of being understood by the intellect, therefore it is difficult to explain.'

'It must be.' (Falsetto.)

'The moment you try to realize it as a concept, it takes flight.'

'Mm.' (On a very high note.)

'Its aim is to irritate, provoke and exhaust the emotions.'

To my utter amazement, Alfred now lost his temper. During twenty-six years of married life I had never seen that before. He said, furiously, 'You have succeeded in irritating, provoking and exhausting my emotions to a point at which I must tell you that, in my view, most Asiatics are incapable of thought. Zen must be simply perfect for them. But you are not an Asiatic; you have studied the great philosophies –'

'Please, Father, say Asian.' David had not even noticed the effect he was having on Alfred.

'I suppose, alone with you and your mother, I may be allowed to use the correct –'

'Not if it hurts my feelings. You see, our baby is one –'

'Adorable!' I said.

'Oh my dear boy, I beg your pardon a thousand times. Well, I've got some papers to read so perhaps I'll go back to the Chancery. Good-bye for the present.'

'He's called 'Chang, Dawn told me,' I said as the door shut on Alfred.

'We named him after the great Zen Master Po Chang. We dropped the Po. You have heard of him?'

'I seem to know the name – I'm awfully ignorant though, about all that.'

'It was Po Chang who placed a pitcher before his followers and asked them "What is this object?" They made various suggestions. Then one of the followers went up to it and kicked it over. Him Po Chang appointed to be his successor.'

'Oh of course! Well, anyhow, I thought the baby a perfect angel.'

'He's everything to us.'

This rule about never asking questions, though I knew it to be sound and would never break it, sometimes made life rather difficult. I was dying to know the origins of baby 'Chang but how could I find out?

'You must have one of your own,' I hazarded.

'We are going to – that's why we got married.'

'When you've got two babies, which makes a family, will you not settle down?'

'The wheel of birth and death, in the face of eternity, is of no more importance than sleeping or waking. Do you not know that new bodies are only created so that we can work out our own Karma?'

'Oh, do shut up and talk sensibly,' I said.

'To talk in terms that you would understand, Ma, I can't approve, I never have, of your way of life. I hate the bourgeoisie. In Zen I find the antithesis of what you and Father have always stood for. So I embrace Zen with all my heart. Do you see?'

'Yes. I wonder why you feel like that?'

'It seems almost incredible that people like you should still be living in the 1950s.'

'You can't expect us to commit suicide in order to fall in with your theories.'

'Oh, I don't mind you being alive, it's the way you live. Basil feels as I do. I've implored him for years to cut the umbilical cord and now at last he has.'

'That's your doing, is it? Thanks very much. He lies on his face on hot sand, instead of reading for his exam. It seems appalling waste of time to me.'

'Time does not exist. People who have clocks and watches are like bodies squashed into stays. Anything would be better than to find oneself in your and Dad's stays when one is old. Dawn and I are looking for an untrammelled future. Where is she?'

'If you go to the room above this one you'll find her.'

He went. Presently I heard his heavy footfall over my head. When David was a child Uncle Matthew used to say he walked like two men carrying a ladder. Greatly relieved, I telephoned to the Chancery. I got Philip. 'Just tell Alfred,' I said, 'that old Zennikins has gone and he can come back and finish his tea.'

Alfred kissed the top of my head. 'To think he took a first in Greats!'

'Let me pour you out another cup – that's cold. I remember, when the boys were little, you used to say if they don't revolt against all our values we shall know they are not much good.'

'That was not very clever, was it?'

'You were very clever – you took a first in Greats yourself. Another thing was: "I hope when they see me coming into a room they will look at each other as much as to say: here comes the old fool. That is how children ought to regard their father."'

'How very odd of me. I've quite forgotten.'

'Yes, one forgets –'

'Hot news,' Northey said, next day. 'David and Dawn are drinking whisky with sweet Amy in the Pont Royal bar. 'Chang has been dumped with the men's coats.'

'How do you know?'

'I've just seen them.'

'And what were you doing at the Pont Royal bar?'

'I was meeting Phyllis McFee, the friend of my far-distant youth in Caledonia stern and wild.'

'Northey, it's not a suitable place for young girls. Please find somewhere else to meet her – why not here? What's the good of giving you that pretty room – ?'

'You're saying all this because you don't like clever little Amy.'

'No, I do not.'

The answers to all the questions we had so discreetly not asked now became available to us in the *Daily Post*.

ZEN BUDDHISTS AT PARIS EMBASSY

Bearded, sandalled, corduroyed, and piped, accompanied by wife Dawn and baby 'Chang, David Wincham, the eldest son of our envoy to France (formerly Professor of Pastoral Theology, Sir Alfred Wincham), is staying with his parents on his way East, where he plans to join a Zen community. During a Parisian tea-ceremony yesterday David outlined his projects.

EXPECTING

'Dawn and I were married last week. We are expecting our first baby in two months. Dawn's father, the Bishop of Bury, disapproves. He wanted her to finish her studies and he was against our adopting little 'Chang, the child of our Zen Master.'

WORLD CITIZEN

'Yes, 'Chang is a Chinese name; our child is a World Citizen. Dawn's father is against World Government. He does not understand Zen nor does he realize the importance of the empty or no-abiding mind. He thinks that people ought to work; Dawn and I know that it is sufficient to exist.'

So David, Dawn, and 'Chang are existing very comfortably at the expense of the taxpayer. I asked when they expect to leave for the East. 'In seven hours, seven days, seven weeks, or seven years. It's all the same to us.'

'If it's seven years,' said Philip, 'your successor will have to give them the entresol.'

As a matter of fact, we heard no more about going East; they settled quite contentedly into the best spare room over the Salon Vert. It seemed that the long maturing of the Sacred Unsubstantiality could come to pass quite as well in the Hôtel de Charost as in a Siberian gaol – better, perhaps, because they were not certain to find a Zen Master in the gaol whereas there was this excellent one at Issy-les-Moulineaux. Dawn felt tired and was not anxious to recontemplate the wisdom of the road. David told Mildred Jungfleisch all this and she kindly passed it on. No explanations were vouchsafed to me or Alfred, but the portents seemed to indicate a good long stay. I bought an Empire cradle which I set up in the Salon Vert and banned the blue plastic one from any of the rooms inhabited by us. This was the only step I took to assert my personality.

13

Valhubert joined the throng of Northey's suitors. No doubt this was inevitable, but it worried me since he was in quite a different category from the others: a man of the world, experienced seducer, with time on his hands; I thought he would make mincemeat of the poor child. Besides I was very fond of Grace, my most intimate friend in Paris. She was obviously changing her mind about Northey; I never seemed to hear her say 'What a darling' any more. The other followers were rather a nuisance; they took up far too much of Northey's time and attention and doubled the work of our telephone exchange but I did not think them dangerous. I used to have long confabulations on the subject with Katie, who, fond of Northey and in a command-ing position, was invaluable to me. She was sensible in a particularly English way in spite of having lived abroad for years. She had been at the Embassy longer than anybody else, since before the war, during which she had worked with the Free French.

'Of course, I don't listen,' she said, 'but sometimes I can't help hearing.'

'Do listen as hard as you can, Katie. It's so important for me to know what she's up to. I'm responsible for her, don't forget.'

'You needn't worry – she doesn't care a pin for any of them; she drags in the name of Philip whenever possible. They must be sick of being told that she worships him, poor things. Of course, the ones who can use the secret line, but I feel it's exactly the same. She's so transparent, isn't she!'

'What do the French think of it all, I wonder?'

'The worst, of course, but then they always do. If she had no followers at all they would say she's a Lesbian or has got a lover in the Embassy. You can't count what they think.'

'Tell me something, Katie. Does she often speak to Phyllis McFee?'

'Who?'

'A Scotch girl who is working here in Paris –'

'Never, as far as I know.'

'That's funny. When she doesn't want to do anything she always drags in Phyllis McFee as an excuse.'

'She's probably shut up in some office where she can't use the telephone.'

'Well –' I said, 'I wonder!'

I did not ask Katie about M. de Valhubert but I knew that he was constantly on the line. I also noticed that Phyllis McFee, whose name had hitherto cropped up at regular but reasonable intervals, now seemed to be Northey's inseparable companion.

'Northey, aren't you rather behind-hand with my letters?'

'Not bad – about twelve, I think.'

'Why don't you sit down and finish them after dinner, then they would be off your mind?'

'Because tonight, actually, Phyllis McFee and me are going to Catch.'

'Catch?'

'That's French for all-in wrestling.'

'Darling, it's really not suitable for two girls to go alone to all-in wrestling.'

'We shan't be alone. Phyllis McFee and me have got admirers. We shall be escorted.'

'How can you bear to watch it?'

'I adore it. I love to see horrible humans torturing each other for a change instead of sweet animals. L'Ange Blanc, the champion, has got the fingers of a doctor, he knows just where it hurts the most –'

'Funny sort of doctor. But there's still the question of the letters. They can't be put off indefinitely.'

'I say, Fan, you know how you're not dining out?'

'You want me to do them? But what do I pay you for?'

'You won't be paying me anything at all until November 28th next year. I've borrowed until then. Fanny – each for each?'

'Oh, very well. Bring me your little typewriter and I'll do them in bed.' Only young once; we did not have these boring jobs at that age. Indeed when we were that age, Polly Hampton, my cousins and I, it was as much our duty to go out with young men and enjoy ourselves as now it was Northey's to write twelve letters. I only wished I could be certain that Phyllis McFee was really going to be of the party and that the escort was not Valhubert. As I wrote my letters I resolved that I would have to speak to Northey; the Foreign Legion policy of no questions may be quite all right with boys; girls are a very different proposition, giddy, poor things, hopelessly frivolous, wayward and short-sighted. Although I hate all forms of interference between human beings I felt, nevertheless, that I had a duty to carry out.

I was busy just then. Mr Gravely, the Foreign Minister, came and went. I saw little of him as the dinner which Alfred gave in his honour was for men only. He seemed a dry old stick. I said to Philip, 'I do love Grace's idea of him being driven to the brothels because his wife didn't come!'

'She's not far wrong. All English politicians want to do dirty things as soon as they get to Paris. Only of course they don't want to be seen by Mockbar. It's a nuisance that the only night club which is fairly respectable should happen to be called Le Sexy. La Tomate sounds quite all right but we really could not let them go there – no, I couldn't possibly tell you. Ask Mees –'

Contrary to all known precedent, Mr Gravely did not fall in love with Northey, in fact he hardly noticed her. He gave her various odd jobs to do for him, speaking in a dry, official, impersonal voice which so took her by surprise that she actually did them all herself, quite efficiently.

The night he left we dined at home. Alfred seemed tired and depressed; the visit had probably added to his difficulties. I had not yet had an account of it. David and Dawn had gone to share a bowl of rice with a friend – they never could say they were dining out, like anybody else. However, when we got to the dining-room we found that my social secretary was honouring us, a very unusual occurrence.

'Your cows, Northey,' said Alfred, 'are a nuisance.'

'I know – isn't it splendid! B.B. has stopped them, Fanny, I quite forgot to tell you. You see what can be done, by making a fuss!'

'Again I say, they are a nuisance. The Irish Ambassador was so friendly to me, everything seemed perfect between us. Now he has been called home by his government for consultation. It's very serious for the Irish – one of their main exports has vanished overnight. They all think it's due to the devilish machinations of the English.'

'So it is and serve them right for being so cruel!'

'All poor peasant communities are cruel to animals, I'm afraid – and not only the Irish. If they can't export cattle to France they'll be even poorer. It's not the way to make them kinder. The result will probably be that they will send the unhappy beasts to other countries where the journey will be longer and the slaughter-houses more primitive.'

'B.B. doesn't think so. He says there are no other practicable markets.'

'You know you should use your, apparently absolute, power to make the French eat frozen food. If they would do that these journeys could all be stopped and the beasts could be killed at home.'

'They won't,' said Northey, 'they call it frigo and they loathe it. B.B. says they are quite right – it's disgusting.'

'All very well – they'll have to come to it in the end.'

After dinner she said she was simply exhausted. 'I must dree my weird to bed – oh the pathos of the loneliness!' She trotted off to her entresol. We too went early to our rooms. Before I went to bed I heard a little cheeping noise, very far off, rather like a nest of baby birds, which meant that Northey was on the telephone. I could just hear her when all was quiet in the house. As I went to sleep she was still at it. I woke up again at three in the morning; she was still piping away.

When she came for her orders next day I said, 'Northey, I don't want to be indiscreet, but were you telephoning practically half the night?'

'The agony of clutching the receiver all those hours! My arm is still aching!'

'Who was it? M. Bouche-Bontemps?' She looked surprised that I should ask but replied, nonchalantly, 'No, poor duck, he is too busy nowadays. It was Charles-Édouard.'

Just as I thought. It was evidently time that I should intervene, unless I were going weakly to let things take their course. I went on, very much against my own inclination, 'Whatever was it all about?'

'My investments.'

'Indeed! Have you investments – ?'

'Yes. He has forwarded me my wages until Alfred's sixtieth birthday by which time you will retire and I shall be out of a job. Now he is advising me how to place the money. He says it's very important because nobody else will ever employ me and I am facing a penurious old age. So I have bought Coffirep, Finarep and Rep France. You can't imagine how they whizz. *Les reps sont en pleine euphorie*, the *Figaro* said, yesterday.'

'I don't think you ought to let M. de Valhubert talk to you all night. Grace might not like it.'

Northey's face closed up in a mutinous expression. 'Who cares?'

'I do, for one. But it's not that, darling, I worry about you. I'm so dreadfully afraid you will fall in love with Charles-Édouard.'

'Fanny! Hoar antiquity!'

'No hoarier than most of your followers – they all seem to be over forty and Bouche-Bontemps –'

'But I'm not in love with any of them. Is this a talking-to?'

'I suppose it is a sort of one.'

'*Quelle horrible* surprise! You never scold me. What's come over you?'

'I'm not scolding, I'm trying to advise. There are sometimes moments in people's lives when they take a wrong direction. I feel that both Basil and David have – but men can more easily get back to the right path than women. You ought to reflect upon what you want, eventually, and steer towards that. Now, as M. de Valhubert has noticed, you don't seem to have professional ambitions, so I suppose you are after marriage?'

'Perhaps I would prefer to be a concubine –'

123

'Very well. In that case the first rule is don't enter a seraglio where there is a head wife already.'

'I see your mind is still running on Charles-Édouard.'

'All this midnight telephoning makes it run.'

'But Fanny, if I wanted to hug Charles-Édouard I would do it in bed, not on the end of a telephone line.'

'I don't say you do want to hug, yet. I'm simply afraid that presently you may.'

'I've often told you I'm in love with Worshipful.'

'Yes, often, indeed! Do you think it's true?'

'St Expédite is covered with candles – why do you ask me that?'

'If you want to marry Philip you're setting about it in a very funny way.'

'I never said I wanted to marry him. Why shouldn't I be his concubine?'

'Philip isn't a Pasha, he's an ambitious English Civil Servant. The last thing he would do would be to saddle himself with a concubine – drag her round after him from post to post, can you imagine it! He'd very soon get the sack if he did. The only thing he might do would be to marry you.'

'Fanny – you said it was hopeless –'

'You are making it quite hopeless by your behaviour.'

'How ought I to behave?'

'Be more serious. Show that you are the sort of person who would make a splendid Ambassadress – pay more attention to your work –'

'Now I see exactly what you are getting at –'

'Our interests happen to coincide. And go slow with the followers.'

'I don't understand why, as I don't hug –'

'I might believe that but nobody else will. With Frenchmen love leads to hugs.'

'They're not in love.'

'What makes you think so?'

'They wouldn't mind a hug or two, I must admit, and they do

sometimes very kindly offer, but they're not in love. I know, because as soon as somebody is I can't bear him. There was somebody at home – oh, Fanny, the horror of it!'

'Dear me, this is very inconvenient. How are we ever going to get you settled?'

'With Worshipful of course, who you say never will be –'

Alfred came in. 'Bouche-Bontemps seems to be on the telephone for you,' he said to Northey, 'in the library. They made a mistake (Katie's day off) and put the call through to me – his secretary was very much embarrassed.' As Northey skipped away, delighted, no doubt, at being delivered from a tiresome lecture, he shouted after her, 'Ask him if his government will survive the debate on the national parks, will you?'

'No. I'm not the Intelligence Service! Ask your spies –!'

'Is that rather cheeky? Never mind. I say, Fanny, our son Basil has appeared. He is dressed [falsetto] like "O Richard, O mon Roi!" What do you think this portends?'

'I hardly care to tell you. He has left the crammer, given up all idea of the Foreign Service and has become a travel agent.'

'Good God,' said Alfred, 'Basil too?'

'But he's not quite as bad as poor darling David,' I hastened to say, 'because there is no bogus philosophy, no wife, no adopted baby involved and at least he has work and prospects of a sort. He doesn't do nothing all the time. Oh, how I wish I knew where we went wrong with those boys –!'

'Perhaps it's the modern trend and not exactly our fault.'

'Where is he now?' I asked.

'Having breakfast with the Zen family in the dining-room. David has come down in his dressing-gown today – he looks ghastly. They started nagging away at each other – I couldn't stand it, I took my coffee to the library.'

'Nagging about what?'

'It seems [falsetto] that Beards never get on with Teds. Well, I must go, I'm due at the Affaires Étrangères.'

'The Eels?'

'Oh yes indeed – the Eels, the European Army, Guinea, Arms to Arabs – I've got a horrible morning ahead.'

'And the young man who pirated Dior's designs?'

'No, Mr Stock copes with that, thank goodness. See you presently.'

My next visitor was Basil. I saw what Alfred meant: with his loose garment, tight trousers and hair curling under at the back he had the silhouette of a troubadour. Although I vastly preferred his appearance to that of David (he was quite clean, almost *soigné* in fact) I wished so much that they could both be ordinary, well-dressed Englishmen. I felt thankful that we had been able to send the two youngest to Eton; presumably they at least, when grown up, would look like everybody else.

Basil plumped on to my bed. 'I say, old David's gone to seed, hasn't he? Of course one knows he's holy and all that – still – !'

'How long since you saw him?'

'About a year, I should think.'

'He told me it was he who advised you to take to the road, or whatever it is you have taken to?'

'The coffee-and-jump, did he just? What a build-up! It's true, he used to bang out long saintly letters in that weird old Bible script of his but naturally I never read them.'

'I worry about you boys. What are you up to, Baz?'

'Well, it's like this. The Spanish season is over, thanks be. I've brought over a flock of the bovines on the hoof – turned them out to graze in the Louvre this morning – this afternoon I shall be flogging them down to Versailles. But these little tours are peanuts; we want to keep the racket going until Grandad can get the hustle on his new phenangles. And oh boy! Is he cooking up some sleigh-rides!'

My heart sank. If I did not quite understand what Basil was saying I felt instinctively against phenangles and sleigh-rides. They were not likely to denote a kind of work that Alfred would approve of. 'Could you talk English, darling?'

'Yes, Mother dear, I will. I gets carried away when I thinks of me ole Grandad. Well then, with Granny Bolter's capital (she sends her love incidentally) he is building a fleet of telly-rest coaches.

Get the idea? The occupational disease of the British tourist is foot and mouth. Their feet are terrible, it makes even my hard heart bleed when I see what they suffer after an hour or two in a museum. By this evening several of them will be in tears. There are always some old bags who flatly refuse to get out of the bus towards the end of a day; they just sit in the car-park while their mates trail round the gilded saloons to see where the sneering aristocrats of olden times used to hit it up. Sometimes gangrene sets in – we had two amputations at Port Bou – very bad for trade – just the sort of thing that puts people off lovely holidays in Latin lands. The other trouble, mouth, is worse. Britons literally cannot digest Continental provender – it brings on diarrhoea and black vomit as surely as hemlock would. The heads I've held – I ought to know. After a bit they collapse and die in agony – no more foreign travel for them. So I reports all this to ole Grandad and 'e strikes 'is forehead and says, "Now I've got a wizard wheeze" and just like that, in a flash, this man of genius has invented the telly-rest coach. When they gets to the place they've come to see – the Prado, say, or some old-world hill town in Tuscany, they just sits on in the coach and views the 'ole thing comfortable on TV while eating honest grub, frozen up in Britain, and drinking wholesome Kia-ora, all off plastic trays like in aeroplanes. If they wants a bit of local atmosphere, the driver can spray about with a garlic gun. You wait, Ma, this is going to revolutionize the tourist trade. Grandad has got a board of experts working out the technical details and we hope to have the first coaches ready by next summer. We reckon it will save many a British life – mine among others, because they will no longer need a courier.'

'Ah! So then what will you do?'

'Specials. Millionaires and things like that. We've got an interesting special coming off next month which I'm partly here to see about. Grandad wants to capture the do-gooders market, he thinks it has enormous possibilities for the future – you know, all those leisured oldsters who sign letters to *The Times* in favour of vice. Now they and their stooges are for ever going abroad, to build up schools the French have bombed, or rescue animals drowning in dams, or help people to escape from Franco gaols. They've got pots of money and Grandad thinks no harm in extracting a percentage.'

'I don't think it's right to cash in on people's ideals, Basil, even if you haven't got any yourself.'

'Somebody's got to organize their expeditions for them. Now me Grandad has thought of a particularly tempting line-up, see – an atom march. These do-gooders are not like ordinary Britons, they have feet of sheer cast iron and love a good long walk. But they've had Britain. They've done John o' Groat's and all that and they know every inch of the way to Aldermaston. So me Grandad thinks they might like to walk to Saclay, where the French atom scientists hang out – make a change. If that's a success they can go on to the great atom town in the Sahara. We call it A.S.S. – they start at Aldermaston as usual – Saclay – Sahara. Well, Ma, I wish you could see the provisional bookings. It is a smashing pisseroo old Grandad's got there. He's busy now, working out the cost. He'll make them pay a sum down, quite substantial – you see it's a different public from our Spanish lot, ever so much richer. Then the idea is to have some treats on the side which they'll pay extra for – interviews with atom ministers and such like. I thought Father would come in useful there?'

'I wouldn't count on it.'

'Oh well then, Northey can –.'

'What can I do?' She reappeared, with Philip. 'Hot news,' she said. 'Bigman's going to fall again (that's French for Président du Conseil) – not national parks, Sunday speed limit – so we shall see more of him. Goody gum trees.'

'It's gum drops, not gum trees,' Basil said, scornfully.

'Oh Lord,' said Philip, 'not another chap in fancy dress? What have you come as, may one ask? Really, Fanny, your children! Do you know, the Ambassador has just been obliged to go to the Quai in a taxi because David sent Jérôme with the Rolls-Royce to fetch his Zen Master?'

'No! It's too bad of David – I can't have him doing that sort of thing. Go upstairs, Northey, and tell him to come here at once, will you?'

'Wouldn't be any use – they'll be Zenning away with the door locked by now. They go back to bed after breakfast to empty their minds again. Suzanne can never get in to do the room until luncheon-time. The mess is not to be believed. Have you been up there, Fanny?'

'I had a feeling I'd better not.'

'I went to have a chat with Dawnie yesterday when David was out. It's rather fascinating. You'd never think so much deep litter could come out of one canvas bag. Then they've stuck up mottoes everywhere: "How miraculous this is: I draw water and I carry fuel" (it would be, if they did) and a picture of a hoop saying "The man and his rice bowl have gone out of sight."'

'When you chat with Dawn what does she talk about?'

'I do the talking. She looks sweet and says nothing. She can explain about the ten stages of spiritual dish-washing but she hasn't much ordinary conversation. I love her and adorable 'Chang. If only David would bugger off and leave them both behind –'

'Northey, if you say that word again I shall send you straight back to Fort William.'

'Northey,' said Basil, 'do you know any atom ministers?'

'Yes, there's a dear one called Busson in the rue de Varennes, terribly excited about his old bomb. He's going to poop it off in 1960.'

'Is he indeed?' said Philip. 'Thanks for the tip, Mees. At last you've produced the solid fruit of all that spying you do.'

'I read it in *Aux Écoutes*, to tell you the truth.'

Basil said, 'Could you get permission for a few people to see him?'

'What sort of people?'

'Britons.'

'Rather,' said Philip. 'He simply dotes on Britons, he's always hanging about here, under the Union Jack, keenly waiting for one.'

'Witty,' said Northey. 'Yes, Baz, I expect so. You must put it in writing. You can get permission for anything in France if you send up a written request. Come to my office and I'll type it out for

129

you.' She gave Philip a long look under her eyelashes which would have transported any of the followers and left the room with Basil.

When they had gone, I said to Philip, 'Oh! the children! What a worry they are. Basil has got some horrible new scheme on foot. Never mind. Meanwhile I've decided that somehow or other I must get rid of the Davids.'

'Now you've mentioned it – I didn't like to – but how?'

'So far I haven't thought of a way. After all, our house is their home. We can't turn them out if they don't want to go, Dawn so pregnant and that darling 'Chang, and let David drag them off to China. Then it's no good arguing with him, he has studied philosophy and knows all the answers.'

'Besides, he's such a humbug. All that rot about time meaning nothing – turns up sharp enough for meals, I notice, and the Guru is on the dot when Jérôme goes for him – won't miss a lift if he can help it.'

'Yes – yes,' I said rather impatiently. Poor David, it was too easy to criticize and laugh at him and really got us no further.

'Need your house be his home now that he is married?'

'I suppose the boys never seem grown up to me. Yes, I like them to feel that it is. Nothing would matter if it didn't upset Alfred, but he has got such a lot of worries now and I can see that David is fearfully on his nerves. I must protect him – I must try and get them to go back to England. David can always earn a living there with his qualifications.'

'What are they using for money?'

'A tiny little pittance I give him.'

'Can't you cut it off and say he must find work?'

'His pathetic allowance? No, really I don't think I could.'

'One doesn't have to be a fortune-teller to see they'll be here the full seven years.'

'I'm not sure, Philip. I often get my own way – Lady Leone left quite quickly, did you notice? Oh!' I said, sitting up in bed and seizing the telephone. 'Davey! We must get him over – I'll ring him up now this very minute!'

14

Davey arrived post-haste, in the early afternoon of the following day. 'Quite right to send for me. Oh – this room?' he said displeased, when I had taken him upstairs. He had had the Violet Room before but it was now occupied by David and Dawn and I had been obliged to change him over. I sat on his bed. 'I'll tell you the reason. It's all to do with why I asked you to come.'

'Don't begin yet. I must go for a walk. The thing about having three kidneys is that you need a great deal of exercise. Until you have had it you are apt to see things out of proportion.'

'That won't do. We are all trying to keep a sense of proportion. Can I come with you? I'd love a walk. Is there anywhere special you'd like to go to?'

'Yes, there is.' He opened his medicine chest and took out a piece of glass. I looked at it, fascinated, wondering what part of his anatomy it could be destined for.

'My housemaid broke this off a candelabra I'm fond of. I want to see if the man in the rue de Saintonge who used to blow glass is still there. I last saw him forty years ago – Paris being what it is I'm quite sure we shall find him.'

'Where is the rue de Saintonge?'

'I'll take you. It's a beautiful walk from here.'

It was indeed a beautiful walk. Across the Tuileries, through the Cour Carrée, and the Palais Royal and then past acres of houses exactly as Voltaire, as Balzac, must have seen them, of that colour between beige and grey so characteristic of the Île de France, with high slate roofs and lacy ironwork balconies. Though the outsides of these houses have a homogeneity which makes an architectural unit of each street, a glimpse through their great decorated door-ways into the courtyards reveals a wealth of difference within.

Some are planned on a large and airy scale and have fine staircases and windows surmounted by smiling masks, some are so narrow and dark and mysterious, so overbuilt through the centuries with such ancient, sinister rabbit-runs leading out of them, that it is hard to imagine a citizen of the modern world inhabiting them. Indeed, witch-like old women, gnome-like old men do emerge but so, also, do healthy laughing children, pretty girls in stiletto heels and their prosperous fathers, Legion of Honour in buttonhole. Most of the courtyards contain one or two motor-cars – quite often D.S.s or Jaguars – mixed up with ancient handcarts and pedal bicycles. The ground floors are put to many different uses, shops, workshops, garages, cafés; this architecture has been so well planned in the first place that it can still serve almost any purpose.

Davey and I walked happily, peering and exclaiming and calling to each other to come and look. I said, 'Bouche-Bontemps and the other Frenchmen I see always talk as if old Paris has completely gone; Théophile Gautier died of grief because of what Haussmann did here; a book I've got, written in 1911, says that Paris has become an American city. Even so, it must have far more beautiful old houses left than any other capital in the world. We have walked for half an hour and not seen one ugly street.'

'What I think sad about modern buildings,' Davey said, 'is that when you've seen the outside you know exactly what the inside will be like.'

'Northey said that, about Notre Dame. But I admit she was in a hurry to get to Lanvin.'

The rue de Saintonge itself is inhabited by artisans. Its seventeenth-century houses, built originally for aristocrats and well-to-do burgesses, have not been pulled down (except for one block where the Département de la Seine has perpetrated a horror) but they have been pulled about, chopped and rechopped, parcelled and reparcelled by the people who have lived and worked in them during the last two hundred years. Here are the trades which flourish in this street:

Workers in morocco, fur, indiarubber, gold, silver and jewels;

makers of buttons, keys, ribbons, watches, wigs, shoes, artificial flowers and glass domes; importer of sponges; repairer of sewing-machines; great printer of letters; mender of motor-cars; printer; midwife. There may be many more hidden away; these put out signs for the passer-by to read.

At the end of the street we came to Davey's glassblower, still there, covered with smiles. He and Davey greeted each other as if it were only a week instead of forty years since they last met. The piece of glass, produced from Davey's pocket, was examined. It could be copied, quite easily, but there would be a delay of perhaps two months.

'That has no importance,' said Davey, in his perfect, literary French, 'my niece here is our Ambassadress – when it's ready you will send it round to her.'

More smiles, compliments, protestations of love: 'How we thought of you, when London was bombed.'

'And how we thought of you, during the Occupation. Thousands of times worse to have them marching about the streets than flying about overhead.'

'Yes, perhaps. My son deported – my son-in-law murdered – *c'est la vie* – !'

Back in the Tuileries gardens we sat down in order to begin our, what statesmen call, discussions about David. I described the arrival of the Holy Family and their subsequent behaviour. Davey was very much interested. 'My dear! The unkind French! So how did they take it?'

'Sweet and polite as they always are, to me anyhow.'

'I wish I could have heard what they said to each other, afterwards. Of course I saw Mockbar's account of the Zen Buddhists and paid no attention, but for once there seems to have been a grain of truth in his ravings. I say, look at that statue of an ancient Gaul. What can he be doing?'

'He seems to be eating a Pekinese – or perhaps he's kissing it?'

'No – it's his own beard, but why is he holding it up like that with both hands?'

'Most peculiar.'

'You might have let me know that my godson was married.'

'Nobody let anybody know. The Bishop of Bury saw it in the paper – Alfred rang him up and they mourned together. Oh, Dave, isn't the modern world difficult!'

'Ghastly. No standards of behaviour any more.'

We sat sadly looking at the Gaul.

Presently Davey said, 'I expect I know what we shall have to do for David. It must be the old, old pattern of emotional instability and absence of rationalism plus a serious defection of the glands. He will almost certainly have to have a series of injections and a course of psychotherapy. I count on the Jungfleisches to find us a good man – where there are Americans there are couches galore. Madness is their national industry. What's the joke?'

'In other words, send for the doctor. Davey, how like you – !'

'No, Fanny. Did I order doctors for Pauline? Did I get rid of her?'

'All right, I admit. And there may be something in what you say. But I'm wondering if he will cooperate. He's become so difficult.'

'He'll be delighted to. He is evidently an exhibitionist – that is shown by the beard, the pipe, the strange clothes and Chinese baby. The more attention paid to him the better pleased he'll be. Say what you like about the modern world, we must give three cheers for science. Look at me! If I'd been born fifty years sooner I'd have been pushing up the daisies by now.'

'Very likely, since you would have been a hundred and sixteen. Uncle Matthew always says you are the strongest man he has ever met.'

'It is too bad of Matthew when he knows quite well how delicate I am.' Davey was seriously annoyed. He rose to his feet and said he must go home and have a rest before dinner.

'We've asked some people to meet you.'

'Oh dear! You always seem to dine alone, so I made a little plan with Mildred. One can count on interesting conversation there.'

*

As Davey and I came to the Place de la Concorde we saw that there was something going on. A mob of men in mackintoshes, armed with cameras, were jostling each other on the roadway outside the Hôtel Crillon. Mockbar leant against the wall by the revolving door of the hotel. I never can resist a crowd. 'Do let's find out who it is they are waiting for,' I said.

'It can only be some dreary film star. Nothing else attracts any interest nowadays.'

'I know. Only, if we don't wait we shall hear afterwards that something thrilling occurred and we shall be cross.' I showed him Mockbar. 'There's the enemy. He looks more like a farmer than a gossip writer.'

'Lady Wincham – how are you?' It was the *Times* correspondent. There was a moment of agony when I could remember neither his name nor Davey's. I feebly said, 'Do you know each other?' However my embarrassment was covered by the noisy arrival of policemen on motor-bicycles.

'Who is it?' I shouted to the *Times* man.

'Hector Dexter. He has chosen Freedom. He and his wife are expected here from Orly any minute now.'

'Remind me –' I shouted.

'That American who went to Russia just before Burgess and Maclean did.'

I vaguely remembered. As everybody seemed so excited I could see that he must be very important. The noise abated when the policemen got off their bicycles. Davey said: 'You must remember, Fanny – there was a huge fuss at the time. His wife is English – your Aunt Emily knew her mother.'

More police dashed up, clearing the way for a motor. It stopped before the hotel; the journalists were held back; a policeman opened the door of the car and out of it struggled a large Teddy-bear of an American in a crumpled beige suit, a coat over his arm, holding a brief-case. He stood on the pavement, blinking and swallowing, green in the face; I felt sorry for him, he looked so ill. Some of the journalists shouted questions while others flashed and snapped away with their cameras. 'So what was it like, Heck?'

'Come on, Heck, how was the Soviet Union?' 'Why did you leave, Heck? Let's have a statement.'

Mr Dexter stood there, silent, swaying on his feet. A man pushed a microphone under his nose. 'Give us your impressions, Heck, what's the life like, out there?'

At last he opened his mouth. 'Fierce!' he said. Then he added, in a rush, 'Pardon me, gentlemen, I am still suffering from motion discomfort.' He hurried into the hotel.

'Suffering from what?' said Davey, interested.

'It means air sickness,' said the *Times* man. 'I wonder when we shall get a statement. Dexter used to be a tremendous chatterbox – he must be feeling very sick indeed to be so taciturn all of a sudden.'

A large pink knee loomed in the doorway of the motor. It was followed by a woman as unmistakably English as Dexter was American. She merely said 'Shits' to the snapping and flashing photographers. Using the *New Statesman* as a screen she ran after her husband. Her place was taken by a fat, pudding-faced lad who stood posing and grinning and chewing gum until everybody lost interest in him. I saw that Mockbar's elbows were getting into motion, followed by the rheumaticky superannuated stable-boy action of his lower limbs, the whole directed at me. 'Come on,' I said to Davey, 'we must get out of this, quick –'

Philip was invited to the Jungfleisch dinner as well as Davey and next morning he came to report. The return of the Dexters had been, of course, the sole topic of conversation. When it transpired that Davey had actually witnessed it he became the hero of the evening.

'They are puzzled, poor dears,' said Philip.

'Who – the Jungfleisches?'

'All the Americans here. Don't know how to take the news. Is it Good or Bad? What does it mean? How does Mr Khrushchev evaluate it? What will the State Department say? The agony for our friends is should they send flowers or not? You know how they can't bear not to be loved, even by Dexter – it's ghastly for them to feel they are not welcoming old Heck as they ought to – at the same time it was very, very wrong of him to leave the Western Camp and it wouldn't do for them to appear to condone. The magic, meaningless word Solidarity is one of their runes; old Heck has not been solid and that's dreadfully un-American of him. But one must remember old Heck has now chosen Freedom, he has come back to the Western Camp of his own accord and they would like to reward him for that. So they are in an utter fix. In the end it was decided that Mildred must have a dinner party for policy makers; Jo Alsop, Elsa Maxwell, Mr Gallagher and Mr Shean are all flying over for it – but most of them can't get here before the end of the week. We shan't know any more until they have been consulted. Meanwhile there's the question of the flowers. Either you send at once or not at all; what are they to do? Davey suggested sending bunches with no cards, so that presently, if they want to, they can say, "Did you get my roses all right, Heck?"

'Isn't Davey wonderful?'

'It went down very badly. They were sharked.'

Davey got to work on his godson. Dr Lecœur came and took many tests, David cooperating quite satisfactorily. The Americans at Mrs Jungfleisch's dinner had been unanimous in recommending Dr Jore, head psychoanalyst to NATO. David brought him to the Salon Vert to have a word with me before taking him up to see his patient. He wanted to get the background first. He was a gangling young man, perhaps really much older than he looked. Davey seemed to like him; I tried to put prejudice out of my mind and do the same. When I had told him all I knew about my son, going back to babyhood, even trying to remember how I had taught him to use a pot ('I suppose I smacked him'), Dr Jore cleared his throat.

'As I see it then, Mrs Ambassadress, though of course I may be wrong since no system of psychiatry is as yet I believe infallible, the human element playing, as it must play in all human affairs, its part, since we are only endeavouring towards daylight and though I think I may say that the system by which I personally am guided is now very largely perfectioned, the foregoing reservation must be very distinctly borne in mind. With this reservation, then, very distinctly borne in mind, what I am about to say may be deemed to approximate the facts as they most probably are. Your son, Mrs Ambassadress, in addition to a condition of aboulia which is probably due to oily terlet training, and which may be possible to combat but which is likely to be difficult, stubborn and lengthy, in short not easy, to overcome, your son has an anoetic Pull to the East. Period.'

'A Pull to the East?' I said.

'Please let Dr Jore speak,' Davey said, sternly.

Dr Jore slightly bowed and went on. 'Perhaps I could put this matter rather more succinctly by stating a paradigm which I believe to be unconfutable. Human beings, in my view and in the view of others more qualified than I, are roughly divided (in respect of what I am about to enucleate, to the best of my endeavour and without having had access to my case), human beings, then, fall into two roughly definable categoremia: those who are subject and liable to a Pull to the East and others, I am happy to say an appreciably larger grouping, who are subject and liable to a Pull to the West. Perhaps I could explain this matter more readily comprehensibly if I were to state that those on the continent of Europe who feel a very compelling wish and desire to visit England, Ireland and the Americas feel little wish or desire to go to Russia, China and the Indias, whereas those forcibly attracted to China, Russia and the Indias –'

'Don't want to go to America.'

'Please let Dr Jore finish what he is saying,' Davey said peevishly. 'It's so interesting, Fanny –'

'Of course,' I said. 'If you go far enough East you come to the West. If you could manage to push my son a little further we might get him to Hollywood. Then he could join up with Auden and everybody,' I said to Davey, 'and Jassy could keep an eye on him. That might be a solution?'

Davey sighed deeply. 'And now, perhaps, we could be allowed to hear what the doctor has to say?'

Dr Jore had shut his eyes while I spoke. He opened them again. 'Mrs Ambassadress, ma'am, you have put your finger on the very heart of the matter.'

I looked triumphantly at Davey who said 'Ssh.'

'This is a point which has by no means escaped the learned professor who was the first to proclaim this doctrine of Oriental versus Occidental attraction. Now this attraction (whether towards the Orient or East or towards the Occident or West) occurs in the persons subjected to its magnetism in greater or lesser degrees and we practising psychiatrists find it possible to cure or check it according to its strength. May I explain myself? If the pull, whether to the East or to the West (a pull to the West, of course, is very much more desirable than its converse, and rarely needs to be cured, though in a few, very extreme, cases it should be checked), if the pull, then, is very strong it is comparatively easy to cure. If it is overwhelmingly strong the patient has only to be encouraged to follow it and in these days of jet travel he will find himself back where he started in a surprisingly short time. Period. In the case, however, Mrs Ambassadress, of your son, the pull, by all the evidence which I have been able to garner, is weak. It has pulled him over the English Channel and across Normandy as far as Paris. Here it seems to have left him. Where there is so little for me to combat, the case is difficult. Therefore when your uncle suggested that I should work in collaboration with a physician I gladly agreed to do so. I feel that by super-adding the action of certain glands it should be possible to augment the will-power of your son, thus giving myself a basis on which to proceed. I must now touch upon another and more serious aspect of the Pull. Should the patient yearn towards the manners, customs and ways of thought of the Eastern Lands – should he sit on the floor eating rice; should the muezzin call for him in the Champs Élysées; should he dream of military deploys in the Red Square and think the bronzes of Démé-Jioman superior to those of Michelangelo – then, what I might call the jet treatment will not be sufficient. Then

139

we must wean him back to the manners, customs and ways of Western Civilization and this we must do by means of his subconscious. Here the silent, long-playing gramophone record during sleep has its role, super-added to a daily personal collocution with myself or one of my assistants. Period.'

Dr Jore shut his eyes again and there was silence. I did not dare to break it. At last Davey said, 'Excellent. That is precisely the conclusion I had come to myself. Now I think you should see your patient in his own surroundings – I'll take you up to his room.'

Dr Jore was with David for about an hour, after which he went to Davey's room for an uninterrupted consultation. David came rocketing down to me.

'I see that you and Uncle Davey think I'm mad.'

'Oh, no, darling – whatever makes you say that?'

'Then why have you called in this ghastly Yank?'

'Davey – you know what he is – thought you weren't looking very well.'

'He's quite right there. I don't feel a hundred per cent. But isn't Dr Lecœur coping with that? Why should I need an alienist?'

'You must ask Davey,' I said weakly. 'He's your godfather, he has taken you on, it's nothing to do with me.'

'You told this doctor about teaching me to pee into a pot, didn't you?'

'He asked.'

'Yes, well, another time please let him ask. After all, this was most private between you and me, I call it wildly indiscreet of you to discuss it with a stranger. Another thing, Ma, if Dr Jore comes here every day like he says he's going to he will drive me mad. Really, properly barking. I am quite serious.'

'I must say I see your point.'

'I heard him telling Davey he's going to empty my mind and refurnish it with contemporary Western ideas. Now my Zen Master empties my mind and fills it with the ancient unlearning of the East. It can't be right for them to go on emptying and filling it in competition with each other?'

'I must say it doesn't sound right. You wouldn't think of giving up the Zen Master?'

'I don't like talking to you about Zen – I know you think it's funny – you're laughing now, Ma, aren't you? That's what makes it difficult to confide in you, you laugh at everything.'

'Darling, never at you,' I said, guiltily.

'In that case I'm the only one. You're nothing but a mocking materialist, like all your generation. If your children are not well-balanced you have only yourself to blame.'

'Oh dear. Do you think that you and Basil are different from other people because I mocked?' I was very much disturbed at this notion.

'Different from other people – different from whom? You go about the world with your eyes shut. If you opened them you would see thousands of people exactly like me and Basil – Beards and Teds abounding in every direction. Next time you go driving in that awful great hearse of yours, just look out of the window. You'll see that we're not as different from other people as all that –'

'Then in what way do you think you are unbalanced?'

'I lack self-confidence and will-power. That's what Dr Jore thought.'

'And you don't feel that he can help you?'

'I've told you, Dr Jore would drive me into a bin. Only two people can help me. Dawn is one and the Zen Master is the other. They understand. I could never give them up, either of them.'

'No, darling, you shan't. I absolutely agree about Dr Jore – he's a bore.'

'There you are, with your scale of false values! You divide human souls into bores and non-bores, don't you? I'm a bore and Basil isn't, that I've always known. You ought to be considering where everybody stands in the universal scheme instead of laughing at them and saying they are bores.'

'Anyway, in this case our different methods bring us to the same conclusion. I say Jore is a bore; you say Jore's standing in the universal scheme is low: we both say Jore must go.'

At this David became more agreeable. He kindly admitted that though I was regrettably frivolous I was not without a certain comprehension. He harrowed my face with his beard and we parted on the best of terms.

Davey was more hurt than surprised when I told him that he must get rid of Jore. In my view, I explained, he was calculated to give anybody who had to see much of him a nervous breakdown and I refused to have one of my own children handed over to him. 'David can't bear him,' I said, 'so I'm sure he wouldn't be much good.'

'He's far better than the Zen Master,' said Davey, who, unlike me, had been allowed to meet this legendary figure.

'That I can easily believe. However, David doesn't think so; people must be allowed to go to hell their own way.'

'It's the greatest pity he has taken against Jore. I thought his diagnosis quite amazing – he hit the nail on the head in one. Mildred says he is intensely brilliant; the Supreme Commander has him every afternoon.'

'How can he bear the dissertation?'

'You must remember, with Americans, that they are fighting to express themselves in a language they've never properly learnt. They need the dissertation; the kind of shorthand that we talk would be useless to them.'

The next evening, Davey was good enough to dine in. We were waiting for Alfred and sipping cocktails.

'Why does one never see Northey?' Davey was asking, upon which the door opened and the pretty face looked round it.

'I say, what's happened to David? He fell on me like a stallion just now, in my office.'

'Oh good,' said Davey. 'Dr Lecœur's super-adding gland injection must have begun to work.'

'Really, Davey, I call that rather inconvenient!' I said. 'What about all the young women in the Chancery? I'm supposed to be responsible for their morals, you know.'

'This is Paris. They must be used to dealing with satyrs.'

'In the Bois, perhaps, but not in the Embassy. Is it necessary to turn the poor fellow into a satyr?'

'Please, Fanny, I must ask you not to interfere any more with my treatment of David.'

'Oh, very well. Do you dine with us, darling?'

'Not really. I'm after *France Soir*. Goody gum trees, the Bourse has found her vigour again – but Ay de mi, the Reps have reacted unfavourably to M. Bourguiba's speech. Now there will be a pause for introspection, mark my words. The worry of it!'

'Where's Baz?' I said.

'Buggered. He'll be coming back next week.'

'Buggered!' said Davey, faintly.

'Now, Davey, you tell her she mustn't.'

'It's all right, I know I mustn't and I'm trying desperately hard not to.'

'Is he bringing the atom marchers next week?'

'No, ruminants until the end of the month. He's been very busy organizing the march – he spent hours yesterday with precious Amy, seeing about the publicity. Anything for me to do, Fanny? Don't say yes, there's a darling, but lend me your little mink jacket, I'm so tired of my bunny.'

'Very well, on condition you reform your language. What are you up to?'

'Phyllis McFee and me are going to the Return of the Cinders with M. Cruas. He's poor, he can't take us to a proper theatre. *Le Retour des Cendres*, Fanny, sharpen your wits – the body of Napoleon coming back to the Invalides. So I go and get the jacket – you are lucky to be so kind – good night –'

'They were talking about her at Mildred's,' Davey said. 'It seems she is in full fling with Valhubert.'

I could not help remarking, 'One can always be sure of some good conversation there –'

'Fanny, be serious. Aren't you worried about it?'

'More worried about Valhubert than the others certainly – but no, you know, not really. Northey is a good little child.'

'There are certain women who go through life in a cloud of apparent innocence under cover of which they are extremely unchaste.'

'Yes. My mother for one. But if Northey's like that I don't see what we can do about it. I did scold her for talking half the night to Valhubert on the telephone – she replied that if there was anything wrong between them she would have been in bed with him, not just chatting. Very true I should think.'

'Yes, there's something in that. How much does she remind you of Linda?'

'On the face of it, very much indeed. But there are differences. She's not nearly so concentrated. When Linda was in love she never bothered about followers – they only cropped up when she was out of love with one man and not yet in with another.'

'But is Northey in love?'

'Oh yes, hasn't she told you? She's meant to be madly in love with Philip – I suppose she is, but sometimes I can't help wondering. She never moons about as Linda used to (do you remember the games of patience, the long staring out of the window, the total distraction from real life?). Northey lives in an absolute rush, with at least twenty different admirers. When she has half an hour to spare I think she does go and have a word with St Expédite about Philip.'

'St Expédite,' said Davey, 'how that takes me back! He's a good saint, if ever there was one – I must go and see him again, but only for old sake's sake, alas! At my age one doesn't have these desperately hopeless desires. So she's in love with Philip – how perfect that would be. Doesn't he fancy her – why not?'

'He adores Grace, unfortunately. But I've begun to think, just lately, that he's getting fonder than he knows of Northey and that finally it may all come right.'

'That makes it important to scotch the Valhubert business now at once. Remember, being in love with Prince André didn't stop Natasha from making a fool of herself.'

'I know. Cressida too. Young women are very silly.'

'I think you ought to have a word with him.'

'What, with Valhubert? Davey, the terror! I really don't think you can ask me to do that!'

'Alfred then? It might be easier for him?'

'Oh no, no! Don't tell Alfred – he has enough to worry him. The children are my affair – I never allow him to be bothered by them if I can possibly help it. How late he is, by the way. What can he be doing?'

'Philip told me he had gone to a football match, but surely that must be over by now?'

When at last Alfred appeared he seemed quite worn out. 'I'm sorry to be late – I had to get quickly into a bath – I was simply soaked with rotten eggs at the France versus England. Lord, how I do hate sport. Then I had an endless visit from the Irish Ambassador about those wretched cows.'

15

For a long time now Charles-Édouard de Valhubert had been urging me to go with him and visit the old Duchesse de Sauveterre at her country house, the Château de Boisdormant. He said she wanted to talk about her grandchild, little Fabrice. We had twice made plans to do this; for one reason or another they had come to nothing; at last a day was fixed which suited all of us. Grace, who was expecting a baby and felt rather sick, decided to stay at home. I had always felt nervous at the idea of a long motor drive alone with Valhubert, who intimidated me, but since my talk with Davey I positively dreaded it. If it was really my duty to speak about Northey, now would be the time. However, sitting in the front seat of a new Jaguar, with Valhubert at the wheel, I soon found that the physical terror far outweighed the moral.

'Have I not a style of my own, in driving?' he said, weaving up the rue Lafayette. 'I don't take the outer boulevards, they are too ugly.'

The style consisted in never slowing down. I began to pray for the traffic lights to go red and stop him; my foot was clamped to an imaginary brake until the muscles hurt. The terror increased when he began to imitate the style of other drivers; the young chauffeur of a Marshal of France, the old chauffeur of an American hostess, the driver of a police car (hands never on the wheel) and M. Bouche-Bontemps. He kept looking at me to see if I were laughing, which, indeed, I was; finally his eyes never seemed to be on the road at all. 'Oh please, do be yourself!' I said, and wished I had not as he spurted forward.

Once outside Paris and past Le Bourget I calmed down. He was in full control of the machine, though he went much too fast. We chatted away enjoyably and I realized that he was not at all frightening, much less than he seemed to be when one met him at a Parisian party. When we passed the cross-roads at Gonesse he recited the names of all the people he knew who had been killed there in motor-car accidents, after which silence fell, because of my inability, since I had not known any of them, to aliment the conversation. Thinking that now was my chance, I bravely forced myself to say, 'I worry about Northey.'

'I love this little girl.'

'Yes. That's exactly why I worry.' I was astounded at my own courage.

'Ah – no!' He looked vastly amused and not at all embarrassed. 'I don't love her – I mean I like her very much.'

'It's not you I worry about. She might love. She tells me she thinks of being a concubine.'

He roared with laughter. 'Not in my harem, I can assure you. Why, she is only two years older than Sigi – and half his mental age.'

'That's no protection, surely?'

'With me it is. I don't happen to be attracted by children – not yet – no doubt that will come, one of the horrors of senility. And I dislike the sensation of doing wrong.'

'I thought it added to the amusement?'

'Greatly, if one is cocufying some old prig one was at school with. But to seduce Northey would do her harm and also lead to trouble. I love Mees and I hate trouble. No, we must marry her to Philip – I'm working for that. If he thinks I am courting her and if she seems to cool off him, that, human nature being what it is, may do the trick. He has sighed after Grace quite long enough, it's a bore. Like this I hope to kill two birds with one stone.'

I was not completely reassured but there was nothing more I could say. It was another beautiful day. (When I look back on our first months in France we seem to have enjoyed an uninterrupted Indian summer.) Valhubert and I were now crossing the Seine-et-Marne country where everything is on an enormous scale. Avenues of poplar trees rush over vast horizons and encircle the globe;

down the roads bordered by them the largest, whitest of horses draw ancient wagons loaded with beetroots the size of footballs; each farm with its *basse-cour*, kennels, cow-byres, stables, barns and sheds occupies enough space for a whole village. The land breathes of prosperity; the predominating colour at that time of year is gold.

'This is the battlefield of the Marne,' he told me, 'where thousands of young men were killed in 1914, on days like this, almost before they could have realized they were at war. The Uhlans, mounted, with their lances, the Cuirassiers glittering in polished armour, went into action on horseback. Those battles were more like a military tournament than modern warfare – to read of them now is reminiscent of Agincourt or Crécy. One can't believe they happened in living memory and that there are still many people we know who took part in them.'

We came to a village of whitewashed houses with red and navy-blue roofs clustered round a twelfth-century church. 'I have an uncle who was wounded here at St Soupplets. When he came to, in hospital, they said "You were in the Battle of the Marne." He was perfectly amazed. He remembered seeing a few Germans round that inn across the road there – and then he was knocked down by a bullet, but he had no idea he had been in anything as important as a battle.'

'Stendhal's description of Waterloo is rather like that – casual and unfrightening.'

'I love this country so much but now it makes me feel sad to come here. We must look at it with all our eyes because in ten years' time it will be utterly different. No more stooks of corn or heaps of manure to dot the stubble with light and shade, no more peasants in blue overalls, no more horses and carts, nothing but mechanicians driving tractors and lorries. The trees are going at a fearful rate. Last time I came along this road it was bordered by apple trees – look, you can see the stumps. Some admirer of Bernard Buffet has put up these telegraph poles instead.'

'It is still very beautiful,' I said, 'I never saw the apples trees so

I don't grieve for them as you do. When I go to the country I always wonder how any of us can bear to live in towns – it seems perfect madness.'

'I'm sure you didn't feel like that when you were Northey's age.'

'Now I come to think of it, when I was Northey's age I did live in the country and my only idea was how to get to London.'

'Of course it was. Young people need urban life, to exchange thoughts and see what goes on in the world – it's quite right and natural. By degrees the tempo slows down and we take to peaceful pleasures like gardening or just sitting in the sun. Very few young people are sensitive to beauty, that's why there are so few poets.'

'Yes. But now it seems almost unbearable to think what one is missing by being in a town as the days and months go by. So dreadful only to know the seasons by the flower and vegetable shops.'

'I call that rather ungrateful. Your embassy is in a forest.'

'I know. Our Oxford house is not, however.'

'When were you born?'

'In 1911.'

'And I the year after. So we remember the old world as it had been for a thousand years, so beautiful and diverse, and which, in only thirty years, has crumbled away. When we were young every country still had its own architecture and customs and food. Can you ever forget the first sight of Italy? Those ochre houses, all different, each with such character, with their *trompe-l'œil* paintings on the stucco? Queer and fascinating and strange even to a Provençal like me. Now, the dreariness! The suburbs of every town uniform all over the world, while perhaps in the very centre a few old monuments sadly survive as though in a glass case. Venice is still wonderful, though the approach to it makes me shudder, but most of the other Italian towns are engulfed in sky-scrapers and tangles of wire. Even Rome has this American rind! *"Roma senza speranza"*, I saw in an Italian paper; all is said.' He sighed deeply. 'But like you with the apple trees, our children never saw that world so they cannot share our sadness. One more of the many things that divide us. There is an immense gap between us and them, caused by unshared experience. Never in history have the past and the present been so different; never have the generations been divided as they are now.'

'If they are happy and good in the new world it doesn't much matter,' I said.

'Will they be happy? I think modern architecture is the greatest anti-happiness there has ever been. Nobody can live in those shelves, they can't do more than eat and sleep there; for their hours of leisure and their weeks of holiday they are driven on to the roads. That is why a young couple would rather have a motor-car than anything else – it's not in order to go to special places but a means of getting away from the machine where they exist. The Americans have lived like that, between earth and sky, for a generation now and we are beginning to see the result. Gloom, hysteria, madness, suicide. If all human beings must come to this, is it worth struggling on with the world? So,' he said, narrowly missed by a D.S. which, at a hundred miles an hour and the law on its side, hurtled at us from a right-hand turning, 'shall we put an end to it all?'

'No,' I said hurriedly, 'we must wait and see. I have a few things to leave in order when I go – Northey – the boys. It may not be as bad as we fear. There may be less happiness than when we were young – there is probably less unhappiness. I expect it all evens out. When would you have liked to be born?'

'Any time between the Renaissance and the Second Empire.'

I trotted out the platitude, 'But only if you were a privileged person?'

He said, simply, 'If I were not, I wouldn't be me.'

Very true. Such men as Valhubert, my father, Uncle Matthew would not have been themselves had they not always been kings in their own little castles. Their kind is vanishing as surely as the peasants, the horses and the avenues, to be replaced, like them, by something less picturesque, more utilitarian.

I said, 'Perhaps the Russians will explore some nice empty planet and allow people like us to go and live on it.'

'No good to me,' said Valhubert, 'I wouldn't care a bit for oceans on which Ulysses never sailed, mountains uncrossed by Hannibal and Napoleon. I must live and die a European.'

We whizzed down the ancient roads leading to the Holy Roman Empire in silence now, each thinking his own thoughts. I was no longer frightened by the speed, but exhilarated, enjoying myself. Up in the sky two parallel white lines drawn by two tiny black crosses showed that young men in aeroplanes were also enjoying themselves on this perfect day. At last a signpost marked Boisdormant showed that we were nearing our destination.

'Madame de Sauveterre – ?' I said. 'Just tell me –'

'You have never seen her?'

'Such years ago. I used to stay with an old woman called Lady Montdore –'

'The famous one?'

'Yes, I suppose she was. When I was about eighteen I met Sauveterre and his mother there. It's the only time I ever saw him.'

'Poor Fabrice! He was the most charming person I have known, by very far.'

'So was my cousin Linda.'

'Le coquin! You say he hid her in Paris for months and nobody had any idea of it.'

'She wasn't divorced. Besides, she was terrified that her parents would find out.'

'Yes. And the war had only just begun and didn't seem serious, then. Life appeared to be endless in front of one. Also I think Fabrice had somebody else – another reason for secrecy. Always these complications!'

'Were you very intimate?'

'Oh, very. His mother is my great-aunt – Fabrice was much older than me, twelve years at least – but as soon as I was grown up we became bosom friends. It was an adoration on my side. Hard to think of him as dead, even now.'

'His mother –' I said, coming back to the point.

'She's a worldly old woman as you will see. Fabrice was the only meaning to her existence. Now that he has gone she lives for money and food, torn between miserliness and greed. Enormously rich, no family, no heir. That's why it's important that she should see the boy.'

'Good of you to take so much trouble. You must remember he may not play up. Children are unpredictable – at his age old people are a bore and money hardly seems to exist.'

'He has good manners and he looks like his father. I'll be very much surprised if he doesn't win her over.'

We were now on a little white, untarred country lane winding between rank hedgerows. The crop of berries that year was rich and glistening; I thought I had not seen so white a road and such scarlet berries since I was a child. Presently we came to a park wall of stones covered with peeling plaster – perched up in one corner of it like a bird's nest there was a little round thatched summer-house.

'Is it not typically French, all this?' said Valhubert. 'What makes it so, I wonder? The colour of that wall, perhaps?'

'And that ruin on the hill, with a walnut tree growing out of it; and the trees in the park, so tall and thin and regular –'

An avenue of chestnuts led from the lodge gates to the house, their leaves lay in the drive, unswept. A flock of sheep, watched by a shepherd with a crook, were cropping away at long dark green grass. The house, an old fortress built round three sides of a square, was surrounded by a moat, the turrets at its corners were entirely covered, even to their pointed roofs, with ancient ivy so that they looked like four huge mysterious trees. Valhubert stopped the engine, saying, 'I don't trust that drawbridge. I think we'll walk from here.'

The oldest butler in the world opened the front door long before we reached it. He greeted Valhubert in the way of a servant with somebody he has known and loved from childhood, hurried us upstairs into a round white drawing-room, inside one of the ivy trees, sunny and cheerful, and vanished at the double.

'She'll be down in exactly a quarter of an hour,' said Valhubert. 'Grace thinks she can't bear to begin painting her face until she actually sees us arriving for fear we should have an accident on the road and then all the powder and paint and eye black would be wasted. She and Oudineau are hard at it now. He's her lady's maid as well as butler, caretaker, wood-man, chauffeur, gardener and gamekeeper. Nobody has ever been so much *à tout faire*. The exquisite luncheon we are about to eat (you'll see how it's worth the journey for that alone) will have been fished, shot and grown by Oudineau and cooked by his son. This Jacques has an enormous situation in Paris, but he is obliged to drive down here and do the cooking when my aunt has guests. I must say it only happens once in a blue moon.'

'Is he a chef, in Paris?'

'By no means! He directs an enormous electrical concern – Jacques Oudineau will produce all the atomic plant of the future. He's immensely powerful and very attractive, one meets him dining out everywhere – that's his Mercedes, parked by the kitchen garden.'

'What a charming room this is!'

'Yes – there's nothing so pretty as a *château-fort* – redecorated in the eighteenth century. This panelling is by Pineau. Look at those heaps of illustrated papers – they go back fifty years and more. One day Grace and I were waiting for her to come down and we began looking at them (I am particularly fond of Matania – orgies – galley-slaves – jousting and so on). Literally showers of banknotes came tumbling out of them, all obsolete. Yes, she's a miser in the true sense of the word.'

Presently our hostess appeared looking, I thought, exactly the same as she had some twenty-seven years ago, at Hampton. She had then been in her fifties; she was now in her eighties; she had seemed old then and not a day older now. She must once have been pretty, with little turned-up nose and black eyes, but almost before middle age, probably, she had become stout; there was something porcine in her look. It was hard to imagine that she could have given birth to the irresistible Fabrice. Almost on her heels, Oudineau reappeared and in a voice of thunder announced, "*chesse est servie.*'

We lunched, in a narrow room with windows on both sides, off Sèvres plates which must literally have been worth their weight in gold. 'They belonged to Bauffremont – you know them very well, my dear Charles-Édouard. I never allow Jacques Oudineau to wash them up; he is quite a good cook, but a most unreliable boy in other ways.'

The luncheon was indeed worth the journey. We began with brochet. Why is brochet so good and pike so nasty, since the dictionary affirms that they are one and the same? Then partridges, followed by thick juicy French cutlets quite unlike the penny on the end of a brittle bone which is the English butcher's presentation of that piece of meat. They were burnt on the outside, inside almost raw. Boiled eggs suddenly appeared, with fingers of buttered toast, in case anybody should still be famished. Then a whole brie on bed of straw; then chocolate profiteroles. I was beginning to get used to such meals, but they always made me feel rather drunk and stupid for an hour or two afterwards.

When she tasted the salad, Mme de Sauveterre said 'Vinegar!'

'Jacques is in despair, Mme la Duchesse, he forgot to bring a lemon.'

'It's inadmissible. This boy always forgets something. Last time it was the truffles. He has no head. Thank goodness I haven't got shares in his concern.'

'Thank goodness I have,' said Valhubert, 'since they double every year.'

The Duchess asked a hundred questions about the Embassy, specially wanting to know what had become of all the English people she had known there in the past.

'Et cette adorable Ava – et la belle Peggy – et ce vieux type si agréable du Service, Sir Charles?'

When she saw how little I could tell her about any of them she put me down for what I am, provincial. Valhubert, however, knew all the answers. He told her that she had met me already, at Hampton, after which she got on to Lady Montdore and her circle. Here I did better.

'Yes, she died before the war, of heart failure while having an operation in Switzerland.'

I did not add that it was an operation for leg-lifting which Cedric, the present Lord Montdore, had persuaded her to undergo against a great deal of medical advice. He said that he utterly refused to be seen with her at the Lido again until it had been done. Her heart, worn out by dieting and excessive social life, had stopped under the anaesthetic. As this happened at a very convenient moment for him, the whole affair seemed fishy and many people openly said that he had murdered her. Soon afterwards the war broke out and he fled to America. 'Darling, you can't really imagine ONE going over the top?'

Indeed it was an unlikely conception. However, having killed Lady Montdore and failed to kill Germans, he was badly received in England when he returned there after the war. He had very soon gone back and settled in his native continent.

'The present Montdore? Yes, he lives in the West Indies. I miss him very much. Polly? She is happy, has thousands of children and has completely lost her looks.'

'Fabrice always said she would. And Lady Montdore's lover – *ce vieux raseur* – I forget his name?'

'Boy Dougdale? He has become one of our foremost biographers.'

'Now tell me about yourself, *charmante Ambassadrice*. I hear you have two boys at school with that little monster of Charles-Édouard's? I don't know much about young people as I never see any, but one hears such tales –'

'Does one?' said Charles-Édouard, amused. 'What sort of tales penetrate to Boisdormant, *ma tante*?'

'You would know how true it is,' she said to me, 'but I am told the boys and girls nowadays are against birth?'

'Against birth?'

'Against being born.'

'My aunt means they don't care whether they belong to good families or not, any more.'

'Oh, I see.' I had supposed she meant something to do with

birth control. 'But do you think young people ever cared about such things?'

'When I was young we did. In any case it is shocking to be against. The grandchildren of a friend of mine actually started a newspaper against birth – horrible, I find, and so of course one of the girls married somebody who wasn't born –'

'Yes,' said Valhubert, with a quizzical look in my direction, 'it won't do. We can't have these goings-on in society, though I must say the unborn young man is rather solid for a disembodied spirit.'

'You laugh now, Charles-Édouard, but when your daughters are grown up you will see these things in a very different light. Tell me more about your boys, Mme l'Ambassadrice, I hear that one of them is called Fabrice?'

'He is the child of my cousin who is dead. I have adopted him.'

Suddenly we both found that we could not go on with this conversation. We looked at Valhubert who came to the rescue. 'When all three of them come over for the Christmas holidays I'll bring them here for a few days.'

'Yes, you must. Old Oudineau can teach them to ride bicycles – children like that very much, I find. Do you heat the Embassy with coal or mazout?'

16

When we got back to the Embassy Philip was crossing the court-yard. Charles-Édouard refused a cup of tea; he said Grace would be longing to hear about our day and he thought he had better get back. He drove straight off. Philip came into the house with me. I said, 'I like Valhubert very much.'

'The thing about lady-killers is that they kill ladies,' he replied, grumpily. 'That ass of a Northey is dining with him again tonight.'

'Oh, Philip – alone?'

'I've no idea. Did you see the papers this morning?'

'Hardly. I was in a rush.'

'Didn't see Mockbar?'

I stood still. We were half-way up the stairs. 'Now what?'

'He has found out that the famous Frenchman who won your mother in a lottery is none other than poor old Bouche-Bontemps. He says he is able to reveal that the French premier is one of the ex-stepfathers of Ambassadress Lady Wincham.' Philip pulled a newspaper cutting from his pocket. 'Here we are – able to reveal, yes – Her sixty-three-year-old mother, he goes on – yes, listen to this, it's stirring stuff – ex-Lady Logan, ex-Mrs Chaddesley-Corbett, ex-Viscountess Tring, ex-Madame Bouche-Bontemps, ex-Mrs Rawle, ex-Mrs Plugge, ex-Señora Lopez, ex-Mrs Chrisolithe, is now married to Pimlico man "Grandad" Markson, 22, organizer of Grandad's Tours. Interviewed in London, Mrs Markson said she had lost touch with husband number four. "We were madly in love," she said. Asked if it was true that M. Bouche-Bontemps won her in a lottery, she said, "I think it was a tombola."'

'So?'

'Bouche-Bontemps is frantic, I've had him on the telephone a dozen times. He says he remembers keenly living with this lady, out of her head, but pretty and funny, and he thinks they were together for two or three months but he certainly never married her.'

'Goodness!' I said, 'that seems to put him in an awkward position, doesn't it? Like when are you going to stop beating your wife? If he married the Bolter it's bad but if he didn't marry her it's worse?'

'No, no. You don't understand the French, as Davey would say. If he married her that's the end of his career but if he only lived with her nobody here would think anything of it. Can't you ring her up and find out?'

'Dear me! But I'm afraid she says [I was looking at Mockbar's piece] husband number four. Come on, we'll put a call through now.'

It was not necessary, however. In the Salon Vert there was a telegram on top of my afternoon letters. 'Never married him darling it was deed-pollers gave no interview have taken it up with Grumpy who promises denial tomorrow in *Daily Post* Bolter.'

'Oh well,' said Philip when I handed him this. 'That will make it much better. If they really deny it in the *Daily Post* the French papers won't copy it. They are far keener on accuracy than ours.'

'Don't you think Mockbar has gone too far? Might he not get the sack?'

'Not he! Much more likely to get a rise so that he can fatten his brats until the next jump in the cost of living forces him to make another scoop.' He lifted up the receiver. 'Katie, get the Président du Conseil for Lady Wincham, will you?'

'Is that my stepfather?' I said and was nearly blown over by a burst of laughter. 'Listen – I've had a telegram from my mother which Philip thinks will make everything all right. She says the paper is denying a marriage. It was only deed-poll she says.'

'Deed-poll,' said Bouche-Bontemps suspiciously, 'what is this?'

'What's deed-poll in French?' I asked Philip and repeated after him. '*Acte unilatéral* but you don't have it here like we do. You know – it means she took your name.'

'Did she? There was certainly no *acte*. But why should she take my name?'

'For the neighbours, I expect.'

'But, *chère Mme l' Ambassadrice*, it was at Harrar! The neighbours were Abyssinians – never mind, go on.'

'Anyhow, the point is there will be a denial tomorrow. Oh dear, I'm so sorry – though it's not exactly my fault.'

'But nothing matters as long as I am not supposed to be *biganme* – what is it in English? – bigamous. That would be very annoying – the Hautes-Pyrénées would not like it and nor would my late wife's family les Pucelards (*textiles Pucelard*) from Lille. The only person who would be delighted is my daughter-in-law who hates me, it would quite compensate her for being married to a bastard. Now, of course, I shall be labelled Intelligence Service but as the only Frenchman of whom that is never said is General de Gaulle I suppose I can bear it. *Sacrée Dorothée* – is she really your mother? How strange! No women could be less alike – though I now see a striking resemblance between her and Mees.'

'Oh don't! I always try not to!'

When I had finished talking to Bouche-Bontemps I went to find Northey. Her room was full of newborn wails. 'Mélusine has had six lovely babies, clever girl.'

'I thought you said she was old?'

'Yes. They are miracle-children.'

'So now what? Hadn't somebody better bucket them at once? Before she has got fond of them?'

'Fanny!'

'I know. But darling duck, we can't keep them here.'

'In this enormous house? I saw a dead rat in the courtyard only yesterday.'

'It was a visiting rat then. There aren't any in the house and we've got a perfectly good cat in the kitchen.'

'Sweet Minet. Very well, if you are so unwelcoming I shall give them away.'

'Yes. You must. Did you enjoy the Return of the Cinders?'

'It was lovely. We all shouted *Vive l'Empereur* – a bit late, but never mind.'

'I hear you are going out with M. de Valhubert again?'

'On business, Fanny. I must have a long serious talk about the *porte-feuille*. If the *assainissement de notre place* goes on like this all my profits will disappear and then what will my old age be like? Can you afford to pension me off? I'm getting seriously annoyed about it.'

'You talk worse pidgin than Grace. Do try to keep to one language at a time. I suppose you read Mockbar this morning?'

'Clever little soul. By the way, Davey asked me to say good-bye.'

'Davey has buggered off?'

'Fanny! Never mind, I won't tell Alfred. Yes. He says he can feel himself getting cancer of the lungs at every breath he takes in Paris.'

'What nonsense! Among all these trees! There's no smell of petrol here.'

'He says it's the scentless fumes, heavier than air, which do all the damage.'

'I must say that's a bit too much. He turns David into a sex-maniac and then leaves us to bear the brunt.'

'He'll bravely come back, when he's decarbonized, to see about David. Meanwhile Docteur Lecœur has given him a calming injection so the idea is that all our virtues are saved for the present. Katie had a ghastly time with him last night – she says it was the nearest thing – That beard and those feet, how can poor Dawnie? Why are Zen-men's feet always so awful?' She shuddered.

'I wish Docteur Lecœur would give Mockbar a calming injection.'

'No, Fanny, he's courting. It would be too unfair.'

'Courting whom?'

'Phyllis McFee, for one.'

'Tell me something, Northey. Does Phyllis McFee really exist?'

Wide-eyed, injured look. 'How d'you mean, does she really exist?'

'You haven't invented her, by any chance?'

'She's my old friend of for ever. (The poor make no new friends – oh don't! That wretched Bourse!) Surely I'm allowed the one?'

'Then I can't understand why you never bring her to see me?'

'She works.'

'What at?'

'World Something.'

'Not in the evening surely?'

'Specially then because, you know, the World is round so it's later in America. When that great throbbing, teeming, bustling heart of little old New York begins to beat, Phyllis McFee, relaxed, efficient, smiling (not to grin is a sin), suitably dressed in her latest Mainbocher, immaculate hair-do, neat ankles and red nails, must be on the Transatlantic line. She has no time to waste on people like you.'

'Bring her to luncheon one day?'

'She's far too busy. She can't do more than *un queek dans un drog* which is French for luncheon in a chemist's shop. Just imagine, scrumptious grub all among the cotton wool – takes thinking of – admit –'

'All right then, don't bring her. I don't mind. She seems to work a good deal harder than some people we know.'

'Is that a hint? Not very kind, Fanny. As a matter of fact, Phyllis McFee has ambitions, she wants to hug her boss (which would be French for employer if it didn't happen to mean bruise). I don't.'

'Another person I never see, while we are on the subject of invisible beings, is M. Cruas.'

'He's timid. He wouldn't like to be seen by you. And speaking as your secretary, quite as much up to date, thorough and efficient as Phyllis, may I remind you that you and Alfred have got the National Day of the North Koreans, after which you dine early with the Italians to go to a lovely play, at the Théâtre des Nations, about refrigerators. Some people have all the luck – !'

Feeling myself dismissed, I went up to my bedroom and tried to forget my manifold worries in a long, hot, scented bath.

It took us some time to get from the North Korean to the Italian Embassy. Between the hours of seven and eight all the Americans who live in Paris bring out motor-cars the size of lorries, shiny, showy and horribly cheap-looking, and sally forth to meet each other, drink whisky and rub up their accents. This also happens to be the time when the Parisians are on the move from work-place to home; the streets become almost impassable.

As we drove towards the Alma, at about one mile an hour, Alfred said, 'You seem preoccupied, darling. Is there something on your mind?'

'Something! About a ton of different things –'

'Such as?'

'Mockbar, to begin with. I suppose you didn't see it –'

'Yes, I did. Philip put it under my eyes. Anything sillier I have seldom read. Bouche-Bontemps says it's quite untrue and he must know. Really – if that's all –'

'Oh, how I wish it were. Northey worries me dreadfully.'

'Northey? Why?'

'Any little girl as attractive as she is must be a worry until one has married her off. The followers –'

'Safety in numbers, surely.'

'There are one or two whom I don't think safe.' I did not want to specify Valhubert to Alfred without more proof than I had that he was really a danger.

'Can you wonder they follow? The other day – it was after your luncheon party – she took Mme Meistersinger downstairs. I'd just been seeing off the Burmese and then had gone into Mrs Trott's room to telephone. When I came out the hall was empty – the footman was putting the old woman into her motor and behind their backs, at the top of the steps, Northey was going through a sort of pantomime of ironical reverences. Oh I can't describe how funny it was! Of course she had no idea anybody was watching. It made me

162

realize that one might be terribly in love with that little creature.'

'We all are,' I said, 'except Philip. One does so long for her to have a happy life, not like the Bolter.'

Alfred now said something extraordinary: 'Deeply as I disapprove of your mother and her activities I don't think she could be described as unhappy.'

I looked at him in amazement. We were all so much accustomed in my family to deploring the Bolter's conduct that one took for granted the great unhappiness to which it must have, if only because it ought to have, led.

'You should try and see things as they are, Fanny. Whether her behaviour has been desirable or not is a different proposition from whether it has made her unhappy. I don't think it has; I think she is perfectly happy and always was.'

'Perhaps. Still, you wouldn't want that sort of happiness for Northey, I suppose. My prayer is that she will marry Philip and settle down.'

'I agree. I don't want it for her. But neither do I want her to marry him because, if she does, mark my words, she won't settle down. She will bolt.'

'Alfred, why do you say that?'

'Philip wouldn't hold her. Not enough fantasy, no roughage. Although vastly superior in every way to Tony Kroesig he is in some sort not the contrary of him. Just as Tony didn't do for Linda, so Philip wouldn't for Northey.'

'I see in a way what you mean – they are both rich, conventional Englishmen – but really it's very unfair to Philip.'

'I'm extremely fond of him, I only say he's not the husband for her.'

'I wonder! Luckily it's out of our hands – something they must settle for themselves. Are you beginning to be interested in people in your old age, darling?'

'Old age?' Falsetto.

'Well, I really think it must be that. You used utterly to despise me when I made these sort of speculations.'

'I'm interested in the children and I count Northey as one.'

'I sometimes wish she was our one and only – no, of course I don't mean that, but I could wish that David and Baz hadn't reached these difficult stages just when you and I have our hands full. We can be of so little use to them, under the circumstances.'

'I don't know. We seem to be lodging David and his family, providing medical attention and everything. Basil comes and goes as he likes – what more could we do? I think it's just as well we are busy; it takes our minds off them. Useless for us to worry and we have no cause to reproach ourselves. They are only suffering from growing pains I think – nothing very serious.'

'I do reproach myself for not having sent them to Eton. If we had they might have turned out so differently.'

'I don't agree. Eton produces quite as large a percentage of oddities as other schools. In any case we weren't rich enough, then. We did our best for them, and that's that.'

'We must count our blessings. How I'm looking forward to going over on St Andrew's Day and taking out the little boys. They are perfect.'

'Perfect?' Falsetto again.

'I mean like other people.'

'Oh. So it's perfect to be like other people, is it? Grace tells me they think of nothing but jazz.'

'That's a phase.'

'So are the eccentricities of Basil and David, no doubt . . .'

'My point is that going to Eton will have minimized the danger of such extreme phases in the case of Charlie and Fabrice.'

'*Unberufen*,' said Alfred, as we drove into the courtyard of the Hôtel de Doudeauville.

17

The word *'unberufen'* rang so unaccustomed on the lips of Alfred that it stuck in my mind. Whether it was the result of old age or of having a new position in the world, he seemed to be mellowing; the Alfred of a year ago would have conducted our conversation in the motor on different, sterner lines and would not have said *'unberufen'*. However, when, the next day before luncheon, Katie told me that there was a personal call for him from Windsor, I knew that he must have unberufened in vain. He had gone to the railway carriage in the forest of Compiègne to celebrate the Armistice; I said that I would take the call. No doubt some sort of worst had occurred; I prayed, wrongly, weakmindedly, that it would prove to be a moral and not a physical worst. For a few seconds there was a muddle on the line: *"allo Weendzor – parlez Weendzor,'* during which time an amazing amount of horrible speculations managed to pass through my head. The moment I heard the housemaster's voice, decidedly peevish but not sad, I was reassured: Charlie and Fabrice were obviously still with us on this earth. He did not beat about the bush or try to prepare me for bad news; he told me that the boys had left.

'Run away?' I said, perhaps too cheerfully, in my relief.

'People don't exactly run away any more. The snivelling boy dragged off the stagecoach by an usher is a thing of the past.'

I laughed hysterically at this piece of light relief, put in perhaps to steady my nerves.

'No, you could hardly call it that. In any case, running away is a spontaneous action with which one can have a certain sympathy. This was a premeditated, indeed an organized, departure. They asked to speak to me after early school and announced it, quite politely I must say. Then all three got into a Rolls-Royce, apparently hired for the purpose, and drove off –'

'All three?'

'Valhubert was with them.'

'Oh, he was, was he! And did they give a reason?'

'The excuse was the food – in other words, no excuse at all because I think I may say the food in my house is excellent. I eat it myself. They pretended that poor little Billy last half – you remember the tragedy – threw himself into the weir on purpose because of it. Nothing could be more far-fetched. They said the choice was between a suicide pact and immediate departure.'

'Naughty!' I stifled a giggle.

'I need hardly tell you that I shall be unable to take them back again after this. The drama was played out in public – half the school saw them go. It seems they stopped in Slough for Fabrice to say good-bye to his mistress and three children.'

'Rubbish,' I said irritably. 'I've heard about this mistress in Slough all my life – ever since my cousins were at school. And the King of Siam's seven wives living over the post-office. Typical Eton tales.'

'That may be. I'm only telling you to show the effect of all this on the other boys and the impossibility of my overlooking their conduct.'

'Oh yes, I see, and I quite realize. Does M. de Valhubert know?'

'Not yet. I shall ring him up now.'

'Just tell me where they've gone, will you?'

'I have no idea.'

'No idea! Didn't you ask them?'

'Certainly I did not.'

My irritation turned to fury. What did we pay the wretched man for? With incredible frivolity he had allowed these children we had put in his care, while we were serving our country overseas, to vanish into the blue. All very well for him to be so light-hearted about it; he had got rid of them for good. My troubles were just beginning, but that evidently left him cold.

'Then there's nothing more to say?'

'Nothing, I'm afraid.' We rang off.

I told Katie to keep the line clear until Mme de Valhubert should ring up. Presently I asked her, 'What's become of Northey? I haven't seen her this morning.'

'She was up all night with the kittens. Mélusine doesn't seem to have any milk – too old probably – so it's the fountainpen filler. Poor Northey's trying to get some sleep; I've taken over for her. Every two hours, and one of them isn't sucking properly. I think this is Mme de Valhubert now – that was her butler's voice –'

'Fanny – you are *au courant*?'

'Yes, indeed. That idiot rang us up first. I'm simply furious –'

'Old Tartuffe! Did you ever hear anything so shameful!'

'It's a disgrace, Grace. I shall tell Alfred he's not to pay a penny for this half.'

'No, don't let's. The boys have never cost him much at any time – Sigi lived on mercy parcels I had to send from Hédiard. The wretch! Calmly telephoning to say he let the boys leave without even having taken the trouble to find out where they were going! I expect they are all being murdered by a sex maniac in the fog at this very minute, poor little things –'

'Oh well, I expect not –'

'You know what England is, darling. I was wondering if couldn't *porter plainte* against the school?'

'What does Charles-Édouard say?'

'He's down in his *circonscription* for the Armistice – and I suppose Alfred has gone to Compiègne? What ought we to do? So dreadful to think of those children all alone in London.'

'We aren't even sure they've gone to London.'

'Knowing Sigi I think they have. Who will feed them?'

'I've a good mind to go over now and see what they are up to,' I said.

'You can't. There's a fog as usual. Didn't you notice, no English papers? Look at it here, such a heavenly day –'

'In any case it wouldn't be much good for me to wander round London looking for them like Thomas à Becket's mother, without a clue as to where they are. I suppose we must wait and consult with our husbands when they get back. We'll keep in touch, but let's anyhow meet tomorrow and talk it over. I should think we'll know more by then.'

'You're an optimist!' said Grace. '*À demain* then, unless there's any news before.'

However, at tea-time she rang up again. 'Almost too irritating,' she said, 'I've just telephoned to my father on the chance he might know something and sure enough he gave them all luncheon at Wilton's. Of course the wicked old man is on their side – he would be. Like all Englishmen he's a schoolboy himself really. What a race! He says they ate everything within sight. They showed him menus of all the meals they've had this half which they kept as *pièces justificatives* and he says he can't think how they stuck it as long as they did. Naturally no mention of the mercy parcels. Clever of Sigi, that was, the way to my father's heart has always been through his stomach.'

'Little brutes!' I said. I had transferred some of my rage with the housemaster to the boys, as, I noticed, had Grace.

'The maddening thing is,' she went on, 'he admits he gave them money.'

'How much?'

'He pretends he can't remember – a few pounds he says. If I know Papa, he'll have had at least £50 on him and if I know Sigi, he'll have wheedled it all. So now goodness alone knows when we shall hear any more of them. They were still alive at luncheon-time, apart from that the situation is worse than if he hadn't seen them.'

'Didn't you ask where they were staying?'

'Naturally I did. He only said not with him. Trust him not to make himself uncomfortable in any way!'

At this point Katie cut in, saying, 'Do we take a reversed charge call from London?'

'Oh yes,' I said, 'that's always one of the boys. I'll ring you up presently, Grace.'

'Ma?' It was Basil. 'Look, Ma, it's like this. Old Charles and Fabrice and Sigi are here.'

'Basil, you are a faithful boy. I've been so worried!'

'Oh, so you knew they'd left the booby-hatch, did you?'

'Yes, their tutor rang up this morning and of course Sigi's mother and I have been in the most fearful state wondering what had happened to them.'

'I suppose you thought the robins had covered them with leaves! Your capacity for worry beats anything I ever heard of. Anyway, knowing you, I thought I'd better ease your mind. They are quite alive and nobody has interfered with them, not yet.'

'So what are they going to do?'

'Live it up here. They've gone to a pop show now this minute to see their idol, Yanky Fonzy.'

'Have they got much money?'

'There you are, being your old bourgeoise self. Money! Didn't you know it doesn't count in the modern world? Everybody's got the stuff nowadays. As a matter of fact, they seem to be quite specially well fixed for it – they've pooled Charles's savings, Fabrice's camera and what Sigi's old ancestor gave them just now.'

'Where are they living?'

'Me Grandad has set them up in a shack he happened to own.'

'Then quickly give me the address – I've got a pencil. Good. Any telephone number?'

'I'm not allowed to give it. They don't want the O.C.s beefing down the line – specially Sigi doesn't.'

The O.C.s, I knew, meant the old couples, in other words us and the Valhuberts. 'Aren't they afraid the O.C.s may arrive and beef in person?'

'Not really. They reckon Father's too busy – Sigi's mother is pregnant – Sigi's father wouldn't demean himself and if you come over they can cope.'

'Oh indeed! Let me tell you, Baz, I've seldom been so furious.'

'That's not reasonable of you, Ma. I don't see 'ow you could expect them kids to go on wasting the best years of their lives in that ole cackle factory.'

'Anyway, darling, it was awfully good of you to telephone –'

★

Alfred surprised me by taking the news very badly indeed. I said, 'I don't know why you should mind this more than you did about David and Baz. After all, they are intellectuals, far more brilliant than the little boys, it is dreadfully sad that they should have become so peculiar. But yesterday you said it was only a phase, growing pains. So it is with the others, probably.'

'I mind less about David and Basil precisely because they are cleverer. They have got their degrees. When they see the futility of their present state they can return to more rewarding occupations. Also there is something in their heads. We may feel annoyed with them for not following the path we had hoped they would, but as human beings they are perfectly entitled to decide for themselves what they wish to do. These boys are only in the middle of their lessons – I don't see how the gap in their education is ever to be filled. There is no philosophical basis for their conduct; it comes from sheer irresponsibility. You know what I feel about education.'

I could see that Alfred, whatever he might say, had counted as much as I had on magic Eton to produce two ordinary, worthy, if not specially bookish young men and was disappointed as well as disturbed by this new outbreak of non-conformism.

The Valhuberts came round and the two stricken families held a conference. Charles-Édouard was in a rage, with Grace crowing over him annoyingly, I thought.

'Of course, poor Charles-Édouard is angry with me for being right all along. Such a pity to send the child to Eton, when we could have kept him here and fed him up and had him taught by the Jesuits at Sainte-Geneviève.'

'My dear Grace, they would never have taken Sigi at Sainte Geneviève. That's a school for clever boys. Franklin, perhaps – not sure. No. I sent him to Eton for the education, not for the instruction. Sigi has the brain of a bird, as even you must admit. I wanted him to be at least a well-dressed bird with good manners. Besides I can only stand a limited amount of his company. Now he'll be back on our hands all the year round unless I can persuade them to take him at Les Roches.'

'If he runs away from Eton he would never stay at Les Roches. It will have to be the Jesuits – you must go and see the Superior at Franklin.'

'When you do, will you be so good as to ask him to recommend a tutor for our two?' said Alfred. 'I suppose we shall have to have them here where we can keep an eye on them; they can at least get a proper grounding in French before they cram for Oxford.'

'Have them here?' I said, quite as much dismayed at the prospect as Valhubert was. It seemed to me we had enough on our hands already, what with the holy Zen family, Northey's caravan of followers and Basil's Cheshire-cat appearances and wild-cat schemes.

'What else can we do?' said Alfred. 'That school they call the Borstal Boys' Eton might take them – think of the friends they would pick up there!'

'Gabbitas and Thring?'

Alfred buried his head in his hands.

Grace now said, with perfect truth, that we were looking too far ahead. We must get them away from London and the shack found for them by my stepfather, under our own influence again, before making these elaborate plans. It was decided that we had better wait until it was reasonable to suppose that they would have run out of cash and that then one of us should go over and bring them back.

'But what about your father, Grace? If he goes on supplying them they won't ever run out.'

'I'm thankful to say he has now left London for a round of shoots and he'll be away at least a month.'

It then became evident, just as the little brutes had foreseen, that I should be the one deputed to go after them. The only alternative was Valhubert and he said himself that he was too angry and would be sure to lose his temper at the mere sight of them. The words 'if you do, they can cope' rang a mocking chime in my ears, but I had no choice; I accepted the mission.

So we planned for our sons, hoping to undo the harm they had done themselves. It never occurred to us that they would refuse to cooperate. We were soon to learn our mistake.

We let the rest of November go by; then I sent them a telegram, reply paid, asking them to dine with me at the Ritz the following day. They were kind enough to accept the invitation quite promptly. Alfred said this showed they were starving and should easily be caught, like animals in the snow.

'The gilt will be off the gingerbread by now – they'll have begun to see what it's like to be alone in London with no money. It was far better not to go at once.'

On St Andrew's Day I arrived at the Ritz. When I had unpacked and had a bath I was still about half an hour too early for our appointment; there was nothing else to do so I went downstairs, sat on one of those little sofas below the alcove, where I have perched at intervals all my life, and ordered a glass of sherry. Never possessing a London house of my own I have always found the Ritz useful when up for the day or a couple of nights; a place where one could meet people, leave parcels, write letters, or run into out of the rain. It now remains one of the few London interiors which have never changed a scrap; the lace antimacassars are still attached to the armchairs with giant hairpins; the fountain tinkles as it has for fifty years; there is the same sound of confident footfall on thick carpet and the same delicious smell of rich women and promising food. As in the Paris Ritz the management has been clever enough not to touch the decoration designed by M. Meuwes, the excellent architect employed by M. Ritz. I have been told that the late Lady Colefax once refused a commission to redecorate the ground floor, saying that it would be wrong to alter any of it.

I sipped my sherry and reflected on the enormous length of human life and the curious turns it takes, a train of thought always set off by a place with which I have been familiar at irregular intervals for many years. Some people, I know, feel aggrieved at the shortness of life; I, on the contrary, am amazed at how long it seems to go on. The longer the better. Paris had cured me of my

middle-aged blight exactly as I had hoped it would; if I was sometimes worried there I never felt depressed, bored, and useless, as at
Oxford. I managed the work far better than I had expected to. I had
neither kissed the President nor extinguished the Eternal Flame nor
indeed, as far as I knew, committed any major gaffe. As I am not shy,
and most of the people I met were engaged in responsible, therefore
interesting, work I found no difficulty in conversing with them. Philip
had provided me with one or two useful gambits. ('I suppose you
are very tired, M. le Ministre' would unloose floodgates.)

Alfred was an undoubted success with the French, whatever
Mockbar might say. He was more like their idea of an Englishman,
slow, serious, rather taciturn, than the brilliant Sir Louis, who had
been too much inclined to floor them on their own ground. Such
worries as I had all came from the children; Alfred's were more
serious. He was obliged to press the European Army upon the
French although personally convinced by now of its unacceptabil-
ity. The Îles Minquiers, too, were still giving him a lot of
uncongenial work. However, Mr Gravely seemed quite satisfied
with the way these things were shaping. The Americans had
assured him that the European Army was almost in the bag. He
thought he had himself persuaded M. Bouche-Bontemps to give
up the Minquiers and that it was only, now, a matter of time before
they became British Isles.

Two men coming out of the alcove and passing my sofa roused
me from these thoughts. 'When I got to the factory,' one of them
said, 'they told me that seven of the girls were knocked up – well,
pregnant in fact. It's the new German machine.'

'You don't surprise me at all,' said his friend, 'these new German
machines are the devil.'

I have overheard many a casual remark in my life; none has ever
puzzled me more. As I pondered over it I saw three figures ambling
towards me from the Arlington Street entrance. They were dressed
as Teddy boys, but there was no mistaking the species. With their
slouching, insouciant gait, dead-fish hands depending from, rather
than forming part of, long loose-jointed arms, slightly open mouths

and appearance of shivering as if their clothes, rather too small in every dimension, had no warmth in them, they would have been immediately recognizable, however disguised, on the mountains of the Moon, as Etonians. Here were the chrysalises of the elegant, urbane Englishmen I so much longed for my sons to be; this was the look which, since I was familiar with it from early youth, I found so right, and which I had missed from the tough premature manliness of the other two boys. Charlie and Fabrice had changed their clothes but not yet their personalities; what a relief!

18

'We didn't think we were late?'

'You're not. I was early.'

'Pretty dress, Mum. We've brought you some flowers.'

'Oh, you are nice. Thanks so much – roses!' (But this was rather sinister. Roses are expensive on St Andrew's Day; they must still have got some money.) 'My favourites! Give them to the porter, Charlie, will you, and ask him to have them put in a vase for me. There – let's go and dine.'

I thought the boys were feeling quite as much embarrassed as I was and I counted on food to unbutton us all. They ordered, as I knew they would, smoked salmon and roast chicken and then politely tried to put me at my ease.

'Did you have a good journey?'

'Was it a Viscount?'

'Have you seen the new Anouilh in Paris?'

'Have you read *Pinfold*?'

I said yes to everything but was too much preoccupied to enlarge on these topics. General conversation was really not possible under the circumstances; I ordered a bottle of wine and bravely plunged. 'Perhaps you'll tell me now what this is all about?'

Charlie and Sigi looked at Fabrice who was evidently the spokesman. 'Are you furious with us?' he said.

'I'm more worried than furious. Your fathers are very angry indeed. But why did you do it?'

'The ghoulishness of the food –' Sigi said, in a high wail.

'It's no good telling me about the food,' I said firmly, 'because I know perfectly well that had nothing to do with it. I'd like the real reason, please.'

'You must try and put yourself in our place,' said Fabrice, 'wasting the best years of our lives (only three more as teenagers – every day so precious, when we ought to be hitting it up as never again), wasting them in that dark creepy one-horse place with Son et Lumière (the head beak) and all the other old weirdies yattering at us morning and night and those ghoulish kids mouldering in the same grave with us. It's a living death, Mum; we've been cheesed off for months. In the end it became more than flesh and blood could stand. Do you blame us?'

I was uncertain how to say what must be said. 'What's that you've got on your jersey, Charles?'

'Yank's the Boy for Me. Do you like it?'

'Only rather. Who is Yank?'

'Who is Yank? Yanky Fonzy of course, the Birmingham-born Bomb. I should have thought even you would have heard of Yank – that lanky Yank from Brum – the toughest guy that breathes. He's a disc star.'

'And he's the boy for you?'

'Oh definitely. Of course he's a man's man, you might not dig him like we do, lots of girls don't and hardly any oldsters. But we're his fans, the screamin' kids who follow him round the Beat Shows. Boy! does he wow us!'

'Oh,' I said, flummoxed.

'You ought to come and see for yourself,' said Sigi. '*Tout comprendre c'est tout pardonner!*'

'Do you think I would understand though?'

'If you saw you would,' said Fabrice. 'Yank, coming right into the attack – treating the kids like a man squeezing an orange. That ole mike is putty in his hands; he rolls on the floor with it – uses it as a gun – throws it around, spins it, snarls into it. Then, sudden, dramatic, he quiets down into a *religioso*: "I count them over, every one apart, my Rosary." From that it's Schehera-jazz: "Pale hands I loved beside the Shalimar." "Oh Shenandoah, I long to hear you." Ending up with the patriotic stuff: "Shoot if you must this old grey head but spare my country's Flag, she said." Something for everybody, see?'

'Oh Mum, do try and realize how it makes jolly boating weather seem like a rice pudding.'

'Perhaps I do. But all this has no connexion with real life, which is very long, very serious and for which, at your age, you ought to be preparing.'

'No. The whole point is that we are too old, now, to be preparing. This is life, it has begun, we want to be living.'

'Dearest, that's for your parents to decide. As we support you we must be allowed to have a say in your activities, I suppose?'

'Ah! But I'm just coming to that. Teenagers are definitely commercial nowadays. It's not like we were back in history – David Copperfield. The modern Copperfield doesn't have to tramp to Dover and find Aunt Betsy – no – he is rich – he earns £9 a week. That's what we are making; not bad for a start?'

'£9 a week?' I was very much taken aback. Starving animals in the snow, indeed! This was going to make my task difficult if not impossible. 'For doing what, may I inquire?'

'Packing.'

'That's nearly £500 a year!'

'Definitely.'

'What do you pack?'

'Shavers – you know, razors.'

'Do you like it?'

'Does anybody like work?'

I snatched at this opening.

'Oh, indeed they do, when it's interesting. That's the whole point of lessons, so that one can finally have work which is more enjoyable than packing.'

'Yes, that's what we've heard. We don't believe it. We think all work is the same and it's during the time off that you live your life. No use wasting these precious years preparing for jobs that may be far worse than packing when we shall be old and anyway not able to feel anything, good or bad. As it is we get two days off and our evenings. In between we are inspired by Yank.'

'But my dear children, you can't go on packing for the rest of your lives. You must think of the future.'

'Why must we? All you oldies thought and thought of the future and slaved and saved for the future, and where did it get you?'

'It got your father to Paris.'

'And what good does that do him? How many days off does he get? How does he spend his evenings? Who is his idol?'

'In any case it's now we want to be enjoying ourselves, not when we are rotting from the feet up at thirty or something ghoulish.'

'Just tell me,' I said, 'were you unhappy at Eton? People hardly ever are, in my experience.'

They looked at each other. 'No – not exactly unhappy. It was this feeling of waste we had.'

'It wasn't the Perthshire Set?' I knew that when they first arrived they had been teased (according to their own statements, discounted by me, positively martyrized) by Scotch boys larger and older than they, one of whom was Sigi's fag-master, who were alleged to have stolen their money and borrowed and broken such treasures as cameras, besides inflicting dire physical torments on them.

'Ay, the gret black monolisks fra' Pitlochry,' said Fabrice, 'a' change heer for Ballachulish.' The others were shaking with laughter at what was evidently an ancient and well-loved joke. 'Nu – now we are na' longer wee bairnies they canna scaith us.'

'You didn't leave because of them?'

'They are still ghoulish (in Pop now) but no, definitely not.'

'And you haven't been beaten this half?'

'Oh definitely. I was beaten for covering a boy with baby-powder and Sigi was for holding a boy's head under the bathwater.'

'Sigi!' There was such horror in my voice that he looked quite startled and quickly said, 'But I didn't hold it for as long as they thought.'

'Mum – nobody minds being beaten, you know.'

'Speak for yourself, Charlie,' said Fabrice, making a face.

'Of course it's rather ghoulish pacing up and down one's room before. But not nearly enough for running away. Our reasons were positive, not negative.'

The others agreed. 'Definitely. It was the feeling that life was passing us by and we weren't getting the best out of it.'

'Packing and rocking and rolling aren't the best, either. They will stop wowing you very soon and then where will you be?'

'By then nothing will matter any more. Our teens will have gone and we shall be old and we shall die. Isn't it sad!'

'Very sad but not quite true. You will get old and die, but after the end of your teens until your death beds there will be endless years to fill in somehow. Are you going to spend them all, all those thousands of days, packing shavers? Is it for this that you were created?'

'You see, you haven't understood, just like we were so afraid you wouldn't.'

'Why don't you come back with me to Paris in the morning?'

They looked at each other uncomfortably. 'You see, we think London is a better town to live in at our age. Paris isn't much good for teenagers.'

'Definitely less commercial.'

'So you won't come?'

'You see, we've signed on for our work.'

It was evidently no good pursuing the subject so we spoke of other things. They asked how Northey was. 'By the way,' I said, 'she's a teenager but she's perfectly happy in Paris; she loves it.'

They said, scornfully but quite affectionately, that she had never acted like a teenager.

'Act is the word,' I said, beginning to lose my temper, 'acting and showing off. If you had to leave Eton why couldn't you have gone at the end of the half instead of having a scene with your tutor and hiring a Rolls-Royce to take you, in full view of everybody? So vulgar, I'm ashamed of you. And how I wish you knew how babyish you look in that silly fancy dress.'

'This dinner party is going downhill,' said Fabrice.

'Definitely,' said Sigi.

'Ghoulish,' said Charlie.

'Yes. I think I'm tired after the journey.' I looked at my children and thought how little I knew them. I felt much more familiar with David and Baz. No doubt it was because these boys had always been inseparable. As with dogs, so with children, one on its own is a more intimate pet than two or three. The death of my second baby had made a gap between David and Basil; I had had each of them in the nursery by himself. I suppose I had hardly ever been alone with either of the other two in my life; I was not at all sure what they were really like.

'Don't be tired,' said Fabrice. 'We thought we'd take you to the Finsbury Empire. It's not Yank unfortunately (he's in Liverpool) but quite a good pop show.'

'Darling – no, I can't anyhow. I promised I'd ring up Sigi's mother and tell the news. She's expecting a baby, Sigi.'

If I'd hoped to soften him with this statement I was disappointed. 'I know!' he said furiously. 'It really is too bad of her. What about the unearned income? There'll be nothing for any of us if she goes on like this.'

'Lucky you're so good at packing.' I felt I had scored a point.

As soon as the children had finished their pudding I paid the bill and said good-bye to them. There seemed to be no point in prolonging the interview only to hear, as I was already sick of hearing from David and Baz, what a ghastly (or ghoulish) failure Alfred and I had made of our lives; how we had wasted our youth and to what purpose? It was true that I was tired and, in fact, deeply depressed and upset. I had been unable to touch my dinner; I longed to be alone and lie down in the dark. First, however, I telephoned to Grace. (Alfred I knew was dining out, I would speak to him in the morning.) She was not surprised to hear about the crooner.

'It went on the whole summer at Bellandargues – lanky Yank the Boy from Brum, till I could have killed them. You didn't quite take it in when I told you. It's an absolute mania. But then, Fanny, aren't they getting hard up?'

'I'm coming to that,' I said, just as Fabrice had, 'hold everything, it's far the worst part. They've got a job – they're quite all right for money and I'd just like you to guess what they are earning.'

'Perhaps – I don't know – they couldn't be worth £3 a week?'

'Nine.'

'Pounds a week? Each? But it's perfectly insane! We shall never get them back now.'

'Exactly.'

'But what do they get it for?'

'Packing, Grace. They pack all day, five days a week, in order to have their evenings free for the Birmingham-born Bomb.'

There was a long pause while she digested this fact. Then she said, 'My dear, the person who gives Sigismond £9 a week to pack for him must be out of his mind. I only wish you could see his box when he comes back from school!'

The next day at Orly the lively face of Northey was in the crowd waiting for friends by the entrance. There was something about the mere sight of that child which made my spirits rise, as that of my own boys, alas, no longer did. She had hopped into the Rolls-Royce when she saw it leaving the Embassy. 'Anything to down tools for an hour or two,' she said, frankly, adding, 'hot news!'

'Don't, Northey!'

'Good news I mean – Coffirep has had children. Oh dear, I'm so over-excited – !'

'Dearest – is that the badger?'

'Fanny, do sharpen your wits and concentrate on my life. Coffirep is my shares – so I'm rich, my old age will be nice, oh do be pleased!'

'I can't tell you how delighted I am, specially about it not being the badger.'

'As if he could all alone, poor duck. In the spring I'll get him a sweet little wife – I'm sure he's made a breeding chamber down there, we don't want him to feel disappointed. Oh, I was dying to tell somebody. Alfred didn't properly listen (he's in a do about the boys); Philip only said he wished he knew if there really is any marketable oil in the Sahara; the holies don't care about money, or so they say. (I note they always make me pay the cab if we go in one.) And Charles-Édouard is shooting, which he calls hunting, in Champagne. It's very dull having nobody to take an interest – thank goodness you are back.'

Not another word about the boys; she was either being tactful or was too much occupied with her own affairs – the latter I suspected. She babbled on until we got home. When we drove into the courtyard I saw a group of people, who were obviously not followers, waiting by Northey's entrance.

'Mr Ward,' she explained, 'has very kindly allowed me to put up a notice in W. H. Smith offering my kittens to good homes. It gives me a lot of extra work, taking up references and so on; they have to be rather special people as you may imagine. They must promise not to – you know – castrate; they must live on the ground floor with a garden (I go myself and see), and above all they must not be related to any scientist, chemist or furrier. The kits aren't ready to leave me and Katie yet; this is only for when they are.'

Of course Mockbar duly informed the world that Envoy's Sons had left Eton because the headmaster had threatened to thrash them and were now employed by the London firm of such-and-such in their packing department. Mockbar hardly annoyed me any more nor even extracted a wry laugh; I was getting used to his style and the observations which punctuated all our doings. His paragraphs no longer made me tremble for Alfred's career. Six million people read them, so one was told, and evidently regarded them as enjoyable fiction. He was too often obliged, by the solicitors of some victim, to withdraw a statement for the public to place much reliance in his word.

A few days later Charles-Édouard left hurriedly for London. To my secret rage and disgust he returned that same evening with Master Sigismond in tow. Grace informed me of this, adding, 'He cracked the whip, darling. Thank God I married a Frenchman. Whatever you may say, they do have some authority in the family!'

'The thing is, Alfred can't go over just now; I don't feel I ought to worry him by suggesting that he should. He's having a difficult time, he's busy.'

'He must be. The English! Words can't express what I feel! They are being quite simply too awful. I'm sure Sir Alfred can't approve. Having that Niam on an official visit! Fanny, it's the limit. He has eaten simply hundreds of Frenchmen and now he's got a loan from Stalin – yes, I know, but they're all Stalin to me, I can't keep learning their new names – so that he can catch and eat hundreds more.'

'Nonsense, Grace. In a profile of Dr Niam I read somewhere, they said he is a vegetarian and very pro-French at heart.'

'At stomach they mean. Oh good, I've made a joke, I must tell Charles-Édouard. I've been too pregnant, lately.'

'They say he's firmly attached to the Western World and has a great sense of humour.'

'Oh, do shut up. Are the English our allies or are they not?'

How I wished I knew what whip, cracked by his father, had brought Sigismond to heel. Cracking whips seemed to be something of which neither Alfred nor I was capable. When our boys refused to listen to reason we were done for. It was beginning to be borne in on me that as parents we were a resounding failure. While all three boys had been in full revolt I could just bear it; now that Sigi had returned to parental authority, the evil conduct of our two was stressed. Surely we, too, ought to be able to find some way of mastering them?

'Hot news!' said Northey. 'Guess why Sigi is here?'

'I thought M. de Valhubert went over and cracked a whip?'

'Yes, well, if you really want to know, he went over because Sigi was in bad with the police. He was caught nicking shavers.'

'Doing what, dearest?'

'They were packing shavers – you knew that, didn't you? And were getting £9 a week, which, incidentally, makes skilled secretarial work in embassies seem rather underpaid but let that pass. Clever Sigi discovered that if you nick a few every day (no, Fanny, *don't* keep asking what things mean, sharpen your wits and listen) you can bump up the screw to quite a pound more. But as he's not used to stealing, so far, he was caught and there was a fearful rumpus. Charles-Édouard had to go and buy him off or he'd have gone to a remand home or something. Can you beat it!'

I felt a glow of superiority. 'Poor Grace,' I said, 'how dreadful.'

'By the way, the old foreign lady is not to be told.'

'Ah! Quite right – of course she mustn't be. So is Charles-Édouard furious?'

'Not a bit. He thinks it's most frightfully funny and he's delighted to have Sigi delivered into his hands. Now he'll be obliged to go to the strict Jesuits after all?'

'I shouldn't think even the strictest Jesuits will do that boy much good – he'll come to a bad end all right.'

Northey bashed me out of my complacency with: 'Charlie and Fabrice have got the knack of it now.'

'The knack of nicking?'

'Yes. Sigi says he invented a foolproof method on the way over and rang them up to tell, very kindly. They'll get lovely and rich, he says, in no time.'

19

Holy David had been looking decidedly better since Docteur Lecœur took him in hand, even slightly cleaner. His interest in secular or non-Zen affairs seemed to be reviving; he came with me to the Louvre one day and saw one or two plays with Dawn. I had become devoted to her, which shows that speech is not an essential factor in human understanding. (Northey said who ever thought it was? Think of creatures and how well we get on with them in silence.) I was very hopeful that if the improvement in David continued at this rate he would go back to his university and resume his career.

Then he told me, casually, one day, that he and Dawn were about to resume their journey to the East. I was sorry, indeed, that it should be East rather than West but to tell the truth I felt such a surge of relief that at first I hardly cared which direction they were taking. David's presence in the house was not convenient. The servants and the whole of Alfred's staff disliked him. English statesmen and important officials who came and went in a fairly steady stream cannot have relished the sight of his gowned form and naked feet at breakfast. He was on his father's nerves. Whenever Mockbar was short of a story he fell back on Envoy's Son for some spiteful little paragraph. How heavenly to think that the Zen family was on the move at last! Concealing joy, I said, 'You'll tell me when you would like Jérôme to take you to the station?'

'Not the station, the road. Send us to Provins; after that we will fend for ourselves.'

'With Dawn in her present condition? Oh no, David, that's not possible.'

'Pregnant women have astonishing powers of survival. That has been proved in every great exodus of history. All the same, I think I will leave little 'Chang here.'

The surge of relief subsided, the joy was extinguished. I might have guessed there would be a snag somewhere. 'No, you can't,' I said, putting up what I really knew would be a perfectly ineffectual resistance. 'Who's going to look after him?'

'Mrs Trott and Katie simply love him.'

'We all simply love him; that's not the point. Neither Mrs Trott nor anybody else here has time to nurse little 'Chang. He's your responsibility; you adopted him; nobody asked you to! Why did you, anyway?'

'We wanted a brother for our baby so that they can be brought up together. It was very bad for my young psychology to be three years older than Basil; Dawn and I don't intend to repeat that mistake of yours.'

'But if he's here and your baby is in the East?'

'As soon as our baby is born it must join little 'Chang. I shall send it to you at once so that they can unfold their consciousness together.'

'So I've got to bring up your family?'

'It will be a boon to you. Middle-aged women with nothing to do are one of the worst problems that face the modern psychologist.'

'But I've got far, far more to do than I can manage already.'

'Cocktail parties – trying on clothes – nothing to get your teeth into. You must try not to be so selfish. Think of poor Dawn, you really can't ask her to carry half the cradle like she used to. 'Chang has put on pounds and pounds and she doesn't feel very well.'

'Leave her here. I'd love to keep her. Then she can have her baby under proper conditions, poor duck.'

'I didn't marry Dawn in order to leave her. I need her company all the time.'

She now appeared with the World Citizen, making furious Chinese noises, in her arms. I thought she looked very frail.

'Dawnie, David has just told me he is on the move again. Why don't you stay comfortably here with little 'Chang and all of us, at any rate until after the baby?'

I had forgotten about the dumbness; her huge eyes projected their gaze on her husband's face and he spoke for her. 'You see she has no desire whatever to stay comfortably here. Dawn has never had such a bourgeois reaction in her life.'

I went to my bedroom and rang up Davey. I begged him to come and save the situation. He was uncooperative and unsympathetic; said that it was impossible for him to move for the present. 'My drawing-room curtains have gone wrong – much too short and skimpy. They must all be made again and I must be here to see to it. That's the sort of thing your Aunt Emily used to do – everything in the house was perfect when she was alive. I do hate being a widower; it really was too bad of her to die.'

'Davey, you haven't understood how serious it is about David.'

'My dear Fanny, I think you are being rather ungrateful to me. You asked me to get rid of him; he is going, is he not?'

'I know – but –'

'If he is going East and not West that is entirely your own fault for not insisting on Dr Jore. I told you that a psychiatrist was needed in conjunction with a physician. Docteur Lecœur strengthened his will-power by working on his glands and correcting his inertia. Dr Jore would have altered the trend of his thought. By rejecting Jore you abandoned him to the Zen Master – the Temple Bells are calling and the flying-fishes play. Another time perhaps you will allow me to know best.'

'I wouldn't mind so much if it weren't for Dawnie. I think he'll kill her, poor little thing.'

'Oh no he won't. Women are practically indestructible, you know.'

'Then think of Alfred and me beginning nurseries all over again. Chinese ones at that.'

'Very tiring for you,' said Davey. 'I must go now or I shall miss the Archers.' He rang off.

David and Dawn left that afternoon. The Rolls-Royce took them to Bar-le-Duc and only returned the next day. David had borrowed money from every single person in the Embassy; all, pitying the plight of Dawn and probably confident of being paid back by me (as of course they were), had produced as much as they had available. It amounted to quite a tidy sum. Mrs Trott found a solid peasant girl from Brittany to look after 'Chang.

'Hot news!' Northey said to Alfred. 'Faithful Amy has had orders from Lord Grumpy to give you treatment number one.'

'Oh, indeed?' Falsetto. 'And how does this differ from that which I have been receiving?'

'Differ? So far you have only had number three, watered down at that by precious Amy on account of loving us all so much.'

'He loves me?'

'Oh yes – he's always saying I like that man. He reveres you. It's very distressing for him to be obliged to write all these horrid and not quite true things about us here when he would give his eyes to be part of the family.'

'Part of the family? In what capacity, may I ask?'

'Perhaps you could adopt him?'

'Thank you. We've got 'Chang and the badger, I don't think we want any more pets.'

'Poor soul.'

FAILURE

It is no secret that Sir Alfred Wincham has proved a failure in Paris and that Whitehall now wishes to replace him with a more dynamic personality. Sir Alfred's well-known aptitude for university intrigue has not carried him very far along the twisting paths of French foreign policy. More professional talent, it is felt, is needed at a time when Anglo-French relations have never been worse.

FRIENDSHIP

In view of M. Bouche-Bontemps' old friendship with Lady Wincham's mother (first revealed in this column) French political circles feel that the Embassy has an unfortunate preference for his party, the L.U.N.A.I.R.

Members of opposition parties are never received there any more. Sir Alfred is out of touch with French public opinion.

RANGOON

Well-informed circles are speculating on Sir Alfred's future, and rumour has it that he may shortly be posted to Rangoon.

Northey and Philip raced each other to my bedroom the morning these delightful paragraphs appeared. She dumped 'Chang on my bed. I always had him for a bit after breakfast and found him delightful company; a contented, healthy baby, easily amused and anxious to please. I thought, when I was with him, that his generation may be on the way to rejecting the anti-charm which is the fashion now, may even develop a sense of humour and seek to attract rather than repel. If my grandchild turned out to be half as nice as the World Citizen I would not be at all sorry to have the two of them for keeps.

'At last Mockbar has overreached himself,' Philip said. 'I think it's actionable; Alfred must speak to his lawyer and we might even get rid of him, who knows?'

'Then the poor little soul will starve,' said Northey.

'No matter.'

'Fanny, you brute. What about his babies?'

'They'll survive,' I said. 'Are Anglo-French relations really so bad, Philip?'

'That part I'm afraid is true. Not Alfred's fault (quite the contrary) but boiling up for a first-class crisis. We are determined to get those bloody islands and to help the Americans re-arm the Germans.'

'Seems mad, doesn't it?'

'Not if we really need them as allies.'

Northey said, 'I wish I knew why people want the Germans on their side. I have yet to hear of them winning a war.'

'They'd be all right with French generals.'

'I wish the whole thing could be settled. The Bourse is strongly disconcerted by all these elements.'

'You can't wish it more than I do,' said Philip.

'I must dree my weird. Shall I leave 'Chang? I've got a lot of work.'

'Yes, leave him. Your work has been very satisfactory of late; you're a good girl and I'm pleased with you.'

'It's the well-known cure for a broken heart,' she said with a tragic look at Philip.

'Go on,' he said, 'I like it.'

I asked her, 'Darling, what are you up to tonight?'

'Docteur Lecœur.'

'*Lecœur soupire la nuit le jour, qui peut me dire si c'est l'amour?*' said Philip.

'Yes, it is.'

'And I suppose,' he went on, 'that every time you pass the Palais Bourbon, the statues of Sully and l'Hôpital get up and bow to you?'

'Yes, they do. It's the English who don't appreciate me. Good-bye all.'

We looked at each other when she had gone, laughing. 'Northey!'

He said, 'The diplomatic hostesses here are furious with Mees because she has got Tony de Lambesc in tow – yes, Fanny – that small, fair chap one sees everywhere. They regard him and me as the only sortable bachelors in this town – we have to do all their dinner parties. There are hundreds of unattached Frenchmen who would like to be asked, but you know what those women are, too timid to try anybody new. They might have to deal with unexpected dialogue and that would never do. The conversation must run on familiar lines, according to some well-worn old formula. Suppose somebody mentions Prince Pierre – of course the correct move is, he simply worships his daughter-in-law! Now a stranger might say do you mean the explorer? or worse still, Prince Pierre in *War and Peace*? and the whole party would feel a wrong turn had been taken – they might even have to begin using their brains. That would never do. They like a gentle game of pat-ball and have no desire for clever young polytechnicians hitting boundaries. Lambesc and I know the right answers in our sleep. But now he's always either taking Mees out or hoping to. He waits till the last moment, praying she'll be chucked; it's no use asking him a week ahead. The only hope is to ring him up at half past eight and get him to come round, disgruntled, there and then. It has upset social life dreadfully. Time Mees got married, that's what it is.'

'Yes, but to whom?'

'Who is there? Bouche-Bontemps is a bit old – that Chef de Cabinet (always forget his name) is too ugly – Cruas is said to be poor –'

'Would that matter?'

'With Mees? She would ruin a poor man in no time.'

'Does Cruas exist? I've still never seen him, have you?'

'Somebody has taught her French; she rattles away at a hundred miles an hour. Then Lecoeur is too busy – Charles-Édouard too much married (worse luck) – the Ambassador to the Channel Islands has a *fort des balles* he adores – Amyas now, what about him? An eligible widower –'

'I'm against,' I said, 'though I may be prejudiced.'

'Then there's Lambesc, but he has his scutcheon to gild.'

I said boldly, 'Why don't you marry her?'

'Well, you know, I might. In spite of the carry-on, I can't imagine life without Mees, now I'm used to her. I suppose she is the last of the charmers. The horsetail girls don't seem to be interested in any of the things I like, least of all sex. They join up with the Teds and the Beats and wander about Europe with them, sharing beds if it happens to suit; three in a bed if it's cheaper like that (shades of Sir Charles Dilke) and probably nothing happens! Sex is quite accidental. Is there a baby on the way or isn't there? They hardly seem to notice. Now Northey is a wicked little thing but at least she is out to please and my word how she succeeds!'

'She's not wicked at all. I even think she is virtuous.'

'Anyway, she's a human being. Very likely I shall end by proposing to her.'

'Only, Philip, don't leave it too long or she'll fall in love with somebody else, you know!'

20

Sir Harald Hardrada now came to give his lecture. It was very brilliant and a great success, Sir Harald being one of the few living Englishmen who, even the French allow, has a perfect mastery of their language. As they detest hearing it massacred and really do not like listening to any other, foreign lecturers are more often flattered than praised at the end of their performance (not that they know the difference). We all went to the Sorbonne where the lecture took place and then Mildred Jungfleisch gave a dinner party. The company was: Sir Harald, M. Bouche-Bontemps, the Valhuberts, the Hector Dexters, an American couple called Jorgmann, Philip and Northey, Alfred, and me. The Dexters had been given a clean bill by the State Department, to the enormous relief of their compatriots in Paris. Having had enough, it seemed, of political activities, Mr Dexter was now acting as liaison between leading French and American art dealers.

Mrs Jungfleisch lived in a cheery modernish (1920) house near the Bois de Boulogne. Its drawing-room, painted shiny white and without ornament of any sort, had an unnaturally high ceiling and stairs leading to a gallery; the effect was that of a swimming-bath. One felt that somebody might dive in at any moment, the Prime Minister of England, perhaps, or some smiling young candidate for the American throne. Almost the only piece of furniture was an enormous pouf in the middle of the room on which people had to sit with their backs to each other. As Americans do, she left a good hour between the arrival of the guests and the announcement of dinner, during which time Bourbon (a kind of whisky) could be imbibed.

Bouche-Bontemps had come to the lecture. He and Sir Harald were old friends. They now sat on the pouf, craning round to talk to each other.

'Excellent, my dear Harald! Nothing could have been more fiendishly clever than your account of Fashoda – you haven't got the K.C.V.O. for nothing! I very much liked the meeting between Kitchener and Marchand on the Argonne front – some time you must read the page from Kipling where he describes the naïf joy of the French poilus as they witnessed it. They thought the hatchet had been buried for ever and that if we won the war, *les Anglais* would become real friends and leave us our few remaining possessions. Never mind –'

'Like all the French,' Sir Harald said urbanely, to the company at large, who were twisting their necks to be in on this conversation. 'M. le Président has the work of our great Imperial protagonist by heart.'

'We defend ourselves as best we can,' said Bouche-Bontemps, 'poor Marchand, I knew him well.'

'Were you already living at Fashoda with the Bolter when he arrived?'

'No. Precocious as I may have been, at six months old I was still living with my parents.'

'You can't imagine how fascinated we all were to learn that the famous Frenchman in her life was none other than yourself. I had always pictured an old douanier with a beard and a wooden leg.'

'Not at all. A jolly young ethnographer. Dorothée – *tellement gentille* –'

'I'd no idea you had this African past, Jules. Whatever were you doing there?'

'In those days I was passionately fond of ethnography. I managed to get on to the Djibouti-Dakar mission.'

'Oh! You rogue! Everything is becoming as clear as daylight. So it was you who took away the Harar frescoes?'

'Took away? We exchanged them.'

'Yes. Kindly tell Mrs Jungfleisch here and her guests what it was you exchanged them for?'

'A good exchange is no robbery, I believe? Harar acquired some delightful wall-paintings in the early manner of your humble servant and the gifted mother of your ambassadress. Oh! How we were happy and busy, painting these enormous frescoes – perhaps the happiest days of my life. Everybody was so pleased – the Fuzzie-Wuzzies greatly preferred our bright and lively work to the musty old things which were there before.'

'We don't say Fuzzie-Wuzzies,' said Sir Harald.

'Indeed?'

'No. Like your foreign policy, all this is old-fashioned.'

'*Hélas!* I am old-fashioned, and old as well. *C'est la vie, n'est-ce pas, Mees?*'

'When are you going to fall again?' said Northey. '(Golly, my neck is aching!) We never see you, it's a bore.'

'With the assistance of the present company it should be any day. What are you preparing for us, Harald?'

Sir Harald became rather pink and looked guilty.

Hector Dexter, who had pricked up his ears at the word frescoes, said, 'And where are the Harar paintings now, M. le Président?'

'Safe in the cellars of the Louvre, thanks to me, where no human eye will ever behold them.'

'I have a client in the States who is interested in African art of unimpeachable provenance. Are there no more ancient frescoes at Harar or in its environs?'

'No,' said Sir Harald, 'the frogs swiped the lot.'

'We don't say frogs any more,' said Bouche-Bontemps, 'it's old-fashioned, like taking away other people's islands.'

There was a little silence. Ice clicked in the glasses, people swallowed, Mrs Jungfleisch handed round caviar. Sir Harald turned from Bouche-Bontemps to the opposite side of the pouf and said, 'Now, Geck, we want to hear all about Russia.'

Hector Dexter cleared his throat and intoned: 'My day-to-day experiences in the Union of Soviet Socialist Russia have been registered on a long-playing gramophone record to be issued free to all the members of the North Atlantic Treaty. This you will be able to obtain by indenting for a copy to your own ambassador to NATO. I was there, as you may know, for between nine and eight years, but after the very first week I came to the conclusion that the way of life of the Socialist Soviet citizen is not and never could be acceptable to one who has had cognizance of the American way of life. Then it took me between nine and eight years to find some way of leaving the country by which I could safely bring Carolyn here and young Foster with me. It became all the more important for me to get out because my son Foster, aged now fifteen, is only ten points below genius and this genius would have been unavailing and supervacaneous, in other words wasted, behind the iron curtain.'

'Why? There can't be so many geniuses there?'

'There is this out-of-date, non-forward-looking view of life. They have not realized the vast potentialities, the enormous untapped wealth of the world of Art. They have this fixation on literature; they do not seem to realize that the written word has had its day – books are a completely outworn concept. We in America, one step ahead of you in Western Europe, have given up buying them altogether. You would never see a woman, or a man, reading a book in the New York subway. Now in the Moscow subway every person is doing so.'

'That's bad, Heck,' said Mr Jorgmann, heavily.

'Why is it bad?' I asked.

'Because books do not carry advertisements. The public of a great modern industrial state ought to be reading magazines or watching television. The Russians are not contemporary; they are not realist; they exude a fusty aroma of the past.'

'So young Foster is going into Art?'

'Yes, Sir. By the time my boy is twenty-one, I intend he shall recognize with unerring certainty the attribution of any paint on any canvas (or wood or plaster), the marks of every known make of porcelain and every known maker of silver, the factory from which every carpet and every tapestry –'

'In short,' said Sir Harald, 'he'll be able to tell the difference between Rouault and Ford Madox Brown.'

'Not only that. I wish him to learn the art trade from the

beginning to the end; he must learn to clean and crate and pack the object as well as to discover it and purchase it and resell it. From flea-market to Jayne Wrightsman's boudoir, if I may so express myself.'

'I should have thought that sort of talent could have been used in the Winter Palace?'

'There is too much prejudice against the West. The Russians do not possess correct attitudes. It was an unpleasant experience to discuss with individuals whose thinking is so lacking in objectivity that one was aware it was emotively determined and could be changed only by change of attitude. Besides, hypotheses, theories, ideas, generalizations, awareness of the existence of unanswered and/or unanswerable queries do not form part of their equipment. So such mental relationships as Carolyn here and I and young Foster Dexter were able to entertain with the citizens of Soviet Socialist Russia were very, very highly unsatisfactory.'

'But, Geek,' said naughty Sir Harald (I remembered that the Russian alphabet has no H), 'one doesn't want to say I told you so – not that I did, only any of us could have if you'd asked our advice – why on earth did you go?'

'When I first got back here some four or three weeks since, I could have found that question difficult, if not impossible, to answer. However, as soon as I arrived here in Paris I put myself in the hands of a brilliant young doctor, recommended to me by Mildred: Dr Jore. I go to him every evening when he has finished with the Supreme Commander. Now Dr Jore very, very swiftly diagnosed my disorder. It seems that at the time when I left this country some nine or eight years ago I was suffering from a Pull to the East which, in my case, was so overwhelmingly powerful that no human person could have resisted it. As soon as Dr Jore sent his report to the State Department they entirely exonerated me from any suspicion of anti-American procedure, deviation from rectitude, improbity, trimming or what have you and recognized that I was, at the time when I turned my back on the West, a very, very sick man.'

'Poor old Heck,' said the Jorgmanns.

'Another Bourbon?' said Mrs Jungfleisch.

'Thank you. On the rocks.'

Sir Harald asked, 'And how does he set about curing a Pull to the East?'

'In my case, of course, I have already undergone the most efficacious cure, which is a long sojourn there. But we must prevent any recurrence of the disease. Well, the doc's treatment is this. I lie on his couch and I shut my eyes and I force myself to see New York Harbour, the Empire State building, Wall Street, Fifth Avenue and Bonwit Teller. Then very, very slowly I swivel my mental gaze until it alights on the Statue of Liberty. All this time Dr Jore and I, very, very softly, in unison, recite the Gettysburg Address. "Four score and seven years ago our fathers –"'

'Yes, yes,' said Sir Harald, almost rudely, I thought, breaking in on Mr Dexter's fervent interpretation. 'Very fine, but we all know it. It's in the *Oxford Book of Quotations*.'

Mr Dexter looked hurt; there was a little silence. Philip said, 'Did you see anything of Guy and Donald?'

'When Guy Burgess and Donald Maclean first arrived we all shared a dacha. I cannot say it was a very happy association. They did not behave as courteously to me as they ought to have. The looked-for Anglo-Saxon solidarity was not in evidence. They hardly listened to the analysis of the situation, as noted and recounted by me, in Socialist Soviet Russia; they laughed where no laughter was called for; they even seemed to shun my company. Now I am not very conversant with the circumstances of their departure from the Western camp, but I am inclined to think it was motivated by pure treachery. I am not overfond of traitors.'

'And how did you get away?'

'In the end very easily. After nine or eight years in the U.S.S.R., the Presidium having acquired a perfect confidence in my integrity, I was able to induce them to send me on a fact-finding mission. On arrival here, as I explained to them, the accompaniment of wife and son lending a permanent appearance to my reintegration in the Western Camp, I would easily persuade my compatriots that I had abandoned all tendency to communism. When their trust in me was completely re-established, I would be in a position to send back a great deal of information, of the kind I knew they wanted, to the Kremlin.'

'*Nom de nom!*' said Valhubert.

Bouche-Bontemps shook with laughter: '*C'est excellent!*'

Alfred and Philip exchanged looks.

The Jorgmanns exclaimed, 'That was smart of you, Heck!' Mrs Jungfleisch said, 'And now don't you want to go and dine?'

We all stood up and, like so many geese, stretched our necks. That hour on the pouf had been absolute agony.

The day after Sir Harald's lecture, Alfred had to communicate a very stiff note indeed to the Quai d'Orsay on the subject of the Îles Minquiers. The French were invited immediately to abandon their claim to these islands which, said the Note, was quite untenable, against their own interests, and was undermining the Western Alliance. Simultaneously an anti-French campaign of unprecedented violence was launched in London. Bludgeon and pin were brought into play. Dr Niam duly paid his official visit which was reported in a manner calculated to infuriate the French. Bouche-Bontemps was rudely taken to task in Parliament and the newspapers for the criminal obstinacy with which he was refusing to make a united Europe. At U.N.O. the English voted against the French on an important issue. After these bludgeonings came the pinpricks. The newspapers said that Spanish champagne was better than the real sort. Tourists were advised to go to Germany or Greece and to miss out expensive France. Women were urged to buy their clothes in Dublin or Rome. Several leading critics discovered that Françoise Sagan had less talent than one had thought.

When some softening up on these lines had been delivered the campaign settled down to its real objective, the Îles Minquiers. Facts and figures were trotted out, heads were shaken over them and judgement severely passed. It transpired that after a thousand years of French administration, the islands had no roads, no post-office, no public services. They sent no representative to Paris; there was no insurance against old age; the children were not given vitamins or immunized against diphtheria; there was no cultural life. The fact that there were no inhabitants either was, of course, never stated. The kind-hearted English public was distressed by all these disclosures. As a gesture of solidarity with the islands, an expedition was organized to go and build a health centre on the Île Maîtresse (Grandad cashed in on this). The Ambulating Raiments were immediately dispatched there. These baleful bales are full of ghastly old clothes collected at the time of the Dutch floods. Since then they have been round the world over and over again, bringing comfort to the tornadoed, the scorched, the shaken, the stateless, the volcanoed, the interned, the farnished, the parched, the tidal-waved; any communities suffering from extreme bad luck or bad management are eligible for the Raiments, which are so excellently organized that they arrive on the scene almost before the disaster has occurred. There is a tacit understanding that they are never to be undone, indeed nobody, however great their want, would dare to risk the vermin and disease which must fly out from them as from Pandora's Box. The recipients take their presence as a sort of lucky sign or sympathetic visiting card. (It is only fair to say that in cases of great distress the Raiments are often followed up by a gift of money.) There was just time to have the bundles photographed, at low tide, on the rocks of the Île Maîtresse before they had to be dispatched to Oakland, California, where a gigantic fire had wiped out acres of skyscrapers.

The French sharply resented all these insults. Their press and wireless, which are at least as clever as ours when it comes to throwing vitriol, now revealed terrifying depths of hatred for their old crony over the way. M. Bouche-Bontemps' government, given up for lost, came unscathed through a debate on vegetables out of season which in normal times would have annihilated it. None of the opposition parties wanted to take over in the middle of such a crisis. When the full perfidy of Albion had been exposed for a few days, French opinion was stirred, flickered, then blazed into fury. Individual citizens began to give expression to the public feeling. The shop called Old England was rechristened New England. The windows of W. H. Smith were smashed. English decorations and medals, signed photographs of King Edward VII and Northey's kittens were deposited at the Embassy accompanied by disagreeable messages. Anglo-French sporting events were called off. Import licences for Christmas puddings were withheld. Grace was beside herself, of course. She announced that she was going to empty the English blood from her veins and have them refilled from the blood bank of the VIIth arrondissement.

Alfred sent an alarmed report to the Foreign Office but was told that these waves of ill feeling come and go and are not to be taken seriously. Philip, however, said that he had never seen the two old ladies so cross with each other.

21

At no season does Paris look more beautiful than early in December. There is a curious light, particular to the Île de France and faithfully interpreted by the painter Michel, which brings out all shades, from primrose to navy blue, implicit in the beige and grey of the landscape and buildings. The river becomes a steely flood which matches the huge clouds rolling overhead. As this is not, like harvest time or the first warm days of spring, one of those seasons that induce an almost animal craving for field and forest, you can sit by the fire, look out of the window and peacefully enjoy the prospect. I was doing exactly this in the Salon Vert one afternoon, reflecting with satisfaction that for the rest of that week we had no social engagements (they had fallen off notably of late). I had been writing to Aunt Sadie, to give her news of us all, specially of her granddaughter Northey, my pen was poised while I searched for some little titbit to end up with.

I became conscious of a clamour outside, an unidentified noise which had perhaps been going on for some time, heard by my ears but not realized by my brain. I went over to the window, looked down at the garden and was very much startled by what I saw there. A large crowd was stamping about on the lawn, pushed forward by an ever-increasing multitude milling in from the Avenue Gabriel; between it and the house, like idle maids flicking dusters, a few policemen were half-heartedly manipulating their capes. For the moment they were holding the crowd in check; one felt that a really determined push would easily submerge them. When the fishwives surged into Versailles, the Queen's first instinct was to find her husband; so, now, was mine. Like Louis XVI on the same occasion, Alfred was frantically looking for me. We wasted several minutes missing each other in the huge house; I ran through to the Chancery – he had left it; he found the Salon Vert empty; finally we met in Northey's office off the anteroom at the top of the stairs.

'Go to the nursery, darling,' I was telling her, 'and fetch 'Chang. There's a riot or something in the garden. We'd better all stay together.'

Alfred said, 'The French have had enough and I don't altogether blame them. I wrote in my last dispatch that it would end like this; now it has. Not a bad thing perhaps, it will shake both the governments into seeing sense. Meanwhile I hope these hooligans will bear in mind that the person of an Ambassador is sacred and the territory of an Embassy inviolable.'

'They haven't remembered about the territory. They are completely ruining all our nice new shrubs – just come and see.'

We went back to the Salon Vert and looked out at the rioters.

'I shall lodge a complaint. The police force is inadequate, in my view. What are they shouting? It sounds like a slogan.'

'Listen – no, I can't make it out.' They seemed to be shouting two words and stamping in unison.

Philip ran in, breathless, having come from his own flat. 'The Faubourg is full of demonstrators,' he said. 'Good Lord – the garden too! We are completely surrounded in other words. They are shouting "*Minquiers Français*", do you hear?'

'That's it, of course,' said Alfred. '*Minquiers Français, Minquiers Français*. I only hope this will show the Foreign Office there are limits of ineptitude beyond which they should not go. Another time perhaps they will listen to the man on the spot.'

I said, 'They are nearly up to the veranda now – ought you not to let Bouche-Bontemps know?'

'All in good time,' said Alfred, 'no need to panic. We are his responsibility.'

Northey appeared, 'Chang in her arms, grumbling about her badger.

'Pity we can't all be safely down there with him,' I said.

'I've just had a word with B.B.,' said Northey, 'he is the absolute, utter limit. Shrieking with laughter if you please. He says we may have to stand a long siege and he hopes we've got plenty of Spanish champagne. He can't get the police to do much, he says, it's only a crowd of children.'

'Yes, they do look young – I was thinking that. Why should these boys and girls mind about the Îles Minquiers?'

'Agitators. You can work up a crowd on any subject.'

'B.B. is delighted. He says the teenagers here are supposed to think of nothing but jazz – look at them now! Riddled with patriotism.'

'So he's not going to rescue us?'

'Not he!'

'Then who will? What about NATO?'

'We only know one thing for certain about NATO – it can't get a force into the field in less than six weeks.'

'Anyhow,' said Philip, 'this is the Supreme Commander's time for Dr Jore – nobody's allowed to interrupt them, they'll be in full flood of Gettysburg at this very minute – can't you hear it? 'Foor-scoor and savan eers ago oor faethers brourt fourth –'

'Don't tell me the Supreme Commander has a Pull to the East?'

'Of course. All Dr Jore's patients have.'

Alfred said, 'You must try and check this latent anti-Americanism, Philip – I've already spoken to you about it.'

'Yes, Sir.'

'Now I'm going to the Chancery to do some telephoning. You take Northey and Fanny to your flat, will you? The rioters can come through the veranda any minute, those feeble policemen aren't going to stop them.'

'*Minquiers Français – Minquiers Français –*' rose ever more insistent from the garden.

'I do wish they would leave off stamping, they are ruining the lawn.'

'The French government will be obliged to make good any damage.'

'Come on,' said Philip. 'Alfred's quite right, you'll be better over there. Besides, I want to see what's happening in the Faubourg.'

We crossed the courtyard, went into Philip's flat and looked out of his dining-room window at the street which was jammed as far as the eye could see with young people stamping and shouting *'Minquiers Français'*. I was glad to notice quite a large force of policemen looking, I thought, very much amused, but keeping the crowd away from our gate and exhibiting more authority than those in the garden.

'Oh do look!' said Northey, 'There's good little Amy – the brave soul.'

'I don't see him?'

'Yes, in the ancient bibelot shop, pretending to be a Dresden figure.' She leant out of the window and waved at Mockbar who looked sheepish and seemed not to see her. Then she shouted *'Aimée!'* whereupon he began scribbling in his notebook.

'He's ashamed of you,' said Phillip. 'Anyway I'm glad to see he's on the job all right. For once we need all the publicity we can get; it's the only way to stop this silly bickering – give Bouche-Bontemps and our Foreign Minister a bit of a jolt. They don't want actual war, one supposes.'

'Can't see that it's B.B.'s fault.'

'He'd much better let the thing go to The Hague and be settled once for all.'

Suddenly the shouting and stamping and clapping subsided and a rather sinister silence fell on the crowd. Philip said, anxiously, 'Don't like this much, I hope they're not waiting for a signal.'

Almost as he spoke, the crowd came violently, terrifyingly to life. It surged in the narrow street as if it must burst apart the houses; the slogan took on a blood-curdling note. 'Chang began to scream at the top of his voice; the din was deafening. The police now joined hands and forced the rioters away from the entrance to our courtyard; to my horror I saw that the huge wooden gates were slowly opening.

'Look,' said Northey, 'the gates – a traitor – !'

'Good Lord,' said Philip and made as though to go downstairs.

'Don't leave us –' I was frightened for the baby who might so easily be hurt if the mob poured in and overwhelmed us. I looked out again. The police seemed to be in control. In the middle of the screaming crowd a London taxi, escorted by policemen, was crawling up the street. It was driven by Payne; Uncle Matthew, deeply interested, craned from the window; on its roof, dressed from head to foot in shiny black plastic material, were our boys, Fabrice and Charlie, with another boy, a stranger to me, dressed in shiny white. This child was waving a guitar at the crowd as though he thought the screams and shrieks were meant for him. The more the people cried *Minquiers Français* the more he grinned and waved in acknowledgement. With a superhuman effort, the police cleared a passage for the taxi, got it into the courtyard and shut the gates behind it. We all ran downstairs.

Uncle Matthew was being helped out of the cab by Charlie and Fabrice. The other boy was fidgeting about, snapping his fingers. He looked cross and impatient.

'Excitable lot, these foreigners,' said my uncle, 'how are you, Fanny? Here are your spawn, safe and sound thanks to Payne. We found them in the aeroplane or at least they found me, I didn't know them from Adam of course. They recognized me and hopped into the cab. Do you know, we flew it over – now your stepfather thought of that, very competent fellow.'

'This is Yanky Fonzy, Mum,' said Fabrice, indicating the third lad. He was an unprepossessing hobbledehoy, with pasty face, sloppy look about the mouth and hair done like Queen Alexandra's after the typhoid. 'Didn't the kids give him a wonderful reception – you heard them screaming, "Yanky Fonzy, Yanky Fonzy"? It's never been like this in London.'

'D'you mean that terrifying riot was all about him?' I said.

'It only was a riot of enthusiasm,' said the youth. 'The kids are never nasty or out for manslaughter. They buy my discs and support me. Why are they shut away from here? Where can I go and wave to them? Why are the arrangements breaking down? Where's my French agent?' He fired these questions at each of us in turn, snapping his fingers. He seemed in a thoroughly bad humour.

This curious new light having been thrown on the situation, Philip burst into a loud laugh and went into the house, no doubt, I supposed, to find Alfred.

'He's not much to look at,' said Uncle Matthew, indicating Mr Fonzy, 'and his clothes would frighten the birds, but I'm bound to tell you he whacks merry hell out of that guitar. We had tunes the whole way here.'

I took Charles by the arm and led him out of earshot of the others. 'Just tell me what this means? Your packing job – have you left it?'

'Definitely. Chucked it.'

'Tell me truthfully, Charlie, you haven't been nicking shavers?'

'Oh no, Mum, hardly at all. But even you wouldn't want us to go on packing for the rest of our lives? It turned out to be rather ghoulish and there's no future in it whatever. No, we've moved on. We're in the Showbiz now where there are fortunes to be picked up. Actually we are Yanky's publicity agents. Grandad arranged it for us – he's a smashing old forebear! It was he who thought of arriving like that with the weirdie in the taxi – oh boy, what a gimmick! Yank's Continental debew has started with a real explosion, hasn't it? – there must be thousands of kids round this dump.'

Fabrice came over to us. 'I say, Mum, the kiddos are yearning for Yank, you know. They may easily turn ghoulish if you keep him shut up in this yard for ever.'

'Definitely,' said Charles.

'But how did they know he was coming?'

'That's all done by Sigi, our Paris agent. First-class organization!' The hobbledehoy was now behaving like a prima donna.

'Where can I go and be with my fans? What's happening here? They'll turn dangerous if they don't see me soon. I say, you kids, something has gone wrong. Please send me my Paris agent at once.'

'Here I am.' Sigi appeared out of the blue.

'Well done, Sigi,' said Fabrice, 'jolly spiffing show.'

'So far,' said Yanky, 'but we must keep up the tempo. Where are the kids now? I want to be with them.'

'They've all gone round to the other side of the house,' said Sigi. 'There's a huge garden and a balcony where you can do your act. I've just been rigging up the mike. Come on, no time to waste. Excuse us,' he said to me, ever polite, kissing my hand, 'but if they don't see him soon they will rush the place.' He ran into the house, followed by the other boys.

I turned to Uncle Matthew, feeling I had not made enough fuss of him in all the commotion. 'How d'you do, Payne?'

'Payne's just had a word with your porter,' said Uncle Matthew, 'it seems the street is clear now so I think we'll be on our way. I never meant to bother you at all – Paris isn't on our itinerary – we came here to oblige those boys.'

'Now you are here, do stay. Where are you off to, anyhow?'

'Ypres,' said my uncle. 'Payne and I thought we'd like to see old Wipers again. A fellow in the House told me there's a sector they've preserved exactly as it was. We had the time of our lives in those trenches when we were young, didn't we, Payne?'

'To tell the truth, m'lord, I'd just as soon see them in present circumstances.'

'Nonsense! It will all seem very dull, though better than nothing no doubt.'

'But there's no hurry, is there? Don't go yet. Now you are here, stay for a few days.'

'Oh my dear child, but where?'

'Here, with us, of course.'

'You haven't got room?'

'Darling Uncle Matthew – in that enormous house? Jérôme, our chauffeur, will show Payne where to put the cab and fill it up and everything.'

'Well, that's very civil of you, Fanny. I do feel rather tired. Will there be a cocktail party?'

'Yes, indeed, nearly every evening. I know we've got some people coming presently.'

Uncle Matthew gave me a superior look, saying, 'I thought you'd find out about them sooner or later. Well, that's splendid. If I could see my room I'll go and sit down for a few minutes, then I'll be ready for anything.'

'Take your grandfather up in the lift,' I said to Northey. 'I think we'll give him the Violet Room. Then will you send Jérôme out to look after Payne, please? I must go and see what those boys are up to.'

On the stairs I was overtaken by Philip. 'That unspeakable Sigi,' he said.

'Where's Alfred?'

'He's gone to the Quai to complain – he went out by the Chancery as soon as the street began to clear. Now listen, Fanny –'

'Yes, but hurry. I must go and stop it all –'

'This is very important though. Don't tell Alfred. I don't believe those journalists in the Faubourg have understood – I hope that at this very moment they are whizzing back stories of a riot about the Minquiers. Alfred has already informed the F.O. If we can keep up the fiction, this so-called riot will have a splendid effect. Both sides will feel they have gone too far and there'll be a beautiful reconciliation.'

'That would be perfect but I'm afraid it's too good to be likely. They are all in the garden still, according to Sigi.'

'Yes, they are, I've just been through to have a look. The boy is crooning and the fans are swooning and so on. But the only people there who look like journalists all belong to jazz papers – they won't get anything into the general news and they don't even know that they are in the Embassy garden. Now I'm off to the Crillon to see the press boys there. So sealed lips, eh? – and shoo Yanky off, that's your job.'

'Yes, indeed. But Philip – you'll have to square Mees or good little Amy will know all. She's taken 'Chang to the nursery I think.'

'Right, I'll do that first.'

I ran on up to the yellow drawing-room where I found the boys making a perfect exhibition of themselves. The French windows were wide open; on the little balcony Yank Fonzy was bellowing into a microphone; behind him on the parquet my boys and Sigi were stamping and clapping while the huge crowd of children in the garden had lost all control. The scene was vividly evoked afterwards in *Le Discophile* and I cannot do better than to quote: '*L'atmosphère fut indescriptible. Ce jazz-man chanta avec une passion qui n'appartient qu'aux grands prédicateurs. On dansait, on entrait en transes, on se roulait au sol tout comme les convulsionaires de Saint Médard. Le gazon était lacéré, les arbustes déchiquetés – affligeant spectacle.*'

I pounced forward and very crossly dragged Master Yanky back into the room, then I disconnected the microphone and slammed the windows on the afflicting spectacle. He was so much surprised at this unaccustomed behaviour that he put up no resistance; in any case his body felt as if it were made of dough. Sigi opened the windows again, went on to the balcony and shouted, '*Tous au Vel d'Hiv*': a cry which was taken up by the crowd and had the effect of clearing the garden. Chanting '*Yanky Fonzy – Yanky Fonzy*' the fans made off in the direction of the river.

'I'm sorry, Mme l'Ambassadrice,' ever polite, 'but it was the best way to get rid of them.'

'And what next?' I said. I was almost too angry with Sigismond to be able to speak to him, but it must be said that he was the only one of the boys in control of himself. The others were still rolling and stamping about like poor mad things, well and truly sent.

'Please don't worry at all, we are going now. I'll take Yanky, Charlie and Fabrice to the Club to meet the Duke. After that we're joining up with the kids at the Vélodrome d'Hiver, where there is the great Yanky Fonzy Pop Session you have no doubt seen advertised on all the kiosks.'

'The Club? The Duke?' I had a horrid vision of Yanky in white leather and my boys in black leather bursting in on the Duc de Romanville at the Jockey Club.

'Le Pop Club de France. We've got a rendezvous with Duke Ellington there.'

'Now listen to me, Sigi, I'm not going to have that boy to stay.'

'No, no.' Sigi laughed inwardly, reminding me of his father. 'He has got the honeymoon suite at the George V. I went there to see that everything was all right, which is why I was a bit late. You can't imagine what the flowers and chocolates are like. I managed to nick some and gave them to the concierge for you.'

'Too good of you. And now be off, I beg, and don't use this house any more for your disreputable activities.'

'Count on me, Mme l'Ambassadrice,' he said, with his annoying politeness.

22

As six o'clock struck, a remarkable demonstration of English punctuality occurred in the Salon Vert. Uncle Matthew stood at the ready by the fireplace, while a procession, of a sort very familiar to me by now, came across the Salon Jaune. Few days ever passed without this sort of influx. First there was Brown, the butler. Two fine, upstanding men, older than they looked, as could be seen by grey flecks in the hair, but without a line on their faces or, obviously, a care in the world, marched close on his heels. Conservatives I knew they were, from one or other of the Houses of Parliament. Two elderly wives panted and limped after them in an effort to keep up, one arm weighed down by those heavy bags which Conservative women affect and in which they conserve an extraordinary accumulation of rubbish and an extraordinarily small amount of cash. Two or three boys, of a demeanour already described, which proclaimed that they had but recently left Eton, trailed along behind them, then two or three pretty, cheerful, elegant schoolgirls who seemed to view their relations rather objectively. They were probably about to be confided to 'families' and I would be asked to keep an eye on them. They looked, and no doubt were, ready for anything and I only hoped that I should not be held responsible when anything overtook them.

Simultaneously Alfred, whom I had not seen since the riot, came through the door which led to his own room and library. I had just time to say, 'Alfred, here's Uncle Matthew who has come for a few days. Imagine, he has brought our two little boys – they all arrived in the middle of the excitement!' when the Conservative wives, breaking into a rapid hobble, managed to catch up with Brown and precede their husbands through the double doors.

'We've brought the whole family!' Loud English voices, familiar since all time. 'Thought you wouldn't mind! Let me see now, I don't think you know my sister-in-law, do you?'

I didn't think I knew any of them, though on the telephone, when they had asked to come, there had been something about having met at Montdore House in the old days; I tried to look welcoming but I was dying for a word with Alfred. 'What would you like to drink?'

'My dear! Liquid fire if you've got it! Vodka – just the very thing! We are utterly, completely, and absolutely whacked! Well, the shops all the morning, only to have a look of course – the prices! Then luncheon, that set us back considerably. Then we went to see Myrtle's Madarm – now here's the name (you know, I couldn't remember it yesterday on the telephone).' Delving among the alluvial deposits in the bag and bringing out a crumpled piece of paper. 'Comtesse de Langalluire – that's a tongue-twister if ever there was one! You've never heard of her? I say, I only hope there's nothing fishy. The flat (Boulevard Haussmann) is none too clean and when we arrived Madarm had gone to the police; one of the girls had escaped.'

'No, Mum, she hadn't escaped at all in the end. You know quite well, she'd only gone out to lunch and forgotten to say.'

'So we saw the Monsewer – a sinister little hunchback.'

'The concierge was sweet.' Myrtle was evidently determined to be confided to Madarm whatever happened.

'There was a son who looked quite idiotic and rather frightening.'

'Yes, but I shan't see anything of him as I'll be out all day at the Sorbonne.'

'However, when Madarm herself arrived we thought she seemed rather nice.'

'She had a crew cut,' said one of the boys.

'Her face was sensible, I thought.'

While all this was going on, the Conservative husbands were expressing amazement at finding Uncle Matthew, whom they knew quite well but who clearly did not know them from Adam.

'This is Lord Alconleigh, Peggy.'

'How d'you do? I'm a great friend of Jennifer's.'

'For pity's sake! What on earth do you see in her?'

'It seems you had a spot of trouble here this afternoon?' the other M.P. was saying to Alfred.

'No harm was done; personally I think it will have a good result. Both sides will have to be more conciliatory – both have been to blame. This may clear the air.'

'Can't see the point of making bad blood over those islands, myself. Massigli tells me they are submerged most of the time.'

'There has never been a more pointless quarrel,' said Alfred, firmly. 'Now I hope the question will be sent up to The Hague and that we shall hear no more about it.'

When everybody was happily chattering, Alfred murmured to me, 'Did you say Charlie and Fabrice are here?'

'Uncle Matthew brought them.'

'How splendid of the old boy. Where are they now?'

'Gone to a concert, with Sigi.'

'Good. That's very good news. Now we must take serious steps – get them into a lycée if we can –'

Brown reappeared, announcing 'Madame la Duchesse de Sauveterre and Monsieur le Marquis de Valhubert.'

'We've just heard about your riot,' said Charles-Édouard, 'we called to see if you were alive. When the concierge said you were at home we came up. Tante Odile is in Paris for a few days.'

'How kind you are.' I was frantic inside because of not knowing what names to put to the loud Conservative voices. To my relief, Alfred did the introducing. When he got to Uncle Matthew, I said, 'My uncle saw more of the riot than any of us because he arrived when it was at its worst and drove through the thick of it, escorted by policemen –'

'I call that very brave,' said an M.P.

'My dear fellow, they were a perfectly harmless lot – just a pack of children. I didn't think much of it – if that's the best they can put on –'

'Never underestimate a French crowd,' said the Duchess. 'I speak with knowledge. Three of my grandmothers perished in the Terror.'

'Three!' said Uncle Matthew, much interested. 'Did you have three grandfathers as well? What happened to them?'

'We say grandmothers when we mean ancestresses,' Charles-Édouard explained.

The Duchess said, 'Oh, various things. One of them was murdered in the Jacquerie, and the best housemaid I ever had was shot dead in the Stavisky riots. So don't talk to me of a French crowd being harmless.'

Uncle Matthew seemed to be struggling to remember something and came out with, 'Joan of Arc – didn't she have a sticky end? I suppose she was a relation of yours?'

'Certainly, if she was a d'Orléans, as most people think nowadays.'

'Really?' said Charles-Édouard, with his inward laugh. 'Why do they?'

'*Voyons, mon cher! La Pucelle d'Orléans!* Did she not sit at the King's table? That simple fact alone is all the proof I need. For a woman who was not born to sit at the table of a King of France would be a greater miracle than any voices, let me tell you.'

'My aunt takes no account of historical characters unless they happen to be relations of hers. Luckily they nearly all are. Charles X was a great-grandfather so that arranges the legitimate royal lines of every country except Russia, while her Murat grandmother brings in Napoleon and the Marshals.'

Mme de Sauveterre asked Alfred to show her his library which had been redecorated during the time of Sir Louis Leone. She said she had seen coloured photographs of it in a magazine which Jacques Oudineau had brought down to Boisdormant. 'He knows I like picture papers so he brings me all the ones he has finished with when he comes to see his father. You wouldn't believe how extravagant he is – *abonné* to everything under the sun and you know the price they are nowadays. People are getting much too rich, it can't be a good thing.'

'I want to see Jacques Oudineau,' said Charles-Édouard. 'I hear he has got a Moreau l' âiné he wouldn't mind selling –'

Uncle Matthew began telling the Conservatives about Yanky. 'Teenage Beats,' I heard him say. 'You must remember the name, Yanky Fonzy, and ask for his records because he gets money for every one they sell. Of course, I'm not saying he's Galli-Curci –'

I took Valhubert by the arm. 'I must have a word with you.' In a loud voice I added, 'Come in here, the National Gallery has sent us a large, dull picture and I want you to advise me where to hang it.' We went into the yellow drawing-room. 'Have you seen Grace this evening?'

'Not yet. When we got back from the country my concierge said there had been this riot so I drove straight on here to see what it was all about.'

I told him everything. He shook with laughter, especially when I got to the Club and the Duke. 'But my dear Fanny, what now? What does Alfred say?'

'You do realize we must never tell him about the riot not being real. He would look the most awful fool if it got out – I haven't told Grace by the way –'

'No, better not. Pity to spoil her fun – an anti-English riot is just her affair – she must be thrilled!'

'She is naughty! Philip says if we can keep up the fiction there's some hope of making them all see sense. As for the boys, Alfred doesn't know the full horror. When these people have gone I shall have to explain about Yanky and the Showbiz. Oh, Charles-Édouard, *children!*'

'Don't worry. They'll soon be off our hands, in prison.'

'Here's Philip, oh good. So what's up?'

'It's wonderful. I've been with the press boys ever since I saw you. The best hoax of all time. Simply nobody has twigged. The stories will be amazing, you'll see.'

The newspapers played up exactly as Philip had hoped they would. The reputable ones stated, quite soberly, correctly as far as it went, that several hundred students had gathered outside the

British Embassy shouting slogans and that after about half an hour they had dispersed of their own accord. These reports were accompanied by editorial comment to the effect that if there was a serious misunderstanding between France and England it was time that it should be cleared up. Perhaps the English had not used the most tactful of methods in pressing their rightful claim to the Minquiers Islands. No doubt it had been necessary to entertain Dr Niam (now in Pekin) but the timing of his visit had been unfortunate. As for the European Army, while we in England realized its desirability and inevitability, we had not shown much comprehension of French difficulties in this respect. All in all, we should do well to keep in with our friends since our enemies were legion. The French papers were even more conciliatory, digging into the history of the Entente and saying that so solid an edifice was not to be shaken by a few students exhibiting bad manners.

The Grumpy group reported the affair in their own inimitable style:

'POST' MAN IN PARIS RIOTS
I WALK WITH THE SCREAMING TEN THOUSAND

According to Mockbar, a fearful mob, baying for British blood, had milled in the Faubourg utterly uncontrolled by the police who looked as if they would join in for tuppence. It reminded him of the worst days of the Commune. No mention of sheltering among the ancient bibelots; heroic Mockbar had swayed to and fro in the thick of young devils who, had they guessed he was a Briton, would have scuppered him then and there. While, inside the Embassy, women wailed and babies wept ('That's you and 'Chang, Northey,' I said), the Ambassador had escaped by a back door and taken shelter at the Quai d'Orsay. His First Secretary was drinking at the bar of a nearby hotel.

Lord Grumpy's editorial said: British lives are threatened, British property is menaced. Where? Behind the Iron Curtain? In barbarous lands across the seas? Not at all. These things occurred in Paris. How did our Ambassador the Pastoral Theologian respond to the outrage? Was he at his post? We think there should be a full inquiry into the events of this black day in the history of British diplomacy. If Sir Alfred Wincham has failed to do his duty, he should go.

Lord Grumpy's remarks, as usual, gave much pleasure. They were read with delight and absolutely unheeded by several million Englishmen. Later in the week, Alfred went home to report on the, now vastly improved, situation and to see, with the Foreign Office experts, what could be done to re-establish the Entente. This was made easier by the fact that Junior across the Atlantic was annoying Mother and Auntie with behaviour learnt, it must be said, at their knees. Under a cunning pretext of anti-colonialism, the Americans were scooping up trade in a part of the world where hitherto French and English interests had been paramount. The quarrel over the Eels began to look silly; as soon as the newspapers had lost interest in them and gone on to more important subjects, the dispute was quietly submitted to The Hague Court where the islands were judged to belong to England. In harmony with the spirit of the age, we then granted them full independence.

During the Anglo-French honeymoon which now began, Basil disembarked his atom marchers at Calais. They were all in fancy dress, the men in kilts, the women in trousers; the weather was clear and sparkling and not too cold; the whole expedition was permeated from the start with a holiday atmosphere. Since atom objectors do not exist in France, literally the only public matter on which all Frenchmen are united being the desirability of a Bomb of one's own, the French immediately assumed that the march was a congratulatory gesture to unite Aldermaston with Saclay. The word *jumelage* was freely used by the newspapers; the two establishments were henceforward twin sisters, friends for ever. When the Britons got off their boat they were met with flowers, flags, speeches and wine; from the moment they landed they hardly drew a sober breath. None of them knew any French so, cleverly prompted by Basil, they concluded that the reception meant that the whole population felt as they did; in a joyful Kermesse they danced rather than marched across Normandy. They were not allowed to pay for a meal, a drink or a bed; Basil and his Grandad, who had extorted huge sums for the all-in trip, garnered a rich profit. At Saclay the Atom Minister himself, sent by Northey, was there to greet them. There were more flowers, more flags, stronger wine and longer speeches. The Britons were cordially invited to go to the Sahara and witness the first French atomic explosion whenever it should take place. In a happy haze of drunken mis-apprehension, they were then driven in official motors, with a circus turn of motor-bicyclists escorting them, to Orly and sent home free by Air France.

'Never, since the war, have Anglo-French relations been so cloudless,' said *The Times*. The *Daily Telegraph* said, 'Sir Alfred Wincham's wise and subtle manoeuvring in a difficult situation has been triumphantly successful.' Lord Grumpy said the cunning French had twisted the lion's tail once more and that their valet, Wincham, ought to be sent, forthwith, to Rangoon. Plans and projects for The Visit were now put into operation.

23

'I wouldn't mind the boys calling me Dad,' said Alfred (who did mind, however, and had made great efforts, successful with David and Baz, to be called Father), 'if only they wouldn't pronounce it Dud.'

It was the morning after the riot; Grace and Charles-Édouard had come round for another conference on what could be done with the children. Our two had had breakfast with Alfred; there had been a long, perfectly fruitless argument on lines which were becoming all too familiar. In a sincere effort to use language that Alfred could understand they explained that members of the Show-biz were the aristocracy of the modern world; that Yanky was its King and that as Yanky's gentlemen-in-waiting they had the most covetable position of any living teenagers. Alfred asked what their plans were for the immediate future. 'Driftin' with Yank to Russia,' was the reply. (Driftin', it seems, is Showbiz for touring.) They were to drift through France, Switzerland, and Czechoslovakia, possibly taking in the Balkans; their final objective was Moscow. 'So lucky we all opted to learn Russian at school.'

'And wherever we appear,' Fabrice said, 'the kids will go scream-ing, raving mad because in those countries everybody has Yanky's discs which they buy on the black market. You should see the fan-mail he gets from iron teenagers.'

Alfred then spoke, in the tongue of our ancestors. He summoned up all his wisdom, all his eloquence, he drew tears from his own eyes as he argued his case for civilization. They listened politely for an hour. When they were quite sure he had finished and that they were in no way interrupting him they replied that his fate had been an example to them. They couldn't help noticing that he had led a sorrowful existence year after year, growing old without having known any pleasure, fun, or enjoyment and that as a result he had landed up in this deplorable, antiquated giggle-academy, the English Embassy at Paris.

'When I left the room,' he said, after telling us all this, 'I heard Charlie say to Fabrice "Poor Dud, he's had it!" I think that pretty well sums up their attitude. We are duds, Valhubert, and we've had it. Yes, even you.'

'I don't know why you should say even me. Specially me, I should have thought.'

'You are a man of action and as such they might have had a certain respect for you. Of course they know quite well that you had a good war, but I'm afraid that means nothing to them because what were you fighting for? They don't care a fig for liberty, equal-ity, fraternity, or any of our values – still less for their King and Country. The be-all and end-all of their existence is to have a good time. They think they could have rocked and rolled quite well under Hitler and no doubt so they could.' Alfred buried his face in his hands and said despairingly, 'The black men affirm that we are in full decadence. Nothing could be truer, if these boys are typical of their generation and if they really mean all the things they told me just now. The barbarians had better take over without more ado. We made the last stand against them. At least we have that to be proud of. But you have fought in vain, my life's work has come to nothing – this job the most pointless part of it, very likely.'

'My dear Ambassador,' said Valhubert, 'you take it all too trag-ically. Young persons in prosperous circumstances live for pleasure. They always have and no doubt they always will. When I think what Fabrice and I were like, right up to the war! Between women and hunting, we never had a serious thought. Of course when we were Sigi's age, our noses were pressed in the direction of a grind-stone by force of economic sanctions. If we could have earned £9 a week packing shavers do you really think we would have stayed at the lycée another hour? And I bet we'd have found some water-tight method of nicking, by the way.'

'I'm sorry, Valhubert, but I cannot agree with you. Many

adolescents, even rich ones, have a love of learning for its own sake. I know, because as a don I have had hundreds of civilized rich young men through my hands.'

'But with these boys you must face the fact that they are not, and never will be, intellectuals. Hard for you, I know – still two out of four in your family took firsts, quite an honourable percentage. The other two never will, in a hundred years. In the end they will probably be the most conformist all the same.'

'But nowadays no respectable career is open to people without degrees.'

'To speak practically. Sigi will be very rich – I have never had to work so I can't exactly blame him if he doesn't, can I? Little Fabrice only has to play his cards well enough to refrain from throwing them in Tante Odile's face to be in the same circumstances.'

'But Charlie must earn his living.'

'Don't you see, darling,' I intervened, 'the point is that he can. He was making this huge amount in London, and now, at sixteen, he is one of the kings of Showbiz!' I trust that a note of pride could not be detected as I said these words.

'You torture me. Have we brought a human soul to this stage of development only to see him promoting pop sessions?'

'But, dearest, how can we prevent it? Charles-Édouard is quite right. We can't do more for the boys now (any of them) than look on at their vagaries with tolerance and provide a background when they need one.' Twinge of conscience here. Had I been nice enough to David?

Valhubert said, 'Exactly. They are grown up. Each man in the last resort is responsible for himself. Let them be – let them go. Sigi tells me they are drifting off tomorrow with Yanky Fonzy, taking 20 per cent of his earnings, plus their expenses and anything else they can nick. All right. Count it as the Grand Tour; they'll see the world; it's better than packing. When they come back, if they are eighteen by then, they can go to the wars like everybody else. Only do send Fabrice this afternoon to see Tante Odile.'

'How French you are, Charles-Édouard,' said Grace, laughing.

'Hot news!' This was Northey, coming in with my breakfast. 'The Bomb from Brum has buggered!'

'Already? And the boys never came to say good-bye?'

'The point is, he has left them behind. There was the most terrific bust-up yesterday at Le Pop Club and he has gone.'

'Can it be true? What has happened?'

'It was all about the publicity. You see when Yank saw those kids in Main Street – biggest outdoor reception even he has dreamed of – he thought he'd never had it so good. He expected to hit the headlines on the front pages. Grandfather in the taxi, he thought, gave that little extra something that journalists love, then the crowds, the police, Alfred going to the Quai (I must say it wrung my withers not telling the dear little soul about it).'

'If you had, Northey –'

'Yes, well, I didn't, did I? So Yank thought the boys were geniuses and honestly, Fanny, in a way they were. You've got to hand it to Sigi – he mobilized that enormous crowd – then the Vel d'Hiv was a whizz, every teenager in Paris must have been there and the receipts broke all records. At the Club they were congratulating Yank on his wonderful agents and he was so pleased he kept signing travellers' cheques, giving them to the boys. Of course he could hardly wait to see the papers. Came the Dawn – *quelle horrible* surprise! As you know, sweet Amy and the rest of them barked up the wrong tree – Yank might have stayed in London for all they knew and the bitter thing was his wonderful riot was put down to those silly old islands. His name wasn't mentioned in the news at all – no photographs of him with the screaming kids – taxi gimmick thrown away. A few paragraphs in the entertainment pages saying that he had arrived in Paris and sang from a balcony in the Avenue Gabriel. There'll be a story in the jazz papers of course, but he always has them on his side and this time he'd counted on the dailies. In short, Sigi did marvels, but he only warned the jazz journalists and he got all of them in the garden. He never thought of telling the others – he had no idea, of course, that there would be such a mob of kids in Main Street. So the whole thing has fallen as flat as a pancake. Yank says that's what comes of dealing with bloody amateurs; he telephoned to London for his old agent he's always had and as soon as he arrived they drifted off –'

'Northey! It's too interesting and unexpected! So how are the boys taking it?'

'If you ask me, they are relieved. They had begun to see that Yanky is a most unpleasant person. And Fanny, it's my opinion they've had about enough of earning their own livings. They admit now that the shavers were a tremendous bore – it seems you are shut up in a horrible sort of place which brings on headaches. Driftin' would have been rather fun, but not with Yank. He has put them right off the Showbiz – and they didn't much care for the people at the Club (except for the Duke, who is heaven). They were all on Yanky's side and made the boys feel inferior. Then one of their friends at Eton has asked them to a boys' shoot in Jan which they long to accept. Apparently it's a spiffing house to stay in, where the oldies know their place. They'd like to become ordinary again, you know – they'd really give anything to go back to Eton.'

'Well, that's out of the question – silly little fools. We shall have to see what can be done with them – Condorcet probably, before they cram for Oxford. Meanwhile it's almost the Christmas holidays and they can go to their old shoot. Oh, darling, you don't know what a weight off my mind this is!'

At dinner that evening the boys were studiously normal. They wore dinner jackets, their hair, which had been standing on end, was now watered and brushed in the usual way; they were clean. They gave us looks which I well remembered from their early nursery days and which I could remember bestowing, myself, on the grown-ups; looks which said if all can be forgotten and forgiven we will be good again. They called Alfred Father, and asked him to explain about the C.E.D. They asked me what books I had been reading – I quite expected them to say 'Have you been abroad lately?' a favourite gambit with people they hardly knew. They were sweet and attentive to Uncle Matthew and told him about the shoot they were going to. His old face lit up because it had once belonged to a relation of his and he had shot there many a time in the past.

'Who has got it now?'

'The father of our friend Beagle. He has made nine (you know, the big ones, millions, I mean), since the war.'

'Like blissful Jacques Oudineau,' said Northey, half to herself.

'Has he indeed? You want to look out, in the Sally Beds, not to shoot up the hill. Feller peppered me there once good and proper. Where's young Fonzy this evening?'

Sheepish looks. 'Gone to Moscow,' said Northey.

'What's he want to do that for? Payne and I had our luncheon at a place where the cabmen eat. They haven't got proper shelters; this is a restaurant. Dangerous good snack. We got talking with a Russian there who seemed heartily dissatisfied with his government – you'd hardly believe the things he told us. Now young Fonzy is a very civil chap. He gave me a lot of his records, signed. Of course the signature doesn't make the smallest difference – I mean you can't hear it – but he meant it kindly no doubt.'

'What have you been doing all day, Uncle Matthew?'

'After luncheon we went to the museum. Saw old Foch's coat and a lot of dummy horses and some pictures of battles we liked very much. Then I came back to see if there would be a cocktail party but you were out.'

'Oh bother, yes – it was a National Day we had to go to.'

'It didn't matter. I was rather tired you know, really.'

After dinner he said it was bedtime and he'd better say good-bye. 'We have an early start – I shan't come and disturb you in the morning, Fanny – I know you've never been much use before seven and I want to be off at half past five. Many thanks. Payne and I have enjoyed ourselves.'

'Come again,' I said.

All three boys were invited to stay at Boisdormant. Before they left I screwed up my courage to have a long-postponed talk with Fabrice. This was a moment I had always dreaded, when I must tell him who his father was. He knew that my cousin Linda was his mother and presumably thought that her husband, Christian Talbot, whose surname he bore, was his father. He had never seen Christian or exhibited any interest whatever in him and since he had asked no questions I had not raised the subject. I found it, for some reason, deeply embarrassing to do so.

'Fabrice, darling, you're sixteen now –'

'Definitely.'

'Which is really grown-up. In fact you have taken charge of your own life; you're not a child any more. So I suppose I can talk frankly to you –'

'If this is a pi-jaw hadn't I better fetch Charlie?'

'No, it isn't. One doesn't pi-jaw with one's fellow grown-ups. I simply want to talk about your parents. Now I've always told you that my darling cousin Linda was your mother.'

'Definitely. And my father was the son of this old woman we are going to stay with.'

'Yes, but how did you know?'

'Mum, you are a scream! Of course I've known since I was nine – from the very first moment I saw Sigi at Easterfields. He had heard the Nannies telling each other when he was meant to be asleep.'

I suppose my feelings on hearing this must have been the same as those of a mother who finds that her girl has been conversant with the facts of life since childhood. Thankful, really, not to have to enter into difficult explanations, I felt slightly aggrieved to think that Fabrice had kept such important knowledge from me all these years and not best pleased at the way in which he had found it out.

'Everything's always arranged by Sigi,' I said, crossly. 'Never mind. So, darling, be very nice to your grandmother, won't you?'

'Then she might adopt me and leave me a lot of money?'

'Oh dear! How cold-blooded you are –'

But I knew that at sixteen people put on a cold-blooded air partly because they are terrified of betraying sentiments which might embarrass them. Fabrice would be incapable now of saying that

Alfred and I were his heart's father and mother; that would come much later, if at all.

He went on, 'Sigi thinks we might make a syndicate for getting what we can out of her. She can take the place of Yanky in our lives.'

'Good luck to you!' I said. 'I expect that Duchess is capable of looking after herself – just like Yanky. You boys aren't quite as clever as you think you are –'

'Don't be ghoulish, Mum.'

They stayed a week at Boisdormant and came back in tearing spirits, having greatly enjoyed themselves. Oudineau had taken them out shooting every day and Jacques Oudineau, who kept a little aeroplane at a nearby aero-club, had allowed them to flop out of it in parachutes to their hearts' content. In the evenings they had listened with real, not simulated, interest to the Duchess's endless tales of her family and the history of Boisdormant. They were taking notes of episodes suitable to be incorporated in the Son et Lumiére and other attractions for tourists which they planned to produce there the following summer. Jacques Oudineau would see to the technical details, Sigi was to be publicity agent in Paris while our boys, collaborating with Basil and Grandad, would supply an endless stream of Britons. Beautiful Boisdormant was clearly destined to wake up one day and find itself the French Woburn. As these activities were not likely to get the boys into much trouble and could easily be combined with their lessons, I could only feel thankful at the turn their lives had taken. Jacques Oudineau, young and dynamic, seemed to have gained a far more complete ascendancy over them in one week than Alfred and I during their whole lives; they could only talk of him. He had decreed that they must now work very hard and pass all the exams with which the modern child is plagued; then he would take them into his business and they would be happy ever after. As for the Duchess, according to Valhubert she found that Fabrice more than came up to her expectations. As soon as she saw Uncle Matthew, she said, she realized that the family was *bien*. Fabrice himself then won her heart by looking like her late son and exhibiting perfect manners. Her will, it seemed, had already been altered in his favour.

24

After Christmas, Philip was posted to Moscow. It seemed to me that everybody had either gone or was going there. M. Bouche-Bontemps, in a fur hat, was conferring with Mr K at the Kremlin; the French papers were full of lines and sidelines on Russia, no photograph without its onion dome. On Boxing Day, David and Dawn had their baby in a snowstorm between Omsk and Tomsk, causing the maximum amount of trouble to Alfred's colleague in Moscow; telegrams flew back and forth. They were illegally on Soviet territory; it was not easy to get permission for them to stay there until David should be out of danger. (The other two had risen above the experience but it had nearly killed him.) However, the kind Ambassadress took them all in; knowing by experience how difficult it would be to budge them again, I felt sorry for the Ambassador. Yanky Fonzy was enjoying a triumphant season at the Bolshoi. Basil and Grandad had just got their visas and were going to Moscow to negotiate a long-term exchange of tourists.

It was more of a blow than a surprise to learn that we were to lose Philip. We had always known that he was due for a move and that he had only been left at Paris long enough to see us comfortably into the Embassy before becoming Counsellor somewhere else. When he came to tell me his news I said, 'Talk about a Pull to the East – I feel as if I were living in the last act of *The Three Sisters*. All we get back from Moscow is Hector Dexter, a very poor exchange for you and Northey.'

'How d'you mean, me and Northey?'

'I naturally suppose you'll be taking her. You're not going to leave her here with a broken heart, Philip – don't tell me that?'

'Oh, dearest Fanny, do I really want the whole of the Praesidium milling round my dacha? Not to speak of faithful wolves and sweet Siberian crows in one's bedroom?'

'As soon as she's married, with a baby, all that will stop, I've seen it so often. How is your love for Grace?'

'Very hopeless, what with one thing and another. My own fault for telling Mees about St Expédite. Every time I go to St Roch, there she is keenly putting up candles. It's quite ridiculous – the saint doesn't know which way to turn, as Mees said herself, last time we met there.'

'Chuck the whole thing and marry her.'

'What a matchmaker you are.'

'It's time the poor duck was settled. Besides, think how lonely you'd be in Moscow, without any of us.'

'Good for trade,' said Philip, 'promotion, important post and so forth, but I can't say I greatly look forward to it. I would certainly find it much jollier if I had Mees there. But what would you do without her yourself?'

'It won't be the same, but I can have sister Jean now. The Chelsea setter has already found another girl with more money and a larger tiara, and Jean is looking for a job.'

'Oh dear – how I hate taking irrevocable decisions!'

'Go on, Philip. No time like the present. She's in her office – go and propose to her this very minute.'

'All right. So long as you realize that it's entirely your responsibility.' He kissed me on both cheeks and went off.

I was now seized by misgivings. Left to himself, would not Philip have havered and wavered and in the end gone away without coming to a decision? I had induced him to propose, deliberately ignoring the wise reflections of Alfred, although I knew that there was a great deal of truth in them. On the face of it, Philip had the makings of an excellent husband. Attractive, kind, clever, gay, and amusing, never boring, he was also very rich. Nevertheless something was missing, some sort of intensity or ardent flame which, had it existed, might well have won over Grace, or, in the old Oxford days, me myself. Furthermore, he had been in love with us as he was not with Northey. She had fallen in love at first sight, so she loved an image which she had invented and which might easily be rubbed away in daily wear and tear. On the other hand, I told myself, there are no rules for successful marriage. Northey and Philip seemed rather suited, she so lively, he so orthodox; her superabundant vitality, the maternal instinct she lavished on creatures, would turn into their proper channel when she had babies; she was accustomed, now, to Embassy life.

Another factor, I must say, weighed with me. Mockbar had, of late, taken Northey as the heroine of his page. It was no secret now to the readers of the *Daily Post* that the Marquis de Valhubert, who had escorted the world's most beautiful women, was her 'friend'. His British-born wife was expecting her fifth child in March; Mockbar gave the impression that, after this happy event, Valhubert would announce his engagement to Northey.

'Really, darling,' Grace said, 'I shall have to find out what sort of thing the bridegroom's wife is expected to wear at a wedding.'

'Poor soul,' was Northey's reflection, 'he has found out the truth about the riots and he is minding. Hard put to it to mollify Lord Grumpy, just as the children are getting to the age of a glass of wine with their food, you know. However, there's hot news today. M. Cruas is engaged to Phyllis McFee!'

I wondered why these characters were suddenly being liquidated. M. Cruas may have been based on fact; Phyllis McFee was certainly a figment of Northey's imagination; both played a useful part in what Philip called 'the carry-on'. During the last week or two they had been unusually busy – hardly a day without one or other being invoked. It seemed rash of her to make such a clean sweep; I felt a little uneasy. 'Is it wise to get rid of them both at a blow?' I asked.

'Much as I shall miss the beloveds, I have their happiness to consider. Each for each is what we teach. They are buggering off on a long, long honeymoon in Asia Minor.'

Everything considered, was it not my duty to Louisa to get this wayward creature married if I could?

Northey stood in the doorway. Her eyes were like blue brilliants; she radiated happiness. She stood quite still and said, 'It's me, Fanny! I'm engaged!'

'Darling – yes, I know. I can't tell you how delighted I am!'

'You know?'

'Philip told me.'

'But I've only just told him.'

I saw that I had been tactless, of course she would not like the idea of Philip having discussed the matter beforehand.

'He was looking everywhere for you and I suppose he felt so happy that he couldn't resist telling me.'

'Oh yes, I see – he did very kindly offer. Only think, Fanny, two short weeks ago I would have accepted.' She shuddered.

'But, darling, I don't quite understand. I thought you said you were engaged?'

'Yes. I'm engaged to Jacques Oudineau.'

read more   🐧

NANCY MITFORD

THE PURSUIT OF LOVE

'Obsessed with sex!' said Jassy, 'there's nobody so obsessed as you,
Linda.
Why if I so much as look at a picture you say I'm a pygmalionist.'
In the end we got far more information out of a
book called Ducks and Duck Breeding.
'Ducks can only copulate,' said Linda, after studying this for a
while, 'in running water. Good luck to them.'

Oh, the tedium of waiting to grow up! Longing for love, obsessed with weddings
and sex, Linda and her sisters and cousin Fanny are on the look out for the perfect
lover.

But finding Mr Right is much harder than any of the sisters had thought. Linda
must suffer marriage first to a stuffy Tory MP and then to a handsome and
humourless communist, before finding real love in war-torn Paris . . .

The Pursuit of Love is one of the funniest and sharpest novels about love and
growing up ever written.

'Utter, utter bliss' *Daily Mail*

NANCY MITFORD

THE COMPLETE NOVELS

Here in one volume are all eight of Nancy Mitford's sparklingly astute, hilarious and completely unputdownable novels:

Highland Fling

Christmas Pudding

Wigs on the Green

Pigeon Pie

The Pursuit of Love

Love in a Cold Climate

The Blessing

Don't Tell Alfred

Published over a period of thirty years, they provide a wonderful glimpse of the bright young things of the thirties, forties, fifties and sixties, in the city and in the shires, firmly ensconced at home or making a go of it abroad; and what the upper classes really got up to in peace and in war.

'Deliciously funny' Evelyn Waugh

'Entirely original, inimitable and irresistible' *Spectator*

'A comic genius' *Independent on Sunday*